Magic in Life

Erasmus Cromwell-Smith

For my Children,
"...Our Blue Unicorns in Life exist, only if we can see them..."

Erasmus Cromwell-Smith Books

In English

(Inspirational/Philosophical)
The Equilibrist series:
- The Equilibrist (Vol. 1)
- Geniality (Vol. 2)
- The Magic in Life (Vol. 3)
- Poetry in Equilibrium (Vol. 4)

(Young Adults)
The Orloj Series:
- The Orloj of Prague (Vol. 1)
- The Orloj of Venice (Vol. 2)
- The Orloj of Paris (Vol. 3)
- The Orloj of Munich (Vol. 4)
- Poetry in Balance (Vol. 5)

(Educational)
The South Beach Conversational Method:
- Spanish
- Inglés
- German
- French
- Italian
- Portuguese

En Español

(Inspiracional/Filosófica)
La serie el equilibrista:
- El Equilibrista (Vol. 1)
- Genialidad (Vol. 2)
- La magia de la vida (Vol. 3)
- Poesía en equilibrio (Vol. 4)

(Jóvenes Adultos)
La serie el Orloj:
- El Orloj de Praga (Vol. 1)
- El Orloj de Venecia (Vol. 2)
- El Orloj de Paris (Vol. 3)
- El Orloj de Munich (Vol. 4)
- Poesía en Balance (Vol. 5)

(Educacional)
El método conversacional South Beach:
- Español
- Inglés
- Alemán
- Francés
- Italiano
- Portugués

(Sci-fi)
The Nicolas Tosh Series:
- Algorithm-323 (Vol. 1)
- Tosh (Vol. 2)

As Nelson Hamel*
(Action-Thrillers)
The Paradise Island Series:
- Miami Beach, Dangerous Lifestyles (Vol. 1)

(Sci-fi)
The Rebel Hacker Series:
The Rebel Hackers of Point of Point Breeze (Vol. 1)

* In collaboration with Charles Sibley.

TABLE OF CONTENTS

In *Geniality*, the preceding book, the story concluded with my father discovering that my mother had left him. That moment is precisely where *The Quibbler* begins.

Even now, I struggle to fully understand why, all those years ago, my mother chose to run away from true love. During their time together, she showed signs of growing fears, but none seemed significant enough to justify, let alone explain, such a heart-crushing and sudden departure. One day, she simply vanished.

By all accounts, theirs was a genuine, infatuated, and passionate relationship. Friends described them as the perfect match, often calling them "lovebirds" in jest. So deeply were they absorbed in their own world that there was little room for socializing or even close friendships, aside from their shared academic duties and tutoring commitments. On the surface, their love seemed idyllic.

As I delved deeper into my father's life, I became determined to uncover what might have driven my mother to walk away from such a profound connection. The more I explored, the more a picture began to form—one that hinted at underlying reasons, perhaps even the true ones, hidden beneath the surface. This book focuses on the years they spent apart, from 1977 to 2017. It explores her family and professional life, his world travels, academic pursuits, and writing career, as well as the invisible yet unbreakable bonds that kept them inexplicably tethered across decades, ultimately leading to their reunion. Like the previous two volumes, this story is told in my father's voice, in the first person.

Due to the success of his unique teaching format, my father, Professor Erasmus Cromwell-Smith, continued to use it for a third consecutive academic year in 2019. That year, he once again began by revisiting the day he discovered Victoria was missing. However, unlike the classes of 2017 and 2018, there was a renewed energy and sense of resolution in his storytelling. My mother's return in late 2017 had completely transformed him, filling his life with the love and presence he had yearned for so long. Her unwavering support rejuvenated him, bringing strength and joy back into his life.

It was during that year, more than twelve months after their reunion, that my mother finally opened up and revealed the real reasons she had left my father in 1977.

Finally, I must acknowledge that I never had the chance to meet my biological parents, yet their absence remains a deep source of pain. Writing these three books has been my way of piecing together their story, weaving it into the lives of my adoptive parents with care and profound love. This final volume has allowed me to bring their narrative to a close, merging their legacy with that of the remarkable couple who raised me. In doing so, I've found a sense of closure—not only for their story but also for my own journey as the author of *The Equilibrist* series.

Erasmus Cromwell-Smith II

Chapter 1

Adversity

Royal Cambridge Scholastic Institute (2019)
(Erasmus and Victoria's Home)

The tick of the cuckoo clock is the only sound resonating through the still darkness of the early morning.

Professor Erasmus Cromwell-Smith has dozed off on his beloved Chesterfield sofa. Resting on his lap is the latest object of his insatiable curiosity: a 17th-century leather-bound book with gold-burnished pages exploring the subject of coherence. Nudged closely to his side, sleeping as soundly as him, is Victoria Emerson-Lloyd, the love of his life. Together, their faces form a portrait of plenitude—a radiant testament to the incomparable beauty of true love.

At the prescribed hour, the cheerful clucking of the cuckoo bird stirs them awake, announcing the arrival of a new day. As they stretch into one another, their shared smiles illuminate the room like the first rays of dawn.

This morning marks the beginning of a new academic year. The illustrious pedagogue is eager to embark on his first class.

"Dear, what will be the subject of your class today?" Victoria murmurs, still half-asleep.

"Adversity, my lady," Erasmus replies, his voice tinged with both seriousness and anticipation.

Not long after, Victoria kisses and waves him off as he pedals through the crisp autumn morning on his trusty, old rusty bike, the fallen leaves crunching under its wheels as he makes his way to class.

Royal Cambridge Scholastic Institute (2019)

(University Auditorium)

The auditorium is filled to capacity, buzzing with palpable energy. Students eagerly anticipate the return of Professor Cromwell-Smith, their excitement almost tangible.

The professor strides in with deliberate purpose, his expression bright and welcoming. Hand on his chin, he surveys the room, pausing momentarily as if connecting with each student individually.

A broad smile spreads across his face, eliciting a mix of chuckles and intense, focused stares from his audience.

"Welcome! How's everyone today?" he greets, his voice resonating through the hall.

"Awesome!" comes the collective reply, mirroring his signature phrase.

"I trust you all had a fun and enlightening summer," he says exuberantly.

Then, shifting his tone to one of firm authority, he continues, "A quick reminder—punctuality is a non-negotiable in this course. No excuses."

"As with the previous two years, we will follow the same format—one last time," he declares. "This year, we're delving into new subjects through narration, readings, and the lens of poetry. The first themes we'll explore are adversity and hardship," he announces, setting the stage for the year ahead.

"Are you ready for the journey?" he asks, receiving a sea of nodding heads in return.

"Adversity," he begins, pacing the floor with deliberate intensity.

"What happens when we face adversity? Have we been taught how to react, how to handle it, how to cope? Are we ever truly prepared?

And what about the aftermath? Suppose adversity strikes, and we overcome it—what then?" His questions linger in the air, inviting reflection.

Pausing for emphasis, he continues, "Today, we'll start right where we left off last year. On the night when the love of my life vanished. That day, adversity struck me unexpectedly, and I wasn't prepared to face it at all."

He stops, letting the weight of his words settle before delivering the opening line.

"It begins like this…"

— ✳ —

Cape Cod, Erasmus' Hotel Room (1977)
(Early Friday Night)

"She's gone, Erasmus," Gina's words reverberate through his mind, a relentless echo that refuses to fade. The weight of those three words settles heavily on his chest, each repetition carving deeper into his resolve.

Erasmus has only one idea in mind. He has to get back to Boston. He must start looking for her. Grabbing his coat, he hastily collects his belongings. The stack of notes and papers from the mentors remains untouched on the desk, their importance now eclipsed by the urgency of his mission. Within five minutes, Erasmus leaves the hotel room with luggage in hand. Right after checking out, he steps into the biting Cape Cod night. The cold wind lashes at his face, a stark reminder of the distance he must cover — not just in miles but across the fragile emotional landscape he now confronts.

As he rushes out, Erasmus runs headlong into "The Riddler," Mr. Ringwald, the antiquarian from downtown Boston.

"Erasmus, young man, what are you up to?" he asks, his gaze flicking to the small suitcase.

"Where are you going, luggage and all, at this hour of the night?" Mr. Ringwald presses, surprise evident in his tone.

Erasmus bows his head in courtesy but doesn't answer and rushes past the startled Riddler. As he walks away, guilt and gratitude war within him. He pauses momentarily, then turns and says, "Mr. R, I've got to go and see about a girl. Sorry."

"THE girl?" the Riddler calls after him.

"Yes, THE girl," Erasmus yells back, a faint smile tugging at his lips. Unexpectedly, Ringwald starts chasing him.

"Erasmus!"

"Yes?" Erasmus responds, slowing slightly.

"Take this and read it when appropriate," Ringwald says, out of breath as he catches up.

"Thank you, Mr. Ringwald," Erasmus replies, accepting the scroll with gratitude.

"For nothing, young man. I've got a gut feeling that you may need it," Ringwald predicts ominously.

"But you don't have to—" Erasmus begins to protest.

"C'mon, take it and use it. Now go. Go!" Ringwald insists.

With determined strides, Erasmus heads toward the train station, his mind racing with possibilities, regrets, and a single burning hope: finding Victoria.

Cape Cod Train Station, Mass. (1977)
(Friday Night)

Erasmus sits alone at the deserted Cape Cod train station. No more trains are scheduled for Boston, but he doesn't care; his nerves and angst have overtaken him completely. Hours later, still in the dark, a Good Samaritan gently shakes him awake.

"Are you going to Boston?"

"Yes."

"Then you better get moving; otherwise, you'll miss the train—it's about to leave."

Erasmus jolts upright and sprints, barely catching the train with no time to spare.

He's sound asleep again when the announcement awakens him.

"We're arriving at Boston's main station."

Erasmus heads straight home, where he methodically tears through the apartment, searching for a note, a clue—anything in writing. An hour later, he sits on the living room floor, staring blankly at the now lifeless surroundings.

'Nothing. Not a word,' Erasmus realizes, the thought stabbing deeply.

'She took everything. I don't even have a number or an address to reference,' he muses in turmoil, chastising himself for missing the signs. He spends an hour or more on the phone with directory assistance, all to no avail. The number is unlisted. Reality finally hits home mid-Saturday afternoon when he visits a professor who taught them both.

Professor Jenkins initially appears startled until Erasmus asks about Victoria's sudden disappearance.

"Oh, I know what you're referring to, young man. She wrote a letter to the admissions office notifying them she was dropping out. She also left a note thanking all of us, specifically her teachers, for everything we did for her. This kind of withdrawal from a highly functional, trouble-free student is rare, but in my experience, it's always due to extraordinary reasons and circumstances."

"Thanks, Professor Jenkins."

"I understand she's from out of state. What are you going to do now?"

"I've got to go and find out about my girl, sir. Thanks for your help, professor," Erasmus says, shaking his former teacher's hand with gratitude.

"Good luck, young man."

Saturday night proves unbearable. Erasmus spends it wide awake, haunted by her absence. By Sunday morning, a fiery determination replaces his despair. He knows he can't stay passive. He needs to act.

Harvard University Campus (1977)

(Sunday Morning, Erasmus and Victoria's Studio)

"Good morning, Gina," Erasmus greets her with forced civility.

"Seriously? What time is it?" Gina snaps groggily, immediately realizing her tone.

"Sorry, Erasmus. That was insensitive of me. How can I help?"

"Do you have her phone number or address?" he asks, desperation lacing his voice.

"No, I'm sorry. For some reason, Vicky never shared her family life or contact information with me," Gina replies, shaking her head apologetically.

"Ok, thanks anyway," Erasmus mutters, dejected.

The following week sees Erasmus in a quasi-catatonic state, hoping she'll somehow return. It isn't until the next weekend that he finally accepts the reality—she's not coming back.

Boston Main Train Station (1977)

(One Week Later, Saturday Morning)

'Eventually, I'll end up hating all train stations,' Erasmus reflects grimly as he boards a train bound for Chicago. Halfway through the long journey, he discovers he's taken the wrong route. Instead of heading through New York to St. Louis—the

correct path to Victoria's hometown of Waterloo, Illinois—he's traveling the long way around. 'Nothing I can do for now.'

Waterloo, Illinois Main Train Station (1977)
(Monday Morning)

'All it'll take is just to be in front of one another, and we will be reunited,' he reassures himself repeatedly.

The old, crumpled, yellowed pages of a station phone book finally come to his rescue. After hours of searching, Erasmus secures an address and phone number. However, dread creeps into his heart when his call meets an ominous recording: the line has been disconnected.

Fighting the sickly feeling in his stomach, he takes a taxi to her address. His heart pounds as he prays for the best while preparing for the worst.

"Young man, they moved out in the middle of the night," Victoria's neighbor announces bluntly. "We're in shock; we've been neighbors all our lives. Old Emerson and I grew up together. There must've been a compelling, private reason for them to vanish like bandits, hiding from everyone. Who knows— maybe their daughter got knocked up while at Harvard," the neighbor speculates, eyeing Erasmus with suspicion, as though he might be the culprit.

En Route by Train from St. Louis Back to Boston
(Via New York – 1977, Monday Afternoon)

Defeated, Erasmus boards the train home. He drifts in and out of restless dreams until a sudden memory strikes him: Mr. Ringwald's scroll. For a moment, panic grips him—did he leave it behind? But relief floods in as he retrieves it from his small suitcase.

Erasmus stares at the scroll, its purpose now clear. With reverence, he prepares to read it. First, he showers, shaves, and

*changes into a fresh set of clothes. Then, with a steaming cup of
tea in hand, he finally sits down, ready to absorb its contents.*

*

"Adversity"

Either by acts of men, nature, or humanity's creations,
fatefully, sooner or later,
weather systems will gather on the horizon,
events will unfold unexpectedly,
and inevitably, one way or another—
with or without warning—
adversity will strike
during our life's journey.

Adversity will affect us—
emotionally, spiritually, physically, materially—
often in any combination.

When we face hardship in life,
there is no choice.
We gather all our strengths, forces, and powers—
those we have and those we summon,
those distinct and those we reach for.

We confront adversity head-on,
without fear or hesitation,
with all our will and desire—
for ourselves or others—
to live and to overcome,
to prevail and rise back up,
to defeat and render adversity
completely annihilated and vanquished.

When we don't confront or face hardship head-on,
we become trapped—

lost in indecisiveness,
drawing circles within our minds,
wasting valuable time,
avoiding or delaying action.

These are moments—some lasting a lifetime—
where we find ourselves lamenting,
feeling sorry for ourselves or others,
procrastinating, commiserating,
while doing little to fight back.

When we behave in such ways,
our failure to act leads us nowhere,
except to an empty place,
where excuses sound hollow—
not only robbing us of our ability to live a life in full,
but also reflecting the attitude of a soldier
who runs away from the battle of life
without ever firing a single shot,
unwilling to face the enemy of adversity
with courage and conviction to defeat it,
or perhaps,
adapt to it.

Getting a grip on adversity is best
when we catch it early on.
When, out of foresight, anticipation,
preparation, and readiness,
we see it coming and are prepared for it,
we prevent it or stop it right in its tracks,
before it happens—right at its onset.

And yet, in many ways, adversity is also an opportunity,
sometimes for renewal and new beginnings,

other times, it marks the beginning
of the end of a bad spell.

How we react and cope with it
determines our success—
in overcoming and turning adversity
into something positive.

Hardship is formative and transformative,
rattling our core as a "comfort buster,"
testing our character, courage, and resilience.

If adversity is avoidable,
it is our existential duty
to do all within our power
to prevent it or stay out of its path.
But if it is inevitable,
we must adapt—
learning to live with it,
as our goal is to outlast and outwill it.

If hardship is irreversible,
we still seek to find and squeeze the most out of life,
wringing meaning from every second
we exist in the universe.

If it is mendable,
we fight like lions,
refusing to give up,
curing ourselves of it,
relentlessly to no end.

Yet, we must beware of "mirages in the desert,"
as hardships sometimes
are nothing but a figment of our imagination—

where we see obstacles and hurdles
where there are none.
We create them out of fear, insecurities,
pessimism, or depression.

Adversity is best faced with existential tools like
hope, conviction, optimism,
ingenuity, faith, and work ethic—
a busy mind and spirit,
all coupled with love.

Sometimes, we encounter the adversity of others
and don't know what to do.
Involuntarily, our perception of them
becomes contagious,
as if those afflicted with hardship
suffer from an infectious disease
we want to stay away from.

On other occasions, we act
as if those under hardship
have somehow suddenly changed—
fallen from their former selves.
We perceive them and behave as though,
because of their circumstances,
they are suddenly not worthy of us.

How wrong we are to conduct ourselves
in such ways.
Inevitably, we too will experience hardship
and may find ourselves
on the receiving end of such disdain—
of the same exact happenstance.

Thus, it is wise and existential
to treat the hardship of others
with the utmost respect,
a kind and giving heart.

Even if their battles are not ours,
it is wise to remind ourselves
that we are still soldiers of the same army,
fighting the same life war of existence.

Against unforeseen mishaps and vicissitudes,
hardship is greatly diminished when thought of
in comparative and relative terms.
No matter how difficult things seem,
they can always be worse.

Adversity is at its worst when it comes unannounced,
catches us unprepared,
and we are unguarded against it.

The best attitude against hardship
is to treat it as an enemy of war—
to whom we never surrender,
against whom we never quit.

On the contrary,
we fight and confront relentlessly,
until we defeat it and render it powerless.

But if we can't,
we adapt—
extracting what life still has to offer,
even within the circumstances,
because life never stops,
even as we overcome adversity.

Adversity must always be treated
as an existential opportunity—
a chance to awaken
from a life of comfort and complacency.

A chance to renew and reinvent ourselves.
But adversity becomes an opportunity
only if we choose to make it so.

*

As the words of the poem linger in the quiet of the train, young Erasmus leans back in his seat, staring at the passing countryside. The rhythmic clatter of the tracks beneath him seems to echo the steady resolve growing within his heart. The scroll's profound message has awakened something dormant, a quiet determination to face life head-on. His weary reflection in the window hints at the transformation taking place—a shift from sorrow to action. The train journey, though physically uneventful, has marked a pivotal turning point, setting him on a path that would ultimately shape the man he would become.

—— �֍ ——

Royal Cambridge Scholastic Institute (2019)
(University Auditorium)

The sudden ring of the bell jolts the professor and his class back to the present. Cromwell-Smith pauses, as if still transported back to that moment, "On that train ride back to Harvard," the professor continues, his voice steady but tinged with the wisdom of time and experience, "I made several pivotal decisions that helped me confront adversity and ultimately overcome how I felt. First, even though my wandering mind was consumed with turmoil, I kept the scroll with me, and as the Riddler had predicted, the moment arrived when I truly needed it. Secondly, despite not being in the mood, I resolved to open and read it. That decision turned out to be transformative, as its words illuminated a path forward—a path of decisiveness I chose to follow. Thirdly, by the time I returned to Boston, I had already resolved to move on with my life while preserving, without bitterness, all the wonderful memories of my time with Victoria. In this spirit, the very same day of my return, I wrote to Mrs. V back in Wales, pouring out my feelings of longing and uncertainty. Her thoughtful reply gave me the encouragement, strength, and clarity I needed," the professor emphasizes, his gaze sweeping the attentive faces of his students.

"Not long after, I graduated from Harvard and made one final trip to my hometown of Hay-on-Wye in Wales before settling permanently in America. While there, I discovered that my childhood mentors had orchestrated a surprise mentoring session for me. It was during this gathering that they imparted the timeless happiness formula—an inspired recipe that became the final touch needed to straighten the course of my life for good. At the end of today's class, I will share a copy of this formula with each of you," he announces, a smile of quiet pride softening his features.

"Adversity is an intrinsic part of life," he continues, his tone now imbued with conviction. "It is often both the ultimate challenge to everything and everyone we hold dear and an opportunity to create something meaningful, perhaps even extraordinary, out of it. Adversity is a double-edged sword— hardship on one side, and on the other, a door that opens to renewal or a new beginning."

He pauses, stepping back from the desk to face his students. "Now, I open the floor for any questions or thoughts you might have on what we've discussed today."

Anna, a Literature and Philosophy major, with short curly brown hair and glasses that always seem to slide down her nose as she ponders deeply, raises her hand. "Professor, in the poem 'Adversity,' you speak of the moment when we don't confront hardship head-on, leading us into indecisiveness. I'm curious about the philosophical implications of this—do you think that avoiding adversity can be considered a failure of character, or is it more about human instinct for self-preservation? Is there a balance between retreat and confrontation in how we deal with personal challenges?"

"An excellent question, Anna," Professor Cromwell-Smith responds. "You're right to highlight the tension between instinctual retreat and the need for confrontation. From a philosophical standpoint, we can view avoidance as a natural response—human beings are wired for survival, and often our first instinct is to shield ourselves from harm. But, as the poem suggests, there's a line where this instinct crosses into passivity, and in those moments, we rob ourselves of growth. It's not about being reckless or overly confrontational; rather, it's about having the courage to face the challenge when it comes, even if that means starting small. I wouldn't define avoidance as a failure of character per se, but as a missed opportunity to engage with life's deeper lessons."

Carlos, a Psychology and Neuroscience major, tall with dark, neatly combed hair and a warm smile that contrasts with his usually serious demeanor, speaks next. "Professor, you spoke about the dual nature of adversity—how it presents both hardship and opportunity. From a psychological standpoint, how do we cultivate the resilience to see adversity not just as a threat but as an opportunity? Is it possible to actively reframe these experiences in a way that promotes psychological growth?"

"Carlos, you've hit the core of the challenge," Professor Cromwell-Smith responds. "In psychology, reframing is indeed a powerful tool—it's about shifting the lens through which we view an experience. Instead of seeing adversity purely as a threat, we can train our minds to view it as an opportunity for growth, learning, or even self-discovery. There's a fascinating process in cognitive psychology called cognitive restructuring, where we intentionally change negative or limiting thoughts into more constructive ones. Resilience isn't a fixed trait; it's a skill that can be cultivated with practice. This can start with acknowledging the adversity, processing it, and then asking, 'What can I learn from this? How can this moment make me stronger, more capable, or more understanding?' Over time, this mindset becomes automatic."

Jane, a History and Political Science major, with long black hair often tied into a neat ponytail, and a focused gaze that reveals her attention to detail, asks, "Professor, the poem seems to suggest that adversity is inevitable and, in some cases, irreversible. Do you think history shows us examples of how societies, as opposed to individuals, handle adversity? Are there historical moments where adversity has been 'irreversible,' and what can we learn from them?"

"That's a fascinating perspective, Jane," Professor Cromwell-Smith says. "You're absolutely right that history is rife with moments of collective adversity—whether that's war, political upheaval, or social injustice. Some of these events, like the fall of empires or the devastation of war, seem irreversible. Yet, what's striking is the resilience of societies that rebuild and transform in the aftermath. Take, for example, the recovery of Europe after World War II, or the Civil Rights Movement here in the United States. These moments of collective suffering and loss became the catalysts for significant change. The key lesson is that while some adversities may be irreversible, the ways in which we respond can reshape the future. It's a testament to the human capacity for reinvention, even when facing what seems like an insurmountable challenge."

David, an Economics and Sociology major, athletic build with a sharp jawline, often seen with a slight frown when analyzing social trends and patterns, asks, "Professor, the poem emphasizes confronting adversity with courage and will, and yet, it also speaks about avoiding unnecessary 'mirages in the desert'—things that aren't real obstacles. How do we distinguish between genuine adversity that requires confrontation and imaginary challenges that we create in our minds due to fear or insecurity? Is there a method to discern this distinction?"

"That's a very insightful question, David," Professor Cromwell-Smith responds. "The line between real adversity and self-created challenges can be incredibly thin. Often, our minds play tricks on us—fear, doubt, and insecurity can make challenges seem larger or more insurmountable than they truly are. One way to distinguish between the two is by questioning the source of the adversity. Is the challenge external—something truly outside our control—or is it rooted in our internal fears, anxieties, or projections? One method I recommend is the 'reality check'—take a step back and analyze the situation from an objective standpoint. Ask yourself: 'Is this something I can control? Is it based on facts, or is it influenced by my emotions and fears?' Real adversity demands action; imagined adversity often requires nothing more than a shift in perspective."

"That will be all for today. I'll see you all next week," Professor Cromwell-Smith concludes, his words lingering like echoes of wisdom. As the students rise and file out of the auditorium, he hands each of them a copy of the happiness formula, his gesture filled with quiet hope for their journeys ahead. As the last of his students exit the auditorium, their murmured conversations fading into the corridor beyond, Professor Cromwell-Smith lingers at the lectern, gazing out over the now-empty seats. The silence feels heavier, more contemplative, after the depth of their shared discussion. Gathering his notes and adjusting his glasses, he allows himself a rare moment of reflection. The echoes of the past and present intertwine, and he silently wonders which seeds of wisdom, if any, have found fertile ground among his students.

Straightening his posture, he walks toward the door, his mind already preparing for the next lecture—a chance to explore life's complexities further and, perhaps, to inspire a few more hearts

The Happiness Formula

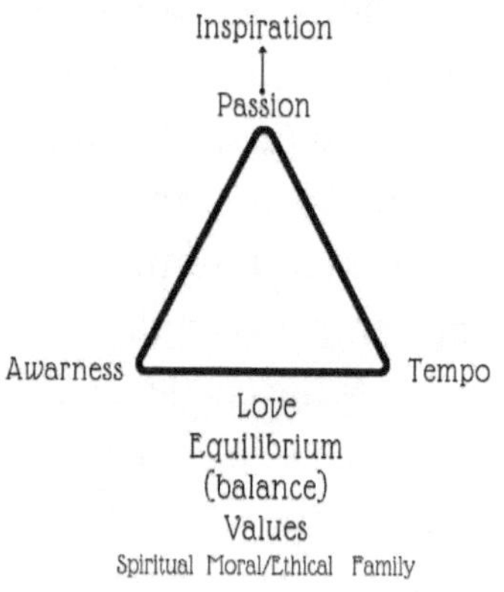

As the professor steps outside, he surveys the campus and feels a quiet satisfaction at the sight of students departing with expressions of gratitude and determination etched on their faces.

Walking toward his old rusty bike, his eyes land on a figure sitting on a bench in the distance. It's Victoria. Her shoulders quake as she cries inconsolably, her sobs audible even from afar. Gulping for breath between tears, she seems consumed by an overwhelming tide of emotion.

Without hesitation, Erasmus strides briskly toward her, his

heart heavy with concern. Sitting down beside her, he doesn't say a word. Instead, he gently wraps his long arms around her, his embrace a mantle of love and protection. The world around them seems to fall away as he focuses solely on her.

'She needs to let it all out,' he thinks, his chest tightening with empathy as her pain seeps into the quiet space between them. After a while, Victoria breaks the silence, her voice trembling.

"Erasmus, I sat through the whole class," she confesses, her words like a fragile offering. Her tear-streaked face turns toward him, her eyes searching his for understanding.

He is momentarily taken aback but quickly collects himself, nodding thoughtfully. After a pause, his voice comes soft and steady, a gentle anchor in the storm of her emotions. "Alright, Victoria," he whispers, his tone inviting yet deliberate. "Why don't you go ahead and tell me what happened while I was looking for you?"

Her tears intensify momentarily as if his words have unlocked the floodgates. Engaging a voice fractured by emotion, she begins to recount the events of that fateful night. The memories spill out, raw and unfiltered, each word a fragment of the pain and guilt she has carried for so long.

Erasmus listens intently, his arms remaining firmly around her, offering silent reassurance as she lays bare the story that has haunted them both for decades.

— ⚓ —

The Emerson-Lloyd Family Home, Waterloo, Illinois (1977)
(Victoria's Arrival from Harvard)

"Victoria, you can't force your entire family to uproot itself from one day to the next. This is our home. It's where we've lived all our lives, where you and your siblings were born, and where

our lifelong friends are," her mother declares sternly, her voice brimming with finality.

Victoria, however, ignores her entirely.

"Mom, Dad, it's your choice: either we do it, or I'm on a train back to Boston today—this time for good," she asserts firmly, her tone unwavering.

Her father's face contorts in alarm. "Victoria Emerson-Lloyd, what sort of trouble are you in?" he demands.

"Love trouble, Dad. If he shows up here, I'm afraid I won't be able to resist him." Her voice cracks under the weight of her confession.

"Victoria, why don't you just tell us what's going on?" her mother presses, her distress palpable.

"The only thing happening here," Victoria cries, her tears falling freely, *"is that I'm marrying the guy you want, not the one I love."*

Her father freezes, visibly taken aback. "I'm lost! We don't want you to do that," he asserts, his eyes darting to his wife, who fixes her gaze on the floor to avoid his accusatory stare.

"Who is he?" her father urges, his tone softening.

"A British student," Victoria murmurs, her voice barely audible, *"about to complete his master's degree."*

Her father's bewilderment shifts to suspicion as he looks between his wife and daughter. "You two need to explain yourselves. What is this, then? An arranged marriage?" he asks, disgust edging into his voice.

"Victoria has made a sensible decision to raise a family with an experienced and well-to-do gentleman from the same region we're all from. The matter is settled, and there is nothing further to discuss," her mother declares, her tone firm and unyielding.

"You told me this was Victoria's decision! It sounds like you're coercing her to marry that man," he accuses, his piercing gaze landing squarely on his wife.

Victoria sits frozen, her mother's words slicing through her. Her emotional outburst has laid bare her true feelings, and all she wants now is to bolt to the train station and return to Erasmus. Across the room, her mother, visibly panicking, scrambles to regain control of the unraveling situation.

"Victoria," her mother interjects hurriedly, "let me speak to your father alone about this." Without waiting for consent, she ushers her perplexed husband into another room.

Victoria, caught in the turmoil, remains seated, her warring impulses raging within her. Moments later, her mother returns, a triumphant smile plastered on her face.

"Victoria, we have a property in Columbia, Illinois, just north of here. We can move there temporarily until you're married. It's also closer to your likely new university in St. Louis. Socially, being away for a few months won't impact us much," she announces cheerfully, her voice brimming with forced optimism.

Victoria shakes herself out of her trance, turning to Erasmus as she continues her tale. "Shortly after I got married, I moved and settled in Columbia, Illinois. That's where all my children were born. Not long after my return from Boston, I also enrolled at the University of Missouri in St. Louis, where I eventually completed my studies in criminal psychology. Years later, after I graduated, I started my teaching career, and then we moved to Boston. Still, to this day, I don't know how she persuaded my father to go along with it."

Her voice trails off, her gaze distant, as if still grappling with the memory of those fateful days.

— ✦ —

Royal Cambridge Scholastic Institute (2019)
(Campus Backroads)

The newly reunited couple strolls through the mushy grass path toward his home. Victoria's face shows visible relief, her shoulders slightly less tense than before. Erasmus, ever perceptive, senses that the real challenge now lies in her finding a way to forgive herself for the choices she made. With quiet determination, he tightens his embrace, a blanket of forgiveness wrapping around her as if to shield her from the storm within.

"I love you," he murmurs softly in her ear, his voice a steady anchor as she trembles, grappling with the uncertainty of her unfinished puzzle.

Victoria slows her steps and turns to gaze at him, her eyes brimming with gratitude and love. But in an instant, those eyes widen with surprise and awe. She notices the tiny scroll in his hand and immediately knows it is meant for her.

"Earlier this morning," Erasmus begins with a tender smile, "before I fell asleep on your shoulder, I wrote this little something for you, my lady."

He holds the scroll delicately, his fingers trembling slightly, and begins to read in earnest, his voice carrying the depth of his emotions…

"How is it that you make me feel so special?"

What are all those little things that you do?
What is it about the way you act?
What are those spellbinding words you say?
What is it about the magical verses you scribble?
All of it makes me feel so special,
my love.

Is it that you make me feel
whimsical,

happy,

loved,

adored, and revered to no end?

Or is it because, every single day,

in the whirlwind of your devotion,

you remind me that I am for you

the most important person in the world,

the very center of your universe?

This is the only way I can explain

how, while basking in joy,

I have no choice but to fee:

motivated,

inspired and

profoundly grateful.

That's how,

you bring out the best in me.

You draw from me all that I can give,

simply because of who you are

and how you make me feel— so special, so unique, my love.

*

Victoria trembles, her breath hitching as the weight of his words envelops her. She sighs deeply, her emotions coursing through her like a tide of joy and release. Without hesitation, she leans in and kisses him passionately, a kiss that seems to transcend time itself. The moment stretches endlessly, an unforgettable union of love, forgiveness, and renewal that neither will ever forget.

Chapter 2

Coherence

Nantucket Island, New England, Mass. (2019)
(Sunday morning, dawn)

As the newly reunited couple sits on the sand with a wool blanket around them, the ocean, just a few steps away, reflects the calm of the air's gentle breeze. They sip their hot teas, warmed by knee-high wool socks—the perfect touch for a crisp 50° morning—while waiting for sunrise to break on the horizon.

A week has passed since their unfinished conversation, and day by day, the ghosts of the past have begun to subside. The joy of being together again gradually erodes lingering guilt and grudges, but Erasmus senses that Victoria is not yet free of the emotional scars she carries. He knows more revelations will surface as she confronts her pain.

"He was a psychiatrist," she suddenly blurts out.

"Who? …" Erasmus begins to ask, but she interrupts, continuing her monologue.

"And he was much older than me."

She pauses, momentarily lost in time. Erasmus clings to her every word, sensing the gravity of her dialogue, though he's unsure where it's heading.

'Maybe this explains her past behavior,' Erasmus reflects. 'No! Could it be?' His thoughts are interrupted as his heartbeat quickens.

"Twenty-eight years my senior," she finally says, her voice tinged with lament.

"Old enough to be my father but chosen to be my husband," she adds bitterly.

The revelation hits him like a thunderbolt. He looks at her, immersed in thought, as if questioning who Victoria really is.

"As I look back, I see now how he manipulated me, how he manipulated my mother, and in a way, my entire family to suit his needs," she continues.

"During the first few years, I fell under his perverse and coercive spell. He persuaded me, therapeutically speaking, that the most effective way to make a clean break from my feelings for you was to focus on every negative thing I could remember about you—and to repeat it over and over."

"Did it work?"

"In the beginning, yes. I created an alternate reality to justify my behavior. But over time, my true feelings resurfaced, and that was the end of that."

'Finally, the truth,' Erasmus thinks, feeling an onslaught of emotions.

"He exploited my vulnerability as his patient, using his intimate insight into my emotional state. He slowly steered me toward him, subtly coercing me with arguments about social convenience and material wealth."

As she speaks, the disjointed puzzle in Erasmus' mind begins to come together, piece by piece, offering clarity.

"Reluctantly, I convinced myself I could control him better than I could control you. His intellect and personality didn't intimidate me like yours did. I didn't feel inadequate around him as I often felt around you. I also believed his economic position was the safer path for me and the children I hoped to have."

Erasmus has a million questions but knows better than to interrupt the cascade of life-altering revelations.

"But, my love, my children and I later paid a heavy price for my poor judgment. I traded true love for a caretaker role," she laments.

"In the end, he was the only winner. By buying me, he pulled himself out of the lonely state of a divorced man who had never experienced a meaningful emotional connection," she asserts with sadness.

"I lived a miserable and unhappy life as a woman, longing for you all these years. Motherhood saved my sanity; my children filled my empty heart with joy. I poured myself into loving and raising them, giving them as normal a life as possible. Outwardly, I pretended everything was fine."

She pauses briefly, her tone darkening. "Before he became ill, he was already just an old man I cared for daily. Over time, my children saw through it. I began speaking openly about you and us—even in front of him. He despised it, reacting sarcastically, saying, 'What does it matter? I got you in the end.'"

Erasmus, now in a trance, reflects, *What Vic's daughter said last year in class about her mother marrying the man her family chose must have been Sarah parroting the family's official story*, he reasons.

"My children loved him like a distant relative," Victoria explains. "There was no affection. I believe his children came only because of my persistence. He was never affectionate or close to them."

"How did you meet him?" Erasmus asks uneasily.

"He was my mother's psychiatrist. She insisted I see him when I turned eighteen, claiming I needed therapy for mood swings and bouts of depression," she recounts.

"After a month, he started asking me out for dinner. By the fifth month, he proposed to my parents. My mother immediately agreed, but my father was hesitant. Eventually, everyone ignored what I wanted.”

She pauses again, the rising sun illuminating the vast ocean around them, creating a stunning backdrop to her revelations.

“Dear, after that scene, I left for Boston. Eventually, we met, and I didn’t have contact with him again until I returned home three and a half years later,” she continues.

“Poignantly, a long time later, when he was terminally ill, he confessed he’d been infatuated with my mother but knew she would never cheat on her husband.”

“In a way, for him, having you was a twisted way of having your mother,” Erasmus states aloud.

“Yes, and sadly, for her, it was the same—a twisted way of having him,” she reveals.

Victoria pauses, the waves lapping at the shore echoing her turbulent emotions. “My doubts, anxieties, and insecurities drove me. My emotions were my undoing. This is simply the story of what happened.”

Erasmus gazes at her for what seems like an eternity. Then, tenderly tightening his embrace under the cozy wool blanket, he whispers, “My lady, that beautiful sunrise is the announcement of a glorious new day. Don’t you think it’s time to move on?”

The soothing notes of Neil Diamond’s “Hello” flow from their portable radio, signaling a renewed sense of life. They cuddle closer as the cool breeze picks up. Their teas, once warm, are now cold, a sharp contrast to their hearts, which glow with newfound warmth. Yet Erasmus notices lingering clouds in her eyes.

‘More is to come,’ he thinks, steady in his resolve. ‘Whatever it is, I’ll be ready.’

As he gently caresses Victoria’s silky-smooth cheeks, the Platters’ “Only You” begins to play. Standing together, their fingers entwine as they sway to the melody, their bodies impossibly close. Their satiated smiles exude peace, love, and joy, as the song's echoes envelop the nascent day.

Nantucket Island's Roads

Later that day, they pedal their way to the island's ferry, which will take them back to the mainland.

"What will be the subject of your class tomorrow, dear?" she asks curiously.

"Coherence."

"That is one anecdote I don't know about, right?"

"Right, it happened after I returned from Wales.

Royal Cambridge Scholastic Institute (2019)
(Next Day, University Backroads – on the way to the auditorium)

As he pedals steadily through the campus back roads, Professor Cromwell-Smith replays all the scenes Victoria described the day before, juxtaposing them with his own tribulations during that period of time.

Not long after, he walks into a packed auditorium, ready and eager to start.

"Good morning, everyone."

"Good morning, professor."

"At some point in time, hopefully sooner rather than later, we all must figure things out in life while looking for coherence. What do we want out of life? What does life mean to us? What is our purpose while we are here on our magnificent planet Earth? And one of the key existential tools that enable this examination is the glue that holds everything together so that things make sense in life. The glue is COHERENCE," affirms the eminent professor in his introductory remarks.

"When Victoria and I were living apart from each other, our lives were turned upside down. Today, I'll be taking you back to a day when I was handed an invaluable—lasting life lesson touching the subject of coherence."

"It begins like this …"

— ✛ —

Waldorf-Astoria Hotel, New York City (1977)

The coffee shop at the Waldorf-Astoria is packed with people from all over the world. Erasmus sips his customary and very British tea with milk while observing the potpourri of clothes, hats, faces, and bodily gestures.

"Erasmus, young man, what a pleasure it is to see you," exclaims the effusive Scottish antiquarian, Colin Carnegie, as he walks quickly toward him.

"Mr. Carnegie, it's so good to see you again."

"This time, it's just a short visit to the Big Apple," he says as he, quite fittingly, orders a hot tea with milk.

"Dear Erasmus, how have you been? Last time I saw you was at Cape Cod, at the New England Antiquarian Conference, where, as I understand it, you pulled a Houdini on all of us by vanishing in the middle of the night," quizzes and declares Mr. C, alluding to the famous escape artist.

"Mr. C, since I last saw you, I graduated from Harvard, went to Wales one last time, spent time with my family, and had a final and memorable session with my three mentors. Once back, I settled in Boston and accepted a teaching position at Brandeis University."

Carnegie stares at him in silence with a solemn smile.

"Extraordinary indeed. Congratulations, young man. But aren't you omitting something pertaining to your update?" states Mr. C, calling him out for deflecting the "escape stunt" aspect of his question.

Erasmus stares at Mr. C with deeply saddened eyes.

"She is gone, Mr. C!"

"She's obviously not here," states Carnegie while acknowledging within himself that, 'they were inseparable,' but there's firmness in his voice as if he's trying to get Erasmus to find courage.

"Unexpectedly, something quite transcendental must have happened, young man. This is the last thing I would've imagined. The two of you literally seemed like you were made for one another."

"My mentors back in Wales gifted me with a profound scribble named, 'the happiness formula.' It has been a great help to me in dealing with her absence, but I need your help on how to accept the loss."

"In moments like this, perhaps it's best to take a step back and contemplate things from a distance. I've got an idea. Come with me; let's take a stroll to my hallowed grounds while in New York," Mr. C announces as he signs the check.

They walk in pleasant weather, blended with the noisy background, through the streets of Manhattan. Erasmus pours out all his love, afflictions, and tribulations to the wise man from the Scottish Highlands. Time flies as they turn onto Fifth Avenue, and shortly thereafter, they enter the hall of the magnificent and timeless New York Public Library. As soon as they walk in, the plaque does not escape Erasmus. It's a dedication to the man who funded its construction and enabled its creation, Mr. C's distant relative, Andrew Carnegie.

'It figures, how fitting, right?' Erasmus mutters to himself.

'Where else would he have taken me other than here,' reflects Erasmus in admiration and with an almost imperceptible smile.

"Impressed?" asks Mr. C.

"Very much so, sir."

"Erasmus, always remember how many lasting good deeds this great Scottish American did and created with his wealth during his life."

"Always do, sir."

Mr. C gets lost inside the library's magnificent Rose Room for a while until he finds exactly what he's looking for. Erasmus sees the energetic man walk back with an enormous, seemingly ancient leather-bound book.

"Erasmus, this is a timeless scribble about one of the most imperative, consequential, and existential tasks every one of us has to perform in life and one you're in desperate need of conducting as soon as possible," declares Mr. C as he starts to read in earnest.

"Coherence"

(Figuring Things Out in Life)

Figuring things out in life
is to clearly define:
what we want out of life,
how we like to live,
who we chose to live with,
where are we heading,
what we believe in,
what we have a propensity for,
what we want to accomplish,
and what we intend to leave as our legacy.

Because, in the end,
we must seek and figure out
what life means to us.
Otherwise,
we wander through it
like lifeless souls

with empty spirits.

Figuring out life's meaning,
allows us to decipher and determine
our purpose and direction are in life.

Otherwise,
we bounce and drift aimlessly through life
like a rudderless vessel
or a craft without its compass.

Life's formula is different for each one of us.
The recipe of "How to Live"
is unique to every individual.
What makes sense for one, few, or many
may not make sense to others at all.

Thus, to avoid living someone else's life—
by copying their "sense-making"—
we must first figure out
what works for us,
then what works for others.

To figure things out in life,
we need coherence—
the glue that connects it all together.

Coherence is connecting in sensical harmony,
our existence with our aspirations and beliefs,
our actions with our dreams and goals,
our vocation, line of work, art or craft,
with our best talents and abilities,
our passions with mundane life,
our convictions and ideals
with what we practice in daily life,
our values and virtues with our faith,

our tempo with our life's clock,
our awareness of every second we have left on planet Earth,
our family, loved ones, fellow human beings
and the objects of our desire,
with the best side of our essence and nature.

To make sense of life
is to coherently connect
our life's meaning
with our life's purpose.

*

"Erasmus, coherence is the glue that creates sensical meaning and purpose in our lives; always remember, in order for us to resolve issues and figure things out, they have to make sense, and this is only possible through coherence."

Mr. Carnegie closes the leather-bound book with a decisive thud, its weight mirroring the gravity of his words. He places it gently on the table, his gaze locking with Erasmus's. "Now, young man, the rest is up to you," he says with a knowing smile, his voice tinged with a mix of encouragement and expectation. Erasmus nods slowly, the profound weight of the moment sinking in as he contemplates the wisdom just imparted.

The dim light of the Rose Room bathes them in an almost ethereal glow, as Erasmus watches Mr. Carnegie stride purposefully back into the labyrinth of bookshelves. Left alone with his thoughts, Erasmus lets the words linger, carving their place into his heart and mind.

— ❖ —

Royal Cambridge Scholastic Institute (2019)

(University Auditorium)

As his class comes back to the present, they find Professor Cromwell-Smith gazing intently at all of them.

The professor pauses, his eyes reflecting a depth of thought as he leans slightly against the lectern. "Mr. Carnegie's words stayed with me," he says, his voice softer now, almost reverent. "His insights on coherence became a compass, guiding me through some of my most challenging decisions." He straightens, his gaze sweeping across the room to meet the students' attentive faces. "Now, let us consider how we might apply such coherence in our own lives," he adds, drawing a contemplative silence over the class before continuing.

"So, what are you all waiting for?" he asks, his tone tinged with a hint of challenge.

Incredulous looks and surprised faces form and project themselves around the packed auditorium.

"Why don't you start figuring things out right away?" he presses, not letting the moment slip by.

"Now, I'd like to open the floor for questions." Professor Cromwell-Smith says, his tone inviting and warm. "Please feel free to ask anything related to the subjects we've covered today."

Charlotte, a fine arts major, known for her deep philosophical insights, raises her hand and is called upon.

"Professor, in the poem *Coherence*, the idea of connecting our aspirations with our beliefs and actions is emphasized. How do we reconcile the contradictions we sometimes experience between what we aspire to and what we practice daily? Can true coherence exist if our actions don't always align with our ideals?"

"An excellent question, Charlotte. The tension between our ideals and our actions is something many of us struggle with, and it's part of the human condition. In the poem, coherence is presented as the glue that holds all aspects of our life together. But it's important to recognize that coherence isn't about perfection; it's about striving for alignment. As we move through life, we must constantly reflect on our actions, learn from our mistakes, and adjust our behavior to better reflect our values. Coherence is an ongoing process, not a fixed state. It's the effort to make our lives and our actions as harmonious as possible with our beliefs, even if we fall short at times."

Benjamin asks the next question.

"Professor, on a previous class, you spoke about the dual nature of adversity—how it presents both hardship and opportunity. From a psychological standpoint, how can we develop greater coherence in our lives when our emotional responses sometimes contradict our intellectual understanding of situations?"

"Benjamin, that's a fascinating question. The emotional and intellectual aspects of our lives don't always align, and this creates what we call cognitive dissonance. In psychology, one way to bring more coherence is through emotional regulation—learning to manage our emotional responses in a way that aligns with our intellectual understanding. It takes mindfulness, self-awareness, and practice. Over time, we can cultivate a sense of harmony by consciously working to bridge the gap between our emotions and rational thought, which is precisely what the poem refers to when it talks about connecting our actions, beliefs, and feelings."

Scarlett, a history major, is next.

"Professor, in *Coherence*, the idea of 'figuring things out in life' is central. You spoke about how coherence connects our existence with our aspirations and values. But sometimes, life presents us with challenges that shake our sense of coherence. How do we restore it when it feels like we've lost our way?"

"That's an insightful question, Scarlett. Life's challenges are often the tests that challenge our coherence—when we feel uncertain, adrift, or disconnected. The poem suggests that coherence is about harmonizing our inner and outer worlds, but when things become unbalanced, we need to return to our values and aspirations. It's about re-centering, reassessing where we've gone off-course, and realigning ourselves with our purpose. When we feel lost, it's often a sign that we've strayed from our core values, so restoring coherence is about taking a step back, reflecting, and making intentional choices to reconnect with what truly matters to us."

Sebastian, an Education major, speaks up next.

"Professor, the poem emphasizes the importance of coherence in making sense of life, but sometimes we're faced with contradictions that challenge that sense. How do we deal with situations where the alignment between our beliefs and actions seems impossible to reconcile? Is it a matter of making compromises, or do we need to revise our beliefs entirely?"

"Another very thoughtful question, Sebastian. In life, contradictions are inevitable—no matter how hard we try to maintain coherence, sometimes our circumstances or actions lead us into conflict with our ideals. The key is to approach this with humility and awareness. It's not about perfection, but about progress. If the alignment between our beliefs and actions feels impossible, we may need to reassess our priorities, reflect on whether our beliefs are still serving us, or whether a shift in perspective is needed. Making compromises can be part of the process, but only if those compromises don't undermine our core values. The goal is to navigate life with intention, and when necessary, to make adjustments that preserve our integrity."

"That will be all for today. I'll see you all next week," Professor Cromwell-Smith concludes, his words lingering like echoes of wisdom. He observes the expressions across the student body morphing into the curious looks of explorers about to embark on journeys into uncharted waters.

As the students rise and file out of the auditorium, he hands each of them a copy of the happiness formula, his gesture filled with quiet hope for their journeys ahead.

As the last of his students exit the auditorium, their murmured conversations fading into the corridor beyond, Professor Cromwell-Smith lingers at the lectern, gazing out over the now-empty seats. The silence feels heavier, more contemplative, after the depth of their shared discussion. Gathering his notes and adjusting his glasses, he allows himself a rare moment of reflection. The echoes of the past and present intertwine, and he silently wonders which seeds of wisdom, if any, have found fertile ground among his students.

Man's endless search for meaning and purpose in life. We all need to figure these two things out first, he reflects, recalling the poignant words of the eminent Holocaust survivor Viktor Frankl.

Straightening his posture, he walks toward the door, his mind already preparing for the next lecture—a chance to explore life's complexities further and, perhaps, to inspire a few more hearts.

Stepping out of the faculty building, his eyes fall on his trusted old bike, ready and waiting for the next journey.

Chapter 3

Virtue

Royal Cambridge Scholastic Institute (2019)
(Sunday Morning, Campus Backwoods)

Erasmus and Victoria meander through the trees, holding hands. His grip is resolute as he strives to make her feel safe and sheltered by his presence. But, above all, he wants her to sense that she is no longer alone.

'Last weekend's shared revelations at Nantucket Island were not her last,' he reminds himself as she leans closer to him while they stroll.

The river emerges into view through the foliage, and a fresh breeze whispers through the treetops. A small clearing reveals itself, and Victoria proclaims it an ideal spot to set up their picnic lunch.

Seated and laughing, the middle-aged couple reminisces about Erasmus' latest absentminded mishap. This one infuriated half the faculty as he introduced six of his colleagues attending one of his classes as his fellow professors visiting from Brandeis University—despite having left that venerable institution decades ago.

Right in the middle of her laughter, he notices something. Behind her broad, radiant smile, he discerns a pair of cloudy, solemn eyes.

'Deadly serious they are indeed,' he murmurs in anticipation. Abruptly, they lock eyes, and she knows he has perfectly deciphered her mood.

'Here we go,' he realizes, bracing himself for her "previous life" dam-bursting exercise.

"Dear, there are still parts of my history that I want to share with you," she declares.

"I know, my lady. Do it at your own pace," he assures her gently, his tone receptive and steady.

"Well, I'm in a hurry, rushing because I feel open and comfortable sharing it with you right now. I also want to put it behind us," Victoria reasons aloud.

"As you wish, my lady. I'm all yours," he replies, smiling and kissing her softly on her lips.

"Well, let me take you back to a crucial moment when an old librarian imparted one of the most profound life lessons I have ever received. This lesson may very well be the reason we found each other again," she says, her words deliberate and weighty.

"It begins like this…

— ✦ —

For almost two decades after I got married, I had been living in Hamilton, Illinois, just across the river from St. Louis, Missouri. On this momentous day, I was supposed to drop off one of my daughters at her college before driving across town to teach a class at the university."

St. Louis, Missouri (1998)

(Mississippi River Bridge, crossing from Illinois to Missouri)

"Mom, I overheard the entire discussion," states Elizabeth, Victoria's 18-year-old daughter.

An eerie silence envelops mother and daughter as they drive through heavy rain across the Mississippi River into St. Louis' city center.

"Your father can be difficult at times, dear," Victoria replies softly.

Victoria's oldest daughter is restless and conflicted. She yearns to speak her mind but respects her mother too much to unleash her full frustration.

"Petulant," Elizabeth blurts out impulsively.

Victoria flinches slightly, taken aback, yet she hesitates to respond with anything but love.

"He loves you all very much," Victoria tries to reassure her daughter again, her tone calm yet strained.

"How do you put up with him?" questions Elizabeth, her restraint breaking as her emotions spill over.

"Family always comes first, Elizabeth," Victoria pleads, but the hollowness of her words does not escape either of them.

"Mother, stop deflecting. Don't you think this is a conversation we need to have?" demands Elizabeth, her voice resolute and insistent.

Tension builds in the family van, the air thick with countless unspoken truths. Visibility is almost nonexistent, and the relentless rain reduces their progress to a slow crawl.

"You're absolutely right," Victoria admits after a pause.

"Perhaps this is an excellent opportunity to do something I've wanted to do for a long time. You still have a couple of hours before your class begins; mine is three hours away. I'm taking you to a very special place where we can sit down and talk about anything you want."

St. Louis Public Library (1998)
(Downtown Area)

After so many years, the old habit persists. Every other week, Victoria visits one of the three librarians in the city. Over the years, they've all become close friends and, in a way, life mentors. Today, for the first time, she isn't visiting alone.

The head of the City of St. Louis' public library, Rebecca Samuels-Ortiz, is a 65-year-old dynamo of energy. With over three decades of experience at the library, she has practically adopted Victoria since they met about a decade ago. At a glance, Rebecca immediately senses Victoria's distress as she approaches, a young woman walking alongside her.

'Another clash with the mind doctor?' Rebecca muses. Then, the striking resemblance between Victoria and the young woman captures her attention.

The two women embrace warmly while young Elizabeth stands by, observing. She feels like she's stepping into a private world her mother has carefully guarded.

"Becca, this is my oldest, Elizabeth," says Victoria, pulling her daughter closer with one arm.

"Dear, Rebecca has been a close friend, mentor, counselor, and crying shoulder of mine for more than a decade," she adds, introducing Elizabeth to the effusive librarian.

Elizabeth and Rebecca exchange a hug. Rebecca, in the purest French tradition, kisses the surprised teenager on both cheeks.

"Your mom has told me so much about you," Rebecca declares warmly.

'Well, she hasn't told me a word about you,' Elizabeth thinks to herself, her skepticism rising.

'Besides, weren't we supposed to have a serious conversation about family matters?' she silently quibbles.

"Nice to meet you," Elizabeth says, outwardly polite but inwardly uneasy.

"The pleasure is mine," Rebecca responds with a welcoming smile.

Elizabeth nods back, her smile warmer than her growing discomfort allows.

Rebecca guides them across the library's main hall to a massive work and reading table. Seated at one corner, Rebecca and Elizabeth exchange subtle, inquisitive glances, as if sizing each other up.

"Victoria, for you to bring your precious daughter here is a remarkable step in the right direction," Rebecca states with conviction. "It's a step toward confronting reality, opening up, and making long-overdue decisions."

Elizabeth's frustration bubbles to the surface. "What are we doing here? I specifically asked Mom for a conversation about serious family matters," she blurts out.

Rebecca, unfazed, continues, her tone soothing yet firm. "But you brought Elizabeth here for a reason, didn't you?"

Victoria's tumultuous gaze mirrors her uncertainty, and Elizabeth is startled by Rebecca's insight. She turns to the older woman, her expression a mix of surprise and curiosity.

"Elizabeth, there are many significant things about your mom's life that you don't know. Some are painful, but many are wonderful," Rebecca begins gently. "You must be patient and allow her to open up at her own pace. Whatever she's ready to share, she will, in her own time. Bringing you here today was a transformative step for her—something she's long meant to do and worked hard to accomplish."

Elizabeth's anger softens as Rebecca's words resonate.

"Thank you for helping me understand," Victoria whispers, her eyes glistening with gratitude as she looks at Rebecca.

Mother and daughter embrace tightly, their bond deepened by the moment.

"Love you so much, Mom," Elizabeth says joyfully.

"Love you too, dear. Love you too," Victoria replies, her voice brimming with relief.

"Victoria, seize the moment. What you've been dreaming of for so long has finally happened," Rebecca declares.

Victoria's eyes widen in intensity, her exhaustion giving way to determination.

"Boston University has offered you a position—it's time for you to pursue your dreams and...find him," Rebecca says with finality.

"I'll be right back," she adds, stepping away to attend to some inquiring visitors.

'Boston? What's going on? Has my mother gone completely crazy?' Elizabeth wonders, her thoughts swirling in a storm of confusion and uncertainty.

"Find who, Mom?" Elizabeth asks, consumed by angst.
Victoria gently presses a finger to Elizabeth's lips.

"All in due time, dear."

Mrs. Samuels-Ortiz strides back with quick steps, a smile brightening her face.

"Elizabeth, be open and understanding with your mom. On this occasion, your best attributes must come to the forefront— tolerance, forgiveness, perseverance, and hope. They are all required of you now," Mrs. Samuels-Ortiz states as an overture.

The erudite librarian fixes her gaze on Victoria for what feels like an eternity. The moment has come to share what they've rehearsed so many times before. Finally, Victoria closes her eyes slowly and nods in consent. Mrs. Samuels-Ortiz then recounts to Elizabeth the story of her mother's love for Erasmus, their breakup, and the circumstances of her marriage to her father. Elizabeth sits motionless, her blank stare seeming to bore into a void as she absorbs and processes the revelations.

"Mom, why did you marry Dad if you didn't love him?" she asks insistently and continues without waiting for a reply. "The

two of you are so different; you never agree on anything. Age-wise, he could be your father," Elizabeth admonishes.

Victoria's world spins as if it's careening out of control, her daughter's mature words slicing through her carefully maintained composure. But life begins to smile upon her for the good deeds she has done over the years and the amends she has sought to make in her pursuit of happiness.

"Mother, then there's all his philandering with patients. How long are you going to put up with it?"

Elizabeth's words are harsh, but Victoria finds great relief in the realization that her daughter is solidly on her side.

"Are you one of his conquests as well?" Elizabeth presses relentlessly. "And what's going on between Grandma and Dad? She adores him, but in a sick kind of way, Mom. If she weren't my grandmother, I would swear she has the hots for him," declares an even more outraged Elizabeth.

Victoria's emotional walls crumble, and she starts to sob intermittently, unsure of how to respond. Her face is soaked in tears as Elizabeth continues.

"Mom, we can do this another time," Elizabeth offers with concern, guilt, and understanding, gently caressing her mom's tear-streaked face.

"Aren't you mad at me?" Victoria asks.

"How could I be? I'm happy you truly do love someone because you don't love Dad."

"Elizabeth, perhaps the most important thing I should add to your perceptive observations is that what your father did professionally—acting as your mom's psychiatrist—was wrong. He exploited a young, vulnerable woman and manipulated both your grandmother and your mom into a situation that nearly destroyed your mom's life," adds Mrs. Samuels-Ortiz.

Elizabeth remains composed, unshaken by the details that have haunted Victoria and Mrs. Samuels-Ortiz for so long. The reason is simple—she already knows much of it. What consumes her mind is one thing—her father's outrageous behavior.

"Mom, you never mentioned his philandering before," Elizabeth declares.

"Call me a fool or naïve, but perhaps it's because I don't love him, so I don't care. But it's mortifying that you, my child, are calling me out. We, as parents, fool ourselves endlessly, believing that our kids don't notice or understand the things we try to hide. How wrong we are. You see it all. You record everything. You even understand things, like this, better than we do. I've come to realize that every word, action, and display that affects our loved ones carries consequences, lying in wait in the future, inexorably catching up with us," Victoria capitulates in surrender.

"Victoria, it's clear that for some time now, your children have understood your situation. Elizabeth's words show they believe you've known all about the mind doctor's behavior and have intentionally looked the other way," intervenes Mrs. Samuels-Ortiz to expose the deeper truth.

Mother and daughter clasp hands, contemplating the erudite librarian before embracing each other tightly, as if holding on for dear life.

As they prepare to leave, Mrs. Samuels-Ortiz interjects with one final reminder.

"Just to remind you, Victoria, Boston University requires your reply right away. Do I have your authorization to give them an affirmative response?"

"Of course you do, Becca. Nothing and no one in the world will stop me from moving to Boston," Victoria asserts with

conviction and finality, despite having no assurance of her husband's stance on the matter.

The old librarian beams with satisfaction, knowing her persistent efforts haven't been in vain. Victoria would never have confronted this issue on her own; she needed the steady push from her trusted friend.

As Mrs. Samuels-Ortiz waves them off, she watches the mother and daughter walk away, pride swelling in her heart. In this one encounter, she has fulfilled two long-standing missions— Victoria has finally shared her story with her children and taken the decisive step to move back to Boston in search of her true love.

— ✦ —

Royal Cambridge Scholastic Institute (2019)
(Picnic in the woods, by the riverside)

"Dear, Mrs. Samuels-Ortiz shared a wonderful ancient scribble with us that day. Its contents not only profoundly moved Elizabeth and me but also fortified my resolve, giving me the strength to make the decisions I eventually took to move closer to you. I would like you to share this with your class if you think it's appropriate," Victoria implores, pulling a small scroll from the picnic basket and offering it to him.

"What is it about?" Erasmus inquires while carefully unfolding it.

"Virtue," she replies with a quiet conviction.

Royal Cambridge Scholastic Institute (2019)
(Campus streets, the next day)

Professor Cromwell-Smith has been pedaling for almost an hour, weaving through the silent, empty campus roads. He's still absorbing everything he learned about Victoria's life, replaying the revelations and their impact on both of them. To his great relief, the previous night, Victoria slept soundly and woke up with a sunny disposition that warmed his heart.

With a lingering sense of fulfillment from their quiet morning together, Erasmus slowly makes his way to campus, the weight of their shared moments guiding him to class. His mind is alight with thoughts of the conversation ahead, eager yet reflective.

It's working, he muses with a soft smile, recognizing that she's steadily putting much of the emotional trauma behind her.

'Nothing compares to the companionship of love for overcoming pain and sorrow,' he reasons, his thoughts carrying him as he parks his old, rusty bike in the faculty parking lot.

Walking through the halls, the morning air feels especially invigorating. He's inspired in an extraordinary way. His admiration for Victoria swells—not just for how she has navigated her life following what he considers a monumental gaffe of existential proportions, but for the way she is now courageously reconstructing her future. She's confronting her past head-on, without glossing over any part of her personal history.

It's a rare and profound kind of bravery, and he treasures it deeply.

Royal Cambridge Scholastic Institute (2019)
(University's Auditorium)

As he enters the classroom, the familiar hum of students' voices brings him back to the present, grounding him in the purpose of the day. Erasmus glances over the eager faces, each student ready to engage with the new subject matter that awaits them.

"Good morning, everyone," he greets with a big, wide smile.

"Good morning, professor," the class roars back in unison.

"Today, we're going to be talking about virtue. I'll take you back to a pivotal moment when Victoria and her oldest daughter were given a timeless life lesson—one that helped them make crucial decisions that changed the course of their lives. These experiences, I believe, were instrumental in leading to our eventual reunion."

He pauses, letting the weight of his words settle over the room, before continuing, his voice calm and deliberate.

"It begins like this …"

— ✳ —

St. Louis Public Library (1998)

Rebecca Samuels-Ortiz has been the head of the St. Louis Public Library for decades. The erudite librarian has served as Victoria's friend and life mentor for over a decade. On this momentous day, Victoria has brought her oldest daughter, 18-year-old Elizabeth, to meet Mrs. Samuels-Ortiz for the first time. It is a day to remember, as Victoria has made the monumental decision to move back to Boston with her family.

Mrs. Samuels-Ortiz, ever attuned to the gravity of the moment, retrieves a cherished manuscript. Her eyes sparkle with anticipation as she addresses the two women before her.

"Ladies, I have here a precious scribble—timeless wisdom that perfectly suits this occasion, especially as you prepare for such an eventful transition," she announces warmly, her tone a blend of solemnity and enthusiasm.

She carefully unfolds the manuscript and begins to read, her voice soft and resonant, espousing love and empathy with every word.

"Virtue"

Just by arriving on planet Earth,
just by being alive,
we are born in grace—
but we are not born in virtue.

Virtue must be acquired over time,
through hard work, dedication and perseverance.

Virtues are not obsequious.
On the contrary,
they must be:
learned and applied,
sought and sweated,
identified and pursued,
nurtured and harvested,
cultivated with discipline,
and developed with sacrifice.

We acquire knowledge
to gain insight, wisdom, and good judgment.

We build brave hearts and fortitude
to nurture courage, tenacity, and valor.

We practice compassion and benevolence
to learn empathy and mindfulness
which perennially results in loving mankind.

We exercise unwavering truthfulness
and unflinching integrity
to cement our honesty, honor, probity, and a good name.

We embrace serenity and silence
to pause, reflect
and become considerate, and thoughtful.

We live with order and neatness
to grow structured, methodical, and organized.

We pursue righteousness and rightfulness
to attain fairness, correctness, and impartiality.

We embody unfaltering hope, boundless generosity,
endless gratitude, and genuine humility
seeking to exceed and surpass
all we have received,
forming our legacy from it.

As our virtues grow,
they mature into a state of noble excellence.

As they evolve,
virtues become the genesis
and enablers of our beliefs and value systems.

Virtues are imperative tools of life,
without chasing and procuring them,
we are incomplete—
not fully functional, coherent, or guided.

Without virtues,
we march through life with blinders on,
unable to extract the fruits of joy
from a life lived in full.

Our virtues form the foundation of our values,
which, in turn,
become the pillars of our character.

Without a solid set of virtues,
our values are incomplete or flawed,
causing seismic faults in our character.

To be virtuous is to be equipped
with a precious set of attributes,
leading us to excellence.

It is to conduct ourselves
by extraordinary standards of nobility,
righteousness, sensibility, and rightfulness.
It is to live under the mantle of inspiration and joy,
guided by a virtuous existence—
a life in full.

*

Mrs. Samuels-Ortiz folds the manuscript gently, the faint rustle of the pages breaking the silence. She looks at Victoria and Elizabeth, her eyes filled with both hope and seriousness. "Victoria, this move marks a new chapter for you and your family. Carry these words with you as a guide, not just for yourself, but for your children as they forge their paths." She offers Elizabeth a warm, knowing smile.

The young woman nods thoughtfully, her mother reaching for her hand in a silent gesture of unity. The atmosphere is thick with unspoken emotions as Mrs. Samuels-Ortiz places the manuscript back in its protective sleeve. For a moment, no one speaks, the weight of the moment hanging gently in the room.

"I'll cherish these words, Rebecca," Victoria says at last, her voice steady but tinged with emotion. The three women share a brief embrace, one that seems to acknowledge the significance of the moment without the need for further explanation.

—✦—

Royal Cambridge Scholastic Institute (2019)
(University's Auditorium)

Professor Cromwell brings the class back to the present with an expression of absolute calm and tranquility. The pedagogue gazes across the room, his students silent and attentive. He lets the moment linger before speaking.

With Victoria's voice still resonating in his mind, the pedagogue feels a gentle pull towards the past. In his reflection, he finds himself transported back to that pivotal moment in St. Louis, where her history had intersected with her future.

"Class, virtuosity is only achieved by deliberate and disciplined effort over a prolonged period of time," he concludes, his words imbued with wisdom. His piercing gaze seems to connect with each of his elated students, leaving a profound impression.

"Now, I'd like to open the floor for questions," Professor Cromwell-Smith says, his tone inviting and warm. "Please feel free to ask anything related to the subjects we've covered today."

Amelia, a performing arts major, raises her hand and is called upon.

"Professor, in the poem *Virtue*, the idea of acquiring virtue through hard work and perseverance is emphasized. How do we reconcile the tension between the virtues we aspire to embody and the imperfections we experience in our daily lives? How do we navigate moments when our actions don't align with our aspirations?"

"Amelia, that's a profound question. The pursuit of virtue requires a continuous effort to align our ideals with our actions. Virtue is something we build over time, but as you've noted, there are moments when our actions don't reflect the virtues we strive for. This is the challenge of being human: we're constantly working to align who we are with who we want to be. In the poem, we see that virtue is not an innate trait but something we must actively cultivate through effort, discipline, and reflection. It's important to acknowledge that perfection isn't required— virtue is about striving, and in moments when our actions don't align with our aspirations, the key is to learn from those moments and keep pushing forward."

James, a Psychology major, asks the next question.

"Professor, in the context of virtue, how do we approach the emotional and cognitive challenges we face when trying to embody virtues such as compassion or courage? For instance, how do we remain compassionate when we feel emotionally drained, or how do we summon courage when fear seems overwhelming?"

"James, that's a great question. The challenge of embodying virtues, especially in the face of emotional or cognitive dissonance, is part of the human experience. In those moments, it's important to remember that virtue isn't about always feeling the right way—it's about acting in alignment with our values, even when emotions are challenging. For instance, compassion isn't just about feeling empathy but about actively choosing to extend care, even when we're tired or overwhelmed. Similarly, courage isn't the absence of fear, but the willingness to act in spite of it. Over time, as we practice these virtues, they become more ingrained in our character. But, like all virtues, they require conscious effort and a willingness to continue cultivating them, even when it's difficult."

Daisy, a philosophy major, asks her question next.

"Professor, the poem suggests that virtues are the foundation of character, yet the process of developing them is a long and demanding one. How can we, as individuals, maintain motivation and resilience in the pursuit of virtue, especially when the results may not be immediately visible?"

"Daisy, that's an excellent point. The journey toward virtue is indeed long and sometimes grueling. It's easy to lose motivation when the results are not immediately apparent. One of the key ideas in the poem is that virtues don't just appear overnight— they are cultivated through consistent effort and practice. The best way to maintain motivation is to recognize that the process itself is a part of the reward. Virtue isn't just about the end result;

it's about who we become along the way. Even small, incremental steps towards embodying virtue are valuable. It's also helpful to remind ourselves of the bigger picture—how living a virtuous life brings meaning, purpose, and coherence to our existence. In those moments of doubt, reflecting on our 'why'—the deeper purpose behind pursuing virtue—can reignite our resolve."

Henry, a creative writing major, speaks up next.

"Professor, the poem emphasizes that virtue is something we must actively pursue and cultivate over time. Given the current challenges and complexities of our world, how do we ensure that the virtues we develop are meaningful in the context of our modern lives? How can we navigate the often-overwhelming nature of modern existence while still prioritizing the cultivation of virtue?"

"Henry, that's a very relevant question. The modern world can be overwhelming, and it often seems like the pace of life makes it difficult to focus on the deeper aspects of our existence, such as cultivating virtue. However, it's precisely in such a world that the pursuit of virtue becomes even more essential. In the poem, we see that virtues are not just abstract ideals; they are the foundation of a meaningful and coherent life. Even in the chaos of modern existence, we can make choices that align with our values. The key is to remain intentional and mindful in our actions—whether it's taking time to reflect, practicing compassion, or maintaining integrity in our work and relationships. In a world filled with distractions, it's easy to lose sight of what truly matters. But by prioritizing the cultivation of virtue, we give ourselves the clarity and strength to navigate the complexities of life with purpose and meaning."

"That will be all for today. I'll see you all next week," Professor Cromwell-Smith concludes, his words lingering like echoes of wisdom. As the students rise and file out of the auditorium, he hands each of them a copy of the happiness formula, his gesture filled with quiet hope for their journeys ahead.

As the bell rings, the students slowly gather their belongings and file out of the auditorium, their faces marked with contemplation. Professor Cromwell-Smith gathers his notes, pausing briefly as he looks out at the now-empty hall. He allows himself a quiet smile, knowing that the words of *Virtue* will echo far beyond this classroom, shaping lives in ways that might only become evident in the years to come.

As the last of his students exit the auditorium, their murmured conversations fading into the corridor beyond, Professor Cromwell-Smith lingers at the lectern, gazing out over the now-empty seats. The silence feels heavier, more contemplative, after the depth of their shared discussion. Gathering his notes and adjusting his glasses, he allows himself a rare moment of reflection. The echoes of the past and present intertwine, and he silently wonders which seeds of wisdom, if any, have found fertile ground among his students.

Straightening his posture, he walks toward the door, his mind already preparing for the next lecture—a chance to explore life's complexities further and, perhaps, to inspire a few more hearts. The professor hurries out of the auditorium with a subtle knot in his stomach. As he departs, he notices the rapt expressions of many students, their faces etched with curiosity and a hunger for further understanding.

There's no path to virtuosity without a preceding stage of self-discovery, he reflects as he steps out of the faculty building, silently wishing that his students would undertake such an introspective journey.

As he approaches the parking lot, his eyes catch sight of Victoria waiting with their bikes. Relief washes over him, and he slows his pace, a broad smile spreading across his face as he takes in the sight of her.

"I'm right here, you old fool," she says playfully, her voice overflowing with affection and a deep understanding of him.

"I just rushed to make sure you were safe," he replies, attempting to justify his now-spent hurriedness.

"Time to go home, my demented Brit."

"Yes, my lady, your whims are my command," he responds with mock chivalry, his grin widening.

As the couple pedals away side by side, a group of students notices them and begins to comment.

"They look like a pair of teenagers, madly crazy in love," one observes, her voice tinged with admiration.

"They have to be," a tall young woman interjects thoughtfully. "After all, they're making up for so much lost time—a lifetime spent apart. What else would you expect

"My take," another student adds, "is that maybe we should try to be more like them all the time, not just when we're trying to make up for lost time."

Chapter 4

Forgiveness

Salisbury Beach, Massachusetts (2019)

Those seabirds sometimes replace the whistling sounds of the autumn wind. The air feels infused with the briny aroma of unspoiled marine life. The sands of the wide beach swallow their feet with every step they take. With his arm wrapped securely around her shoulders and hers snugly around his waist, they walk endlessly against the fading light, as if lost in their own intimate sunset.

Their weekend escapades feel second nature to them, an unbroken thread from their youthful days to their rekindled love. Erasmus senses the unspoken tension building within Victoria. Her eyes, though often warm and reflective, betray a lingering unease. Her hesitation is palpable, but her resolve quietly prevails.

"Dear, one more event happened right after my youngest child, Sarah, found you," Victoria begins, her voice tinged with gravity.

"It was one of the most difficult moments I've ever faced with any of my children. But it needed to happen. I hadn't moved in with you yet. One morning, Sarah came into my bedroom and simply let out everything she had been holding inside," she says, her words weighed by the memory.

"It began like this …"

—✳—

Victoria Emerson-Lloyd, Family Home (2017)
(Boston, Massachusetts)

"Mom, this may surprise you because I've always wholeheartedly supported your re-encounter with Professor Cromwell, but it wasn't like that initially. When the three of us decided to go and look for him, I was the only one who hesitated a little, but not for long. Later, when I finally met him as my teacher, the whole experience was amazing. The feelings that made me hesitate originally just disappeared," Sarah declares, her voice quivering slightly yet firm with conviction.

Victoria sits motionless, absorbing her daughter's words.

Sarah, usually so spirited and light-hearted, has never spoken with such solemnity.

"Mother, this may be a simplistic way of looking at things—after all, I am only a teenager—but your love life reminds me of a movie I adore," she ventures, laying the groundwork for her thoughts.

"As in The Vow, at some point in your life, you broke away from what you were supposed to be in life—another unhappily married career woman, raised in an environment where appearances and wealth trumped everything, and love was a rational decision of convenience. But at some point, you were brave and bold enough to leave home, abandon your prescribed career, and set out to pursue what you were meant to be. Life smiled at you, and true love found you. Unfortunately, when life-altering decisions came your way, you ran away and literally had an attack of complete denial. You seemed to have forgotten all you had loved and enjoyed while on your own—being your true self under the mantle of true love. You erased the important little things: the endless gestures, the intensity, and the magnificence of a well-lived life. It all simply vanished. You replaced history with an alternate reality—a complete fiction of your imagination. Sadly, you returned to your old ways and, for a while, tried

once more to be what your family and social environment expected of you—what you were 'supposed' to be all along. Of course, by doing so, you ran yourself off an emotional cliff, almost destroying your life until you snapped out of it and went back to your true love. You were so fortunate to find him again because, Mom, I'm a diehard fan of Professor Cromwell-Smith," Sarah concludes passionately, her words tumbling out like a torrent.

The stillness in the room is palpable, amplifying every breath and every movement. Victoria begins to cry softly, her arms crossed as she gently rocks herself.

"Enough," interrupts Elizabeth, Victoria's eldest daughter, entering the room and wrapping her arms protectively around her mother.

"No, dear. Let her be. She's right, you know," Victoria counters gently, pushing Elizabeth aside with care.

She approaches Sarah, who sits huddled on the sofa, her face buried in her hands. Kneeling in front of her, Victoria tenderly places her hands on Sarah's head, smoothing her hair with loving strokes.

"Look at me, dear," Victoria whispers, her voice firm yet overflowing with love. At first, Sarah peeks through her fingers hesitantly, but her eyes widen in surprise as they meet her mother's gaze—brimming with acceptance and warmth.

"What you've just released, vented, is essentially all true. You've seen through me in a way I would've never imagined. Dear, I work hard every single day to make amends for the bad choices I've made. I also promise to keep pushing forward until we can all leave the past behind us," Victoria says with conviction, her voice steady even as her eyes glisten with unshed tears.

Mother and daughter embrace tightly, their connection renewed as if an immense barrier has been shattered. In their union, the weight of guilt and misunderstanding begins to lift, leaving room for healing and hope.

— ✦ —

Salisbury Beach, Massachusetts (2019)

Night has set in, and a full moon shows the way for Erasmus and Victoria.

"My lady, your daughter was a bit too harsh on you. I can understand why she felt that way, and I don't excuse your actions, but she ignored your circumstances," states a solemn Erasmus.

"Dear, you know what? She wanted to hold me accountable and for me to take some responsibility instead of deflecting everything on her dad. And she was right in pointing that out to me because it gave me the courage and determination to share everything with you in the last few weeks," says Victoria with a relieved, big, broad smile.

"But the most beautiful thing coming out of that conversation with Sarah is that she adores you, my absentminded Brit." Victoria celebrates by laughing and kissing Erasmus all over his face.

"My lady, let me suggest something to you. Tomorrow in class, I'll take everyone to a moment when I received a great life lesson about forgiveness. Please join me as I'm certain it'll be of great help to us, and hopefully, once and for all, we'll put closure to the open wounds about our broken past that still linger," pleads Erasmus.

"I'll bring Sarah along. I'm sure it'll also be helpful for her," Victoria enthusiastically declares.

The moment she hears the unmistakable, inseparable tune coming out of their battered radio, it triggers her feelings; she looks at him with inviting eyes.

"Aren't you going to ask me to dance?" she sweetly asks as the contagious slow dance rhythm of Aretha Franklin's "Giving Him Something He Can Feel" can be heard softly in the background as it makes its way through the star-studded sky and silver-lined blackness of the dormant ocean. Faraway in their own bubble of love, impossibly paused, they dance under the mantle of a radiant New England night.

Royal Cambridge Scholastic Institute (2019)
(Next Day, University Auditorium)

As Erasmus pedals through the quiet, misty streets of the campus, his mind shifts from the peaceful morning he shared with Victoria to the task ahead—teaching the concept of forgiveness. With each turn of the pedals, he is reminded of the lessons he himself has learned in the past few weeks and how they will guide today's class. The journey, though familiar, feels different today; it is not just the route he is taking to class but also the path he is walking emotionally.   Erasmus reaches the university auditorium, the familiar building now filled with the quiet hum of students settling in for class. His footsteps echo through the hall as he enters, his heart still stirred by his earlier conversation with Victoria. As he walks towards the lectern, he reflects on how much he has grown, and how today's lesson will hopefully guide his students toward the same healing he has found. He smiles briefly, nodding to a few familiar faces in the front row before he begins.

"How's everyone today?" asks the professor.

"Insanely awesome," is the collective response.

The class buzz sounds more like a murmur as everyone notices the presence of Victoria and her youngest daughter, Sarah, sitting on a couple of chairs provided by the professor.

"Forgiveness," Erasmus begins, his voice steady but filled with the depth of the experience he's shared, "is not merely a concept we learn about—it is a practice, an essential part of life that allows us to move forward." He pauses, letting the weight of the word settle in the room. "It is also one of the most challenging virtues we can cultivate, but it is the one that opens doors to healing and peace." His gaze sweeps the room, meeting the eyes of his students.

"Our willingness and ability to forgive are crucial elements of a happy and wholesome life," the professor declares.

"Holding grudges, resentment or ill feelings against others sends us in the opposite direction, disconnecting our gratefulness and indulgence for the privilege of being alive," he continues.

"Today, I'll be taking you back to a moment in my life when I learned the true meaning of forgiveness. A remarkable reunion with a very influential person in my life. That day, she provided me with the type of understanding I needed and a lifelong lesson about the existential virtue of forgiveness. It begins like this ..."

—◆—

Boston (1979)

He doesn't know if it's a curse or a blessing that he has a few free summer weeks before the commencement of his teaching career. He prefers not to revisit any places he and Victoria frequented, nor is he inclined to meet with the antiquarians they had previously visited. To keep himself occupied, he starts to write—first a diary, then essays, short stories, and poems. Soon, he's toying with the idea of writing a novel. As the days pass, some of his emotional roadblocks begin to fade. That's how the idea of visiting one of his most trusted mentors takes shape and evolves until he finds himself on his way to see her.

Train Ride from Boston to Lanesville, Massachusetts (1979)

Leaving Boston's central station early, he's inundated with mixed emotions as the train carries him to Lanesville. The ride through the magnificent countryside stirs memories of Victoria—their bikes in tow, the picnic baskets, the overnight stays at bed-and-breakfasts, and particularly their visits with Mrs. Peabody, the ebullient antiquarian. His thoughts play like a movie, scene by scene, including every dialogue he and Victoria had shared with her. He recalls the last set of poems Mrs. Peabody sent to Victoria and how much they had both cherished them.

Lanesville, Massachusetts (1979)

(Mrs. Peabody's Antique Book Shop)

The quaint train station at Lanesville reinforces the feeling of nostalgia. After leaving the station, he pedals along the New England coast's shoreline road, looking forward to meeting his trusted mentor and friend. However, a little while later, he's disappointed—the shop seems empty as he steps inside the vast and chaotic space. After searching the store in vain, Erasmus sits, waits, and being his usual self, when not occupied with either mind or body, promptly falls soundly asleep!

He dreams of faraway places, traveling in search of Victoria, only to be turned away each time by cruel strangers who refuse to reveal her whereabouts. The intruding sound begins faintly, far off, and repeats every few seconds until it finally pulls him from his deep sleep. Slowly, he opens his eyes.

"It seems as if a full orchestra is needed to wake your highness up," an amused Mrs. Peabody announces.

Still groggy, Erasmus smiles warmly.

"I step out for a few minutes to get myself some breakfast, and voila, I find an intruder, a little bear, snoozing in my shop," she says in jest.

"Well, it's to be expected if Mama Bear leaves her shop unlocked when she's out of town; it shouldn't be a surprise, right?"

"The advantage of small-town living, young Erasmus, but you urbanites wouldn't understand that, right?" she teases, immediately realizing her mistake.

"Oops, I forgot you're a country boy as well," she adds, smiling along with him. But his sad eyes give away something deeper.

"Dearest young man, I know you're going through a hard time with what has happened between Victoria and you. I've corresponded with your steadfast advocate, Mrs. V, who is back in Wales. I've also consulted with a few of your small legion of antiquarian followers here in New England," she says, her tone softening.

"Mrs. P, I'm struggling to keep my head and heart free of anger or resentment. I only want to preserve the good memories, but sometimes it's hard," Erasmus confesses.

"I can completely understand and empathize. I, too, went through a breakup with my second husband under very similar circumstances," she replies, her eyes drifting back in time.

"Let me think, young man," she says, pacing back and forth until suddenly her eyes light up.

"I've got the perfect prescription to treat what ails you. Let me go and fetch it," she offers.

Mrs. Peabody's large frame and size sharply contrast with her surprising agility, which never ceases to amaze Erasmus.

'How can she kneel, climb, bend, and move with such ease and speed?' he marvels once again.

'She defies gravity,' Erasmus muses.
Soon, she's returning with an item in hand.

'Exactly as Victoria always said—within her chaos and piles of books, she knows exactly where everything is and finds it within seconds,' he notes.

"Erasmus, this is a timeless scribble. It's one that helped me get through the abandonment by my second husband. Let me read it to you."

As she begins to recite the poem, the words have an immediate soothing effect on Erasmus' restless spirit and melancholic heart.

"Forgiveness"

What is it to forgive?
Is it to erase from our memory those feelings—
fused anger and hurt,
lingering resentments,
or existential wounds,
caused by the acts of others or life vicissitudes?

Or is it to pardon transgressions
or betrayals by those we trust?
To absolve disloyalty from those we count on.
To excuse the consequential untruths
from those we blindly believe in.

Or is it to acquit the irreplaceable losses
caused by those we rely on?
To the offenses to our decency,
dignity, honor, and self-respect,
perpetuated by those we follow?
Or is it, perhaps to forgive ourselves first?

Yet the problem with forgiving our own acts,
is that we seek recognition and pardon from others first—
as though absolution from their words and gestures
could assuage the guilt we carry.

But guilt cannot be deceived
by fantasies or falsehoods.
The feeling of culpability dissolves
only when our conscience
allows it to,
when we genuinely accept responsibility.

Because
where forgiveness truly happens first, is within us,
and only through a genuine acceptance of responsibility
our feelings of guilt are first assuaged and then go away.

And this is how the stern watch
of our conscience is appeased,
opening the doors for us to be absolved.
Then and only then, what others think or say,
brings completeness
to forgiveness' virtuous circle,
one built out of authenticity and truthfulness.
Once inside this loop,
we can finally reach atonement.

When do we sincerely forgive?

Sometimes, we pretend to forgive, but we really don't,
denying its actuality.

Sometimes, we are simply unwilling to do so.

Both attitudes are poisonous to the spirit
and destructive to the soul,
because the longer they linger,

the more our true selves erode,
the more profound our sadness becomes,
and the more devastating the damage is
to our ability to live a life in full.

To truly forgive,
we must be genuinely willing and disposed
to have the courage to face the pain, the wound,
the offenses or their personas straight in the eye,
confronting them.

Then, whatever or whoever
is afflicting us,
we must let go,
foregoing at whatever pace our heart permits.

But, regardless of anything or anyone,
we must always seek finality and closure
to reach atonement.

What does it take to forgive?"
How do we know, in fact, we have forgiven?"
We recognize it because of our ability to forgive
is a requirement of our personal growth,
as well as for the enrichment and evolution
of our entire self.

Without the capacity to forgive,
our virtues and values have flaws,
and our meaning and purpose in life are clouded and murky,
preoccupied with overcoming the haze.

And without forgiveness,
we are plying through stuck in reverse,
lacking oxygen or inspiration
to breathe and infuse life into our spirit and soul.

Forgiveness is also a precondition
to experience the joy of living,
Without it, happiness is hampered,
limited and handicapped.

The genesis of the noble virtue of forgiveness
is the magical elixir of compassion and piety,

With compassion, we connect and empathize
with the pain and sorrow of
those in need of atonement.

With piety, we are illuminated and enlightened by grace
enabling us to devote ourselves,
with dutiful respect, sincerity, and veneration
to the atonement of ours and other's faults.

When we forgive,
we throw a spreading aura,
a mantle of goodness on everyone
and everything around us.

When we forgive,
our life renews itself
and our "existential time machine's" hands,
move forward in the right direction.

When we forgive,
right from our very own center of the earth,
a torrent of lava explodes into the sky,
freeing our core, our essence,
from life's emotional anchors,
ballasts and dead weights.

When we forgive,
we become worthier, thus more likely,

to be rewarded with forgiveness as well.

When we forgive,
we elevate ourselves to a state of
compassionate and pious grace,
where we can seek atonement for our spirit and soul.

*

As Mrs. Peabody concludes, her words resonate deeply, transcending the confines of her antique bookshop.

"Erasmus, forgiving is both empowering and liberating. You don't need to question how or why you feel as you do now because it is perfectly human to feel angry and dejected after what happened to you. What you need to focus on is taking ownership of the part and role you played and what you learned from it. You also mustn't stand still or allow yourself to get stuck in a quagmire; instead, you must keep moving forward. The trigger to do this is to forgive her and forgive yourself. That's how everything in life restarts and renews itself."

— �֍ —

Royal Cambridge Scholastic Institute (2019)
(University Auditorium)

Professor Cromwell-Smith returns his class to the present with a benevolent look in his eyes.

In the stillness of the classroom, Erasmus' thoughts drift to the past—the poignant moments he and Victoria shared as she faced her own emotional struggles. As he begins to speak, he recalls the lessons he learned from Mrs. Peabody and how her words on forgiveness helped him heal. His voice softens as he speaks, bridging the gap between the past and the present, tying his personal journey to the lesson he is about to share with his students.

"Forgiveness is one of the most powerful tools we can use to navigate life's undesirable outcomes. Without it, we risk carrying emotional anchors or roadblocks that hold us back."

"Questions, anyone?" Asks the professor with pensive tone.

Samantha is a philosophy major with a keen interest in ethical dilemmas, particularly around forgiveness and personal growth. She has shoulder-length blonde hair and often wears a thoughtful expression, reflecting on complex concepts during class. "Professor, the poem discusses the need to forgive not only others but also ourselves. How do we begin the process of self-forgiveness when our actions have caused harm to others, especially when those feelings of guilt persist despite our best efforts to move forward?"

"That's a very insightful question, Samantha. Self-forgiveness often starts with acknowledging the responsibility for our actions and feeling genuine remorse. However, it is essential to not get trapped in guilt, because it can paralyze us. True self-forgiveness involves accepting that we made mistakes, learning from them, and then allowing ourselves to move forward. The poem emphasizes that real forgiveness begins within, and that's where we need to focus first—on accepting our responsibility and letting go of the emotional weight that holds us back."

Jared is a psychology student known for his analytical mindset. With short brown hair and a tendency to take detailed notes, he is deeply engaged in understanding human behavior and emotions. "Professor, the poem mentions that 'guilt cannot be deceived by fantasies or falsehoods.' How do we differentiate between genuine guilt and the guilt we impose on ourselves due to societal expectations or unrealistic self-judgment?"

"Jared, that's an excellent observation. Genuine guilt arises when we acknowledge that we've done something that conflicts with our values, whereas imposed guilt often stems from external pressures or distorted self-perceptions. The poem suggests that guilt dissolves when we take responsibility, but it doesn't mean we should carry it endlessly. Instead of suppressing or ignoring guilt, we need to confront it honestly and understand whether it's stemming from a true moral misstep or if it's been exacerbated by external expectations."

Rachel is an English literature major with a love for poetry and a passion for finding deeper meanings in texts. Her curly hair frames her face as she leans forward in her seat, eager to engage in the discussion. "Professor, in the poem, forgiveness is described as 'empowering and liberating.' Could you elaborate on how forgiveness serves as a tool for emotional freedom, particularly when we are forgiving someone who has wronged us deeply?"

"Rachel, that's a powerful question. Forgiveness, especially in cases where we've been deeply wronged, can feel like an emotional burden being lifted. The poem highlights that forgiveness frees us from emotional anchors and allows us to move forward. When we choose to forgive, we release the hold that anger, resentment, or bitterness may have over us. It doesn't mean we forget or condone the wrongs done to us, but by forgiving, we regain control of our emotions and start the process of healing."

Michael is a history student who enjoys reflecting on the past and its influence on present-day decisions. With glasses and a quiet demeanor, he is often the first to notice historical patterns in personal experiences. "Professor, the poem speaks about the importance of forgiveness in order to avoid emotional stagnation and the erosion of our true selves. In your opinion, how can societies or nations use forgiveness on a larger scale to heal from historical trauma and prevent societal divisions?"

"Michael, that's an insightful way to expand the conversation. Societies that carry the weight of historical trauma—such as war, injustice, or oppression—must recognize the value of collective forgiveness. The process involves not only acknowledging past wrongs but also creating opportunities for dialogue, healing, and reconciliation. Societal forgiveness isn't just about letting go of the past but also about fostering unity and progress. The poem's message can be applied to larger contexts, where forgiveness opens the door for societal healing and a better future."

As the class draws to a close, Erasmus feels the echoes of his own journey within the room. He gives his final remarks, offering the students a simple yet profound piece of advice.

"Forgiveness," he says, "is the key to not only personal growth but also to living a life of peace and purpose. I encourage you all to reflect on your own capacity for forgiveness, both toward others and yourselves." With a final nod to his students, he watches them gather their belongings. He lingers for a moment, taking in the quiet, knowing that today's lesson may have planted seeds of healing in his students' lives, just as it did in his own.

"And that'll be all for today. It's a wrap. I'll see you all next week," declares the eminent professor as he concludes the session.

Victoria and Sarah smile proudly, their hands tightly clasped in a gesture of raw emotion and connection. As he approaches mother and daughter, they embrace in a spontaneous public display of family reconciliation.

The entire student body watches, rewarded with the poignant image of their beloved professor walking out, holding hands with each of his two ladies. To all present, it is a symbolic gesture—a living testament that, for him, forgiveness begins at home.

Chapter 5

Reciprocity

Charles River, Boston, Massachusetts (2019)

As dawn breaks on a cloudy day, Victoria and Erasmus walk, hands intertwined, along the misty river surrounded by fog patches. Nature gives off the smell and feel of a new day. Erasmus knows Victoria's pained past has all but run its course. Her troubled history is now out in the open, and the winds of a new life are blowing away her troubled past, allowing the two of them to address the wounds and scars from a distant perspective as they move forward. But he knows that there's still one more fuzzy cloud to visit – her life in Boston before they reunited.

'All in due time,' he tells himself.

As if she were reading his mind, Erasmus feels the tightening of her hand. A glance confirms the determined and stern look in her eyes – the same look that has preceded her recent outpourings about her life without him.

"Dear, right after that memorable encounter with Mrs. Samuels-Ortiz at the St. Louis Public Library, my husband was diagnosed with cancer. That tragic event turned our lives upside down, and everything else took the backstage," Victoria says.

"What happened with your plans to resettle in Boston?" asks Erasmus.

"That turned out to be one of the few good outcomes resulting from his illness, as I didn't have to create an excuse or try to force the inevitable. We just simply moved upon my decision that Boston was the right location to treat his illness," she replies.

"Did he interpret it that way?" asks Erasmus.

"Outwardly, yes, but I sense he knew my true reasons. As a matter of fact, after that meeting with Mrs. Samuels-Ortiz, I lost any fear of speaking up, voicing my desires in front of him. Little by little, I started to mention you in our family conversations. At first, he tried to stop it, but to no avail; he couldn't stop me from finally voicing my true feelings. You and I at home became fair game," she replies.

"But your actual move to Boston took a long time. I mean, decades had gone by the time you moved over here," he states.

"Thankfully, Rebecca Samuels-Ortiz took the initiative. She did what she thought was best for my future. She wrote and applied to several universities. I consented to her pursuing that initiative, not believing that it would ever pan out, but it did. At that point, there was no turning back. That's exactly what I needed – a slight push to break away from the chains of my thinking and upbringing," Victoria recounts.

"But wasn't it a bit of a quixotic quest? You had no idea where I was or if I'd started my own family," Erasmus says.

"That's true, but it felt as if I was getting closer to you. I knew it was all a fantasy, but it was one that I clung to for a long time. I never let go of it until I moved the family, at which point I was preoccupied," she elaborates.

"But once here, some more years rolled by," laments Erasmus.

"Yes, my love, that's sadly true. His illness took over, and everything else was held in abeyance. It would take five more years until he passed away for me to become alive again," she replies in angst.

Victoria's face turns deeply sad and inundated with anxiety. As she begins to cry inconsolably, Erasmus embraces her with a deep sense of his own guilt.

"I'm sorry, Victoria, we shouldn't have…" he says, ashamed.

"Shhhh, let me continue," she whispers, her satiated eyes exuding love for him as she places a couple of her fingers on his lips.

Like their joined life together, the river fog is slowly lifting, providing them with a clearer picture of their surroundings.

"Dear, after he passed away, I went through a very trying period of doubt. For the first time, I felt it was too late for us to resume. I believed there was no chance in heaven that you would want anything to do with me. I started to visualize you having a new life, married, and with kids. So, I did nothing," she concedes.

"How did you find out that your kids were searching for me?"

"That's another rabbit hole worth exploring," she announces with a spark in her voice.

"It all happened on an early morning surprise visit by my three kids," she says before earnestly starting to narrate.

— ✦ —

Emerson-Lloyd Family Home, Boston, Massachusetts (2017)
(Victoria's kids' family intervention)

"It seems like she's given up, guys," points out Elizabeth, her tone laced with concern.

"I agree. It's been three months, and she's sadder and more depressed than ever," notes Bart, his brow furrowed in thought.

"She's certainly not grieving Father," says Sarah, her voice steady but tinged with frustration.

"We all know that," retorts Bart, leaning back with a resigned sigh.

"After a lifetime of obsessing over it, it's like the dream has disappeared," states Elizabeth, her gaze distant.

"That may be true, but she's still in love with Erasmus," declares Sarah, her voice carrying a quiet certainty.

"If that's true, why has she given up and quit then?" asks Elizabeth, her words cutting through the tense atmosphere.

"Perhaps in her mind, too much time has passed them by, and the duration of our father's illness lasted for so long that she believes it's now too late," Bart reasons, his voice low and reflective.

—◈—

Charles River, Boston (2019)

While sitting by the riverside, Erasmus and Victoria huddle close under their trusted wool blanket. Their body language exudes a deep sense of immersion and intensity, as though the world around them has faded into irrelevance. Every word exchanged carries weight, reverberating in the quiet intimacy of the moment. Victoria speaks in a calm voice, a whisper tinged with absolute peace and contentment, her words flowing gently like the river beside them.

—◈—

Emerson-Lloyd Home, Boston (2017)

"So, what're we going to do about it?" probes Bart.
"Maybe we should do nothing. After all, it's her personal life," ventures Sarah.

"Isn't mom's personal life, at least in part, ours as well? Or do we want to see our mother all alone and miserable for the rest of her life?" challenges Elizabeth.

"She's dedicated her life to us. She's been impeccable and raised us with boundless love and affection. She cared for our father with absolute abnegation and devotion throughout his illness. It's now her time—her moment, and we must help Mom make it happen," asserts Bart with conviction.

"What about the memory of our father? Wouldn't we be betraying it?" an incredulous Sarah questions, her voice tinged with guilt.

"Get a hold of yourself. What memory? A man who hardly ever paid attention or professed love to us, his own kids. His sole interest and focus in life, besides his profession, were women, which, by the way, didn't include Mom. But it did include Grandma. Seemingly, she was one of the few female patients that got away, even though she initiated the poisonous relationship," argues Elizabeth with biting clarity.

"I agree. By now, we all know about his manipulative, controlling approach to engineering their marriage, and it was absolutely wrong. When a mind doctor exploits the emotional vulnerability of his patients, it's not only a violation of a doctor's oath but also deeply immoral," Bart declares emphatically.

"God forgive me for speaking the truth, but he was a malignant narcissist, one of the most dangerous human beings on our planet. People like him destroy lives, scorching the earth in their path and, in our mother's case, without a moment's hesitation. Now, we have a chance to get her life back—a life she lost in her youth. An existence wherein her heart, all her dreams, innocence, and zest for life reside," asserts Elizabeth, her voice brimming with resolve.

"Except for respect, which I'm uncertain he deserves, we don't owe him anything. We all, including Mom, were his victims, and yet dutifully and faithfully, we remained his family to the very end of his life. We owe him nothing more, nothing else," concludes Bart with finality.

Victoria's kids come together in an emotional embrace, shedding a few tears.

"Agreed. Now let's start looking for Erasmus Cromwell-Smith," Sarah declares, finally making up her mind.

— ✦ —

Charles River, Boston, Massachusetts (2019)

As the sun ascends, the fog gradually lifts, unveiling the river and its serene surroundings in their full splendor. Erasmus tenderly caresses Victoria's face, his touch both reassuring and affectionate. Tears cascade down her cheeks, glistening in the early morning light. With a trembling voice yet an unwavering resolve, she begins to narrate in earnest...

— ✦ —

Emerson-Lloyd Family Home, Boston, Massachusetts (2017)

"Where do we begin? Maybe he's no longer in the area? What if he has a family, a wife, kids?" Elizabeth asks, her voice tinged with angst.

"We should still pursue our goal, resolve to find him, and bring closure to this situation," Bart concludes firmly.

"But we'll only tell her about his status if he's available, right?" Sarah asks, her youthful innocence shining through.

"Absolutely," Bart replies with conviction.

"Deal," Elizabeth affirms, her tone resolute.

— ✦ —

Charles River, Boston, Massachusetts (2019)

With the temperature rising, Victoria and Erasmus' blanket now serves as their floor mat. Like the awakening nature around them, their own veils of uncertainty are lifting. At last, they have achieved clarity and transparency after revisiting what had been left unresolved. After a brief pause, Victoria resumes her narration, her voice imbued with a cadence of joy and renewed purpose.

— ✦ —

Emerson-Lloyd Family Home, Boston, Massachusetts (2017)
(A Few Months Later, Victoria's Bedroom, Dawn)

Elizabeth, Bart, and Sarah tread cautiously into their mother's bedroom, as if walking on pins and needles. Bart, trailing behind, wrestles with a tangle of strings attached to a dozen colorful balloons, which pop and squeeze through the door in a chaotic display.

"Hey, guys," whispers Victoria as she awakens, her face lighting up with joy. The trio leans in to kiss her cheeks, their love radiating through the room. Her gaze sharpens as she notices the balloons, her curiosity piqued.

"Bart, those are truly beautiful. Come over here, please," she says, extending her arms to hug her son as he hands her the strings.

"Mother, today I'm a balloon salesman," Bart announces with a broad grin, casually dropping one of Erasmus' childhood poems in front of her.

The memory strikes Victoria like lightning. A wave of emotion washes over her, and she struggles to maintain her composure, forcing a smile. But her children catch the subtle tremor in her demeanor, the telltale sign of memories stirring within.

"Or maybe I'm the boy in the picture," teases Bart, alluding to another of Erasmus' cherished childhood poems.

Victoria's expression transforms as a surge of warmth and nostalgia overtakes her. Her mind races. 'They don't know. How could they know? How would they know?' A feeling churns in her gut, rising to the surface, betraying her outward calm.

"How do you…" she begins to ask, but her voice falters, caught in the storm of raw emotions. Tears glisten in her eyes as she gazes at her children, her hands trembling.

And then it happens—the words she has yearned to hear for decades pierce the air, cutting through the weight of time.

"Mom, I found him! ... I found your blue unicorn," Sarah announces, tears of joy streaming down her face.

Victoria's hands fly to her mouth, her entire body trembling. She struggles to speak, her voice barely a whisper. "You found him?" Her words are knotted, stuck in her throat, yearning for reassurance that this long-dreamt reality has come true.

"Where is he?" she blurts out suddenly, her voice cracking. In a frenzy, she leaps from the bed and embraces her children, her actions frantic and irrational, driven purely by instinct.

"Get dressed, Mom. I'll take you to him," Sarah says, her voice steady and resolute.

Victoria, dazed yet determined, rushes to her dressing room. She moves with a sense of frantic urgency, as if time itself is her enemy. "Mom, you have to promise to do exactly what I say," Sarah insists, her tone commanding as Victoria searches for something to wear.

"All right," Victoria replies, her tone tinged with puzzlement as she hurriedly dresses.

"You can only reveal your presence when he's finished. Today is the final class of the academic year," Sarah instructs.

A brief silence follows as Victoria processes this revelation. "Is he a profess—wait a minute, is he your teacher?" she asks, her voice rising with incredulity.

"Yes, he is. Mom, do you promise...?" Sarah persists.

"Promise," Victoria replies, her excitement bubbling over. "Does he know I'm coming?" she hesitates, her nerves breaking through.

"No, Mom, it's a total surprise," Sarah reassures her.

Hurry up then. We don't want to be late for his class. You don't want to make him wait any longer for you," Victoria exclaims, her eagerness evident.

As Victoria readies herself, an extraordinary sound fills the room—her singing. It's a melody her children haven't heard in years, the familiar humming of their mother from their childhood. Overwhelmed with emotion, the siblings hug each other tightly, tears of joy cascading down their faces.

"Guys, I think we finally have our mom back," Sarah says, her voice breaking, and her siblings nod in agreement.

On the way to the university, Victoria is consumed by a torrent of emotions—joy, anxiety, and anticipation. Her heart, dormant for so long, now races with life. But doubts linger. 'How is he? How does he look? Is he in a relationship? Would he want me back?'

"Mom, relax. Enjoy the moment," Sarah says soothingly. "I'm certain that the professor is still as much in love with you as you are with him. A crazy love, I should add, but true love after all. I've witnessed it firsthand, listening to how he's described the two of you, class after class." Sarah's voice is steady and reassuring as she holds her mother's hand, squeezing it gently, offering unwavering support.

—✳—

Charles River, Boston, Massachusetts (2019)

Erasmus and Victoria are overcome with deep emotions as they reflect on the day they reunited after being apart for more than 40 years.

The middle-aged couple walks through the woods, heading home. Their hands are clasped tightly, her head gently resting on his shoulder. Both wear serene smiles, knowing that the burdens of the past have finally lifted, leaving their shared joy untarnished by lingering shadows.

"Dear, what's your class going to touch upon today?" asks Victoria, her voice soft as they step across their home's entrance into the outer hallway.

"Reciprocity," Erasmus replies with a thoughtful smile. "Which is what life offers you after a life of sacrifice, unyielding convictions, and unwavering loyalty. And, in the end, it paid you back in spades."

Royal Cambridge Scholastic Institute (2019)
(Campus Streets followed by Auditorium)

Erasmus zigzags on his old rusty bike as he pedals toward the faculty building. He takes a deep breath, his heart filled with warmth, still soaring from the joy of an unforgettable morning. Slowly but steadily, he approaches the parking lot, locks his bike, and strides purposefully toward his class.

'Her children's instincts weren't just right—they were uncannily precise, perfectly attuned to the moment and the circumstances,' he reflects, a broad smile spreading across his face as he navigates the bustling halls of the institution.

The distant rumble and murmurs of the class grow louder as he nears the auditorium, and he can feel their energy surging through the walls. Stepping into the lecture hall, the pedagogue shakes off the quite reverie f his earlier thoughts. The buzz of student chatter fills the room like a vibrant chorus, the excitement is palpable, with a purposeful stride and a puzzled look, he walks to the front, ready to lead the next intellectual journey. Then he spots the source of the commotion. Sarah, Bart, and Elizabeth sit proudly in the front row, their wide grins delivering an unmistakable message: *Erasmus, we're part of the team now.*

The professor nods ever so slightly, acknowledging their presence with a grateful smile.

"How's everyone today?" he asks, his voice momentarily thick with emotion.

"Insanely awesome!" comes the boisterous response from the students, amplified by his self-invited guests.

"Reciprocity," Erasmus announces as he regains his composure, his tone resonant and steady.

"While on a trip to the Far East, I learned that mutuality is an intrinsic and crucial part of life. Inevitably, as part of the circle of life, everything we give comes back to us, and everything we take is taken away from us as well."

He pauses, allowing the weight of his words to settle.

"It begins like this …"

— ✦ —

Ginza District, Tokyo, Japan (1997)

Every summer for the past twenty years, I've traveled to Japan to deliver a seminar on Western poetry at Tokyo University. While in Japan, I've savored hiking the mountains around the capital on weekends. My favorite, by far, is the legendary Mount Fuji. I also delight in visiting the exquisite Kyoto Gardens, marveling at their serene beauty and intricate design.

On one particular trip, a Friday evening seminar ran late, causing me to wake up at noon on Saturday for the first time ever in Tokyo. Left with no clear plans, I found myself meandering through the bustling Ginza shopping district. Amid the dazzling neon lights and crowds, my attention was drawn to a low-rise building of about fifteen floors, showcasing the shape and logo of a renowned Japanese consumer electronics brand. Intrigued, I ventured inside, discovering that the entire structure was a demo center for the brand's latest innovations.

Floor by floor, I explored the futuristic showcase, marveling at gadgets yet to be released to the public. On one of the upper levels, I entered their high-fidelity sound room. From that moment, every visit to Tokyo included a ritual stop here, where I could immerse myself in hours of undisturbed tranquility.

The sound room was extraordinary—its purity so profound that the melodies seemed to emerge from a cocoon of absolute silence. Listening to chamber music in this room was transcendent, as if I were seated in the front row of a concert hall with flawless acoustics.

Vivaldi's Four Seasons, a perennial favorite of mine, played in harmony with a video showcasing the breathtaking beauty of Kyoto. The gardens and seasonal landscapes, rendered in vivid splendor, synchronized perfectly with the symphony's movements, each season vividly coming to life.

It was during one of these meditative sessions, completely enraptured by the interplay of Kyoto's imagery and Vivaldi's composition, that I met Atsushi Sanada. His presence was striking: a long, salt-and-pepper goatee framed his face, his bundled ponytail matched his serene demeanor, and his tiny round-rimmed glasses complemented his colorful wool turtleneck cardigan. Like me, he appeared completely transported, deeply engrossed in the music's exquisite sound.

"Do you feel the silence within the music?" he asked unexpectedly, his voice calm and his English flawless. His friendly gaze and unhurried manner drew me out of my reverie.

"Absolutely," I replied, already captivated by his insight. "That's why I make it a point to come here whenever I'm in Tokyo."

"Then you are fortunate," he continued, as if lost in his own thoughts. "To perceive such silence within sound is a rare gift."

He paused, his gaze contemplative, before speaking again.

"Here is an ancient writing I've carried with me for years. It offers clarity for moments like this. It's a loose translation from Japanese." He handed me a tiny scroll, his manner reverent.

With a sense of trepidation and wonder, I unfolded the delicate scroll and began to read...

"Silence within the Music"

There is stillness in the air,
no sound within the music.

Fidelity proclaims perfection,
the notes exude glory.

Purity fills the air—
violins weep,
cellos cry,
trumpets sing,
and the piano chants
to the deepest ends of our hearts.

There is perfection in the room,
absolute serenity in harmony,
flawless stillness,
with room to spare,
to meditate and wonder,
to no end.

There is silence within the music,
there is silence as it plays,
there is silence in the air.

*

The wise man was no longer in the room when I finished reading. Anxious to return the scroll, I darted through the demo building, frantically searching for him. Arriving at street level, the swirling doors propelled me into the bustling rhythm of the Japanese metropolis. There he stood—calm and poised on the sidewalk, smiling at me.

"Atsushi," he introduced himself, extending his hand.

"Cromwell-Smith," I replied, clasping his hand firmly and returning the scroll with a slight bow of gratitude and respect.

"Care for a quick bite?" he asked.

"It would be my pleasure, Mr. Atsushi."

Before long, we stood in front of a series of vibrant window displays showcasing intricate "wax" replicas of various dishes. Each item bore a small sign with its name, description, and price—a masterpiece of Japanese efficiency. Within minutes, we were seated at a counter with our chosen meals and generous servings of sake.

"Thank you for sharing the poem with me," I said, my voice earnest.

"You're welcome. It was an instinctive reaction to your tranquil state of contemplation," Atsushi replied softly, his penetrating gaze offering a glimpse of wisdom beyond words.

"Mr. Cromwell, what brings you to Japan?" he inquired.

"Each year, I teach a seminar on Western poetry at Tokyo University."

His almond-shaped eyes narrowed briefly in curiosity, then widened as a warm smile spread across his face.

"Serendipitous! You must visit my store," he exclaimed, his enthusiasm palpable.

"What's your trade, Mr. Atsushi?" I asked, intrigued.

"Call me Atsushi, please," he urged, his manner disarmingly relaxed.

"And how should I address you?" he queried.

"Erasmus," I replied, making a conscious effort to shed my cultural stiffness.

"Well, Erasmus," he said with a playful nod, "I deal in ancient writings and manuscripts, much like the one you read."

His revelation caught me off guard, igniting my curiosity. My eyes widened, betraying my excitement.

"Serendipity indeed, Atsushi. Are you an antiquarian?"

"A Japanese version of one," he replied with a modest smile.

"Then our stars are perfectly aligned," I declared.

"And why is that, if I may ask?" he prodded.

"I was born and raised in Hay-on-Wye in Wales, famously known as 'book town,' surrounded by an abundance of antique bookstores. My proclivity for the world of books shaped my childhood and teenage years. I practically grew up inside those establishments, mentored by seasoned antiquarians who became lifelong influences."

Atsushi's lips tightened in a thoughtful smile as he nodded repeatedly, his satisfaction evident.

"My humble shop has been in the family for four generations," he shared, his words kindling my growing fascination.

"Atsushi Sanada Shop of Antique Writings" (est. 1870)

Not long after, with plenty of green tea on hand, I find myself seated on a mat on the pristine wooden floor of the impeccable shop. My eyes wander in amazement at the sheer volume of scrolls meticulously displayed around me.

"Erasmus, what occupies your time when you're not visiting Japan?" Atsushi asks with a playful tone.

"I teach poetry and English literature at a New England college. I also write poems and fiction novels," I reply.

"Interesting. My initial impression of you was that your body language exuded serenity and meditation, but your restless eyes betrayed a sense of being lost and in pain. It felt as though you were searching for something—perhaps meaning or purpose— or mourning someone?" Atsushi observes with remarkable precision.

"Aren't we all?" I respond rhetorically, hoping to sidestep his probing insight.

"Indeed, we all are, Erasmus. But more specifically, are you?" he persists, cutting through my deflection with surgical precision.

"Yes," I admit after a moment. *"A bit lost, searching for meaning and purpose, and, yes, mourning as well. I am in pursuit of my true self."*

"One of the keys to living a fulfilling life is reciprocity. It's all in the balance of give and take," Atsushi begins, his voice steady and deliberate. *"Too often, we focus on what we want or need to gain, ignoring what we have to offer, which is where true fulfillment begins. Your quest for identity must include a conscious effort to cultivate mutuality and a predisposition to generosity. Whatever you hope to receive from life or others, it will only come to you consistently once you learn to give first. This profound understanding is earned through life's experiences,"* he explains with a wisdom that feels both ancient and immediate.

"Atsushi, let me share an anecdote about reciprocity with you," he offers, his tone tinged with enthusiasm. *"Years ago, just before I opened my shop, I struggled to gather the resources needed. One of my uncles, a wealthy man, had the means to help me. I approached him for support, but his reaction was unexpected and disheartening. Instead of aiding me, he invested significantly more to establish an antique scroll shop of his own—directly in competition with me. To make matters worse, he sought my advice and help to launch his store."*

"What did you do?" I ask, my bewilderment evident.

"Of course, I helped him," Atsushi replies with a calm smile. *"I put forth my best efforts and my heart."*

"Did he compensate you for your efforts?" I probe further.

"I didn't want him to."

"But did he offer?"

"No, but that was irrelevant to me."

"Did he, at any point, support you in setting up your shop?"

"Not at all. On the contrary, he criticized me harshly, insisting I wasn't cut out to be my own boss. He even campaigned within the family, claiming my efforts were unnecessary because his shop was already established. He thought if I failed, I would end up working for him."

"What happened next?" I ask, leaning in, captivated.

"I managed to open my shop. My uncle, lacking genuine passion for antiquities, eventually lost interest and moved on," Atsushi explains.

"And your family?" I inquire.

"Over time, they came to embrace my work and my store. Today, they fully support me, but it was a long journey. As for my uncle, his actions have left a lasting impression—not a favorable one—within the family."

"But why did you help him? I don't understand," I admit.

"You see, Erasmus, his actions defined him. They reflected who he truly was. My actions, on the other hand, reflect who I am. I didn't allow his choices to dictate my own. I compartmentalized his behavior and rose above the fray, responding with maturity and pouring my heart into helping him."

"But his selfishness was cruel," I argue.

"Be that as it may, once again, his actions defined him, not me."

"What reciprocity did he offer you in return for your generosity?"

"Nothing. And that, Erasmus, lies at the heart of reciprocity. True giving doesn't come with the expectation of something in

return. It's not transactional. But let me share something that will illuminate this concept further."

Atsushi stands gracefully and moves toward a row of aged yellowish scrolls. He carefully selects one, studies it for a moment, and then returns with a look of quiet satisfaction.

"Let us share an exquisite example of ancient Japanese wisdom," he says, his voice imbued with tranquility as he begins to read, translating the words into English with seamless fluency.

"Reciprocity"

Nature blossoms as water drops.
All the world's colors light up around us
as the sun shines.
The entire universe high above glows,
as night falls.

Our entire self gets to live another day,
hence continues,
as we breathe.

Reality's images come to life for us to enjoy,
as we are able to see.

Our entire world exists as we think and comprehend—
consciousness, the genesis of human life.
The whole gamut of the worlds of physics and biology
can only be calculated, measured,
and understood through reciprocity.

At the heart of life's virtuous cycle
lies reciprocity.

If constant motion is the roar
of nature's engine at work,
reciprocity is the essential fuel

that powers it.

When we reciprocate with one another,
we appeal to the better angels within ourselves
and over humanity.

The true essence of receiving anything in life
lies in what we have given beforehand.

In truth, we have not truly given anything,
if nothing comes back.

Inexorably, sooner or later,
if we do good things and do them right,
if we perform good deeds,
life will respond in kind,
rewarding us in spades.

But if we don't, one way or another,
life will find its balance—
often in the most unexpected ways.

Everything and anything we have taken or received
without reciprocity in return
will be taken back, confiscated,
even yanked from us.

If we shoot arrows or throw stones,
we should expect them to rebound,
perhaps with greater force.
If we gift good deeds, books, and roses,
they will return to us in droves.

Mutuality is an immutable correlation—
greater than one,
never a one-way street.

Generosity and reciprocity are inseparable,
each intrinsic to the other.
Together, they create endless virtuous circles,
positive, upward spirals,
of endless giving and receiving.

To reciprocate is to express eternal gratitude
to humankind, life, and The Creator,
it is in essence, a way of paying,
for the privilege of being alive.

All of this comes,
with the lingering, handsome reward:
that everything we have contributed
to life itself and to others,
will, in due course, return to us
as blessings multiplied

*

As Atsushi gently rolls the scroll closed, the shop falls into a contemplative stillness. He places the scroll back on its shelf with reverence, turning to Erasmus with a serene smile. "Erasmus, reciprocity is the essence of balance—not just in nature but within ourselves. If you nurture this principle, it will guide you toward harmony—always remember, in life, begin by asking yourself what you have to offer or contribute before you craft your wish list of desires."

Erasmus bows slightly in gratitude, his eyes drawn to the intricate calligraphy of the scrolls around him, each holding its own mysteries. Outside, the muted hum of Tokyo's bustling streets contrasts sharply with the tranquil haven of Atsushi's shop.

Breaking the silence, Atsushi gestures toward the teapot resting on a low wooden table. "Let us share tea before you go,

Erasmus. Even a brief moment of communion can teach us more about giving and receiving."

The two sit on cushions, sipping the warm green tea in quiet reflection, the rich aroma mingling with the scent of aged paper and cedar. Erasmus, his heart full, feels the wisdom of reciprocity settle deep within him.

— ✦ —

Royal Cambridge Scholastic Institute (2019)
(University Auditorium)

Professor Cromwell-Smith prepares to shift from his personal reflections to the heart of today's lesson. He clears his throat, drawing his students' attention, back to the present. "The word 'reciprocity' should resonate consciously within each of you, from the moment you awaken to the moment you rest. What you give is precisely what you'll receive. Without giving, there's no reciprocal action to sustain the cycle in the long run!"

His voice echoes in the hushed room, the students sitting upright, their attention unwavering. "Let this principle guide you not just academically but in every facet of your existence," the professor concludes, his gaze meeting each pair of eyes in turn, ensuring the message lands firmly in their hearts.

With the story of his experiences shared, Erasmus looks around the room, his gaze inviting questions. The class is silent for a moment, before eager hands begin to rise.

Clara, a senior majoring in philosophy with a focus on ethics, speaks up with a deep sense of curiosity. "In the poem 'Reciprocity,' you mention that what we give is exactly what we'll receive. Could you elaborate on how reciprocity plays a role in personal growth, especially when we face life's most challenging moments?"

"An excellent question, Clara. Reciprocity, at its core, is about balance—what we put out into the world, emotionally, intellectually, or spiritually, inevitably comes back to us. During tough times, when we feel vulnerable or lost, embracing reciprocity can guide us toward healing. The more we give of ourselves—whether in love, forgiveness, or simply understanding—the more we open ourselves up to receiving the same in return. It's not about expectation, but about trust in the process of life and relationships. Growth comes when we learn to give without calculating, knowing that the universe operates on a balance that goes beyond us."

Mark, an English literature major with a particular interest in contemporary poetry, raises his hand with evident eagerness. "The poem 'Silence within the Music' speaks about the stillness found in sound. I was struck by how this theme resonates with the concept of inner peace. Could you explain how silence, or moments of stillness, contribute to a deeper understanding of reciprocity?"

"A thoughtful observation, Mark. Silence is often the space where true understanding begins. In both music and life, silence allows us to pause and reflect. In the poem, the silence within the music signifies a deeper connection, a moment of pure being. Similarly, in life, moments of stillness give us the opportunity to process, to listen, and to truly receive. Without these pauses, the flow of reciprocity becomes disrupted. By embracing silence, we make room for others to give to us, just as we offer ourselves in return. It's in those silent spaces that the most profound exchanges occur."

Olivia, a psychology major studying human behavior, raises her hand, her expression thoughtful. "The idea of forgiving oneself in 'Forgiveness' resonates deeply with me, especially the notion that forgiveness can't truly happen until we accept responsibility. How do you think this acceptance impacts our relationships with others, particularly when we've wronged them?"

"That's an insightful question, Olivia. Self-forgiveness is the foundation of all other forms of forgiveness. When we accept responsibility for our actions, we free ourselves from the shackles of guilt and defensiveness. This act of acknowledging our mistakes, without excuses or deflection, opens the door to healing. Only then can we approach others with sincerity and empathy, without being burdened by our own unresolved feelings. This process doesn't just heal the self, but it also enables more authentic relationships with others. When we forgive ourselves, we create the emotional space to truly forgive others and accept their forgiveness in return."

Alex, a political science major who often explores the intersection of personal values and social dynamics, speaks up with intensity. "In the poem 'Reciprocity,' there's a line that says, 'The true essence of receiving anything in life lies in what we have given beforehand.' Can you discuss how this principle applies to societal structures and our role in fostering mutual benefit in the broader community?"

"A very timely and significant question, Alex. This line speaks to the larger social fabric and how individual actions contribute to the collective well-being. In societal structures, reciprocity is often about giving to the community—whether through service, advocacy, or simply kindness—and in return, we create stronger, more resilient connections. It's easy to fall into the trap of taking more than we give, but true societal progress happens when we all recognize our responsibility to contribute to the greater good. By embracing this, we create systems that are not just transactional but transformational, where mutual benefit thrives, and everyone has a stake in the well-being of others. Reciprocity, then, becomes the foundation of social harmony and progress.

The professor pauses, letting the weight of the statement settle over the room. Glancing at the clock, he gives a small nod and says, "That's it for today. See you all next week—class dismissed."

As the class comes to an end, the students slowly gather their belongings, still processing the weight of the pedagogue's words. A quiet reflection lingers in the air, marking the conclusion of another transformative session. Professor Cromwell-Smith exits, his students are left reflecting on whether there's more they could offer to their seasoned, insightful professor.

"My reward," he declares, seeming to read their collective thoughts, "is your enthusiasm and dedication to this class. Your reciprocation is evident in the self-satisfaction I derive each week we convene here," he says, his voice carrying an air of reassurance as he walks toward the exit.

The student body absorbs his words, their admiration deepened. They realize that their collective effort and his relentless dedication are part of an enduring exercise in reciprocity.

Out in the hall, Elizabeth, Bart, and Sarah await him. For a moment, the group remains motionless, unsure of how to proceed, until Sarah steps forward with a radiant smile and hugs Erasmus tightly.

Erasmus, visibly moved, extends his arms, wordlessly inviting Elizabeth and Bart to join. What follows is a spontaneous "pile-on" of hugs, laughter, and unrestrained affection. The hallway echoes with their shared warmth, a poignant display of love and gratitude that requires no words.

Chapter 6

Defiance and Curiosity

Royal Cambridge Scholastic Institute (2019)
(Victoria & Erasmus' Campus Home)

Time has lost meaning as the magic of Michel Legrand's music envelops their cozy campus home. Erasmus and Victoria sit tightly squeezed together on their beloved Chesterfield sofa, each holding a mug of hot tea. Their faces radiate bliss, their shared contentment so tangible it feels almost like something they can taste.

"If not for your children, perhaps we wouldn't be together right now," Erasmus reflects, his thoughts lingering on last week's surprise visit by the three of them to his class.

"They put their hearts and souls into trying to find you," Victoria responds softly.

Erasmus looks at her, puzzled, his mind assuming it was Sarah's solo effort that led to their reunion.

"In the beginning, they needed a little push," she reveals, a knowing smile forming on her lips. "They got it from the most unexpected place of all."

As the morning light peeks through their windows, Erasmus takes a moment to absorb the joy of their shared morning. With a contented sigh, he prepares himself for the class ahead, the warmth of his connection to Victoria fueling his steps toward the university auditorium.

Royal Cambridge Scholastic Institute (2019)
(Class Auditorium, Next Day)

Entering the bustling auditorium, the energy of the class contrasts with the quiet contemplation of the previous night. Erasmus, though grounded in the moment, feels a shift within him as he steps into the space where he has the chance to impart the wisdom he has gained from both his personal experiences and his life lessons.

"How's everyone today?" asks the spirited professor with a twinkle in his eyes.

"Insanely awesome!" is the collective response.

"Class, sometimes in life, we must rise to the occasion and defy the circumstances and odds we are presented with. There are moments when we must stand up to what seems inevitable, affirming that we're not yet ready to surrender."

A silence falls over the room as the professor intentionally pauses, allowing his words to resonate deeply in the imaginations of his students.

"Last night, Victoria shared an extraordinary anecdote with me about the incredible lengths her kids went to in their effort to find me. It carries two crucial life lessons about what to do when fate seems to be in charge," Cromwell-Smith declares, his voice full of intrigue and warmth.

"The story begins like this …"

—✦—

St. Louis Public Library (2017)

The head librarian, Mrs. Rebecca Samuels-Ortiz, is in for the surprise of her life.

"Becca," comes a soft voice from behind her. She turns, and her jaw drops, her eyes reflecting total surprise.

"Elizabeth-Victoria?" she murmurs, confused, as she steps forward and embraces her effusively.

"Where's your mom?" she asks, noticing two youngsters with shy expressions standing a couple of steps behind.

Samuels-Ortiz recognizes them immediately.

"You must be Sarah and Bart," she exclaims excitedly, approaching them with a broad smile.

"We came without her," replies Elizabeth.

Mrs. Samuels-Ortiz now looks baffled as she leads them to her office's conference table.

"There must be a very good reason for all of you to have made this trip all the way here—especially without her."

"Becca, you understand Mom in ways we don't. We need your insight and reaffirmation to ensure that what we're doing for her is the right course of action."

"And what exactly would that be?"

"We've decided to locate Erasmus," states Elizabeth firmly.

Samuels-Ortiz's eyes precipitously sparkle, and her soft words are filled with loving conviction.

"Nothing would make your mother happier than having a second chance at being with her true love."

"What about Erasmus, Mrs. Samuels-Ortiz? Perhaps his life has gone in a different direction, and maybe he even has a family. Why should we interfere? Isn't fate already set?" Sarah challenges their hopes, her expression concerned.

The old librarian pauses, immersed in deep thought as she contemplates her mentee's offspring.

"You may very well be right, Sarah, but there are moments in life when we must challenge fate's seeming inevitability. Please allow me to share an old writing that fits this occasion."

The trio nods their heads ever so slightly. Almost simultaneously, Victoria's faithful friend disappears into the labyrinthine shelves of her office in search of the scribble.

"This is a tradition that Erasmus brought from Wales, one your mother adopted for life," she explains as she returns with a thick

*leather-bound book with gold burnished pages. Opening it to a
marked page, she begins reading earnestly.*

"Defiance"

When it arises for legitimate and valid reasons,
defiance is a deliberate and positive attitude—
an existential tool that empowers us
to challenge and confront
any kind of hardship.

It is an indomitable force,
so potent that, regardless of
life's obstacles,
unbearable circumstances,
material or emotional shortcomings,
even profound pain and sorrow,
once unleashed,
it ensures that neither
our resilience,
our will,
nor our desire to live,
much less our fighting spirit,
can ever be bent or tamed.

When we resist
in defense of freedom, dignity, and justice,
when we stand for the sake of truth,
when we oppose
oppression, persecution, and tyranny,
when we antagonize
bigotry, hate, and discrimination,
when we remain steadfast
behind virtue, values, and principles—

defiance becomes intrinsic
to what drives and sustains us.
It becomes the very means
by which we withstand,
outlast,
and ultimately prevail.

Defiance is the purest expression,
the release valve within life's turmoil,
igniting the inner fires
that lie at our very core.
Those flames that can never be extinguished,
as they burn and churn,
fueling our deepest passions,
our most unshakeable convictions,
and our firmest beliefs.

Defiance is our fiercest, most primal display—
a sheer force of will and steely resolve
against anything or anyone,
no matter how difficult or unsavory,
that life hurls our way.

Defiance is the attitude
that defines us best,
as true-life warriors—
those who not only
refuse to be conquered by hardship
but who face it square in the eye,
attacking relentlessly,
treating it as an enemy in war,
fighting until it is
vanquished, obliterated, and defeated.

Defiance is an existential weapon
we always carry within us—
a force to bend and break
hardship's aim and pain.
In defiance, we turn the tables,
facing life's vicissitudes head-on.
It is how we drown and conquer our fears,
how we defeat
some of life's greatest impostors.

"That's what you are doing, kids. You're defying fate."

Elizabeth and Sarah, in rapture, begin to cry again. Bartholomeus sobs quietly while smiling. Their eyes reflect profound gratitude, but before they can respond, the old librarian continues.

"There's another attitude that applies perfectly to this situation. An attribute you must cultivate and exercise to energize your efforts until you succeed."

She turns to a different page in the leather-bound book, marked precisely for this moment. Fixing her gaze on them with intensity, the erudite librarian begins to read steadily, her voice carrying weight and emphasizing every word.

"Curiosity"

When we itch to explore,
when we crave adventure,
when we feel an inkling to discover,
when we cannot wait to incessantly
dig, search, find, check, investigate,
analyze, study, experiment, and validate.

When we are unafraid of change,
the unknown, the unseen,
anything or anyone new.

When we are
keen to break the mold,
swim against the stream,
oblivious to conventional wisdom,
improvising and adapting on the spur of the moment.

When we can contemplate life
with candid, innocent, and dreamy hearts.

When we are not intimidated by:
how high, how deep, how low,
how big, how small, how impactful,
how irrelevant, how celebrated,
how despised, how demanding,
how patient, how calm,
how passionate, how defeated,
how triumphant
we may be, go, or become.

Then, we are in possession
of the magical elixir of curiosity—
a whimsical, existential-inducing bug
that carries us on a riveting journey,
lifting us above mundane reality,
wrapped in the mantle of an endless pursuit,
to be awed, amazed, or simply blown away
by the acquisition of precious
knowledge and experience.

Curiosity takes us
to countless labyrinths, mystical places,
memorable people, and transcendental moments.

Curiosity engages us with restless spirits
and a soul soaked with "the light and energy of life."
As an agent of change and the pursuit of wisdom,
curiosity is one of the most valuable
existential tools we possess.

Through curiosity,
we constantly refine our life's purpose,
revisit, renew, and define our meaning.

With curiosity,
we remain goofy, loose, and foolish.
If we deploy and employ curiosity,
we are always ready for "change,"
readily embracing evolution as well.

*

Prevailing over their intense emotions, Victoria's children are now smiling and visibly relaxed. Mrs. Samuels-Ortiz observes them with a satisfied expression, knowing she has fulfilled her mission with flying colors. As the group lingers in the comforting silence of shared understanding, the old librarian glances at the photograph on her desk—a younger Victoria holding a wide-eyed Elizabeth as a baby. "Your mother," she says softly, "would be so proud of the strength you've shown today—your curiosity to uncover the truth and your defiant refusal to accept her apparent fate. Both of these attitudes are driving you. You're not only honoring her but also charting your own paths," she concludes with conviction.

The trio exchanges heartfelt goodbyes with the woman who has shaped so much of their mother's life. As they leave the library,

*the faint chime of the entrance bell seems to echo with promise—
a sound that lingers in Rebecca's ears long after the door closes
behind them.*

—✤—

Royal Cambridge Scholastic Institute (2019)
(Class Auditorium)

As the professor's narration shifts back to the present, he
pauses, seemingly lost in thought for a moment. "Mrs. Samuels-
Ortiz's wisdom wasn't confined to the walls of her library," he
says, his voice softer now. "It transcended generations, shaping
not only Victoria's children but also every soul fortunate enough
to cross her path. In her ability to wield defiance and curiosity as
tools for transformation, she left a legacy that reminds us all to
never accept the limits life imposes without question." The
professor clears his throat, the weight of his reflection
dissipating as he meets the eager gazes of his students.

"Class, curiosity is indispensable when we must or wish to
decipher, analyze, or uncover decisions we're about to make or
actions we're about to take, as we carefully weigh the
consequences of our choices. On the other hand, defiance, when
guided by just and rightful reasons, becomes a necessary stance
to confront adversity, hardship, and especially the concept of
fate," the pedagogue pauses, letting the weight of his words
settle in the room. The quiet hum of anticipation fills the air. He
smiles, a knowing glint in his eye, before offering the class a
lesson in resilience: "Defiance and curiosity are not mere
concepts," he says. "They are tools that allow us to challenge
fate and the constraints of life itself."

A few hands are raised.

"Professor, haven't our studies shown us that fate is a completely false notion?" asks Kieth a History with long, jet-black hair pulled back in a ponytail.

"Spot on, Keith" the professor affirms with enthusiasm. "That is precisely the attitude we must take toward fate. The power of now—our ability to make decisions in the present—is what shapes our future. Fate is not some predetermined force; it is simply the consequence of the choices we make in the here and now. There is no fate," he affirms softly, the truth resonating in the quiet that follows. "Your actions shape your future—your curiosity and defiance are your most potent tools."

Ella, a philosophy major known for her insightful questions, asks with a thoughtful expression, "Professor, in 'Defiance,' you describe defiance as a force that can overcome adversity. How do you differentiate between healthy defiance that leads to growth and defiance that becomes destructive or self-destructive?"

"That's a very astute question, Ella," Erasmus responds, his eyes meeting hers with a look of respect. "Healthy defiance is rooted in a deep sense of purpose. It comes from a place of knowing what is right, standing up for personal values or the greater good. Destructive defiance, on the other hand, often arises from a place of resistance to growth or change. It's the refusal to see beyond one's immediate circumstances and can be driven by anger or fear. The key is self-awareness and a willingness to consider the consequences of one's actions."

Ella nods thoughtfully, her eyes still fixed on the professor as she considers the response.

Alexander, an engineering major with a penchant for asking probing questions, raises his hand with a contemplative look. "In 'Curiosity,' the poem speaks of the pursuit of knowledge and exploration. How do we maintain curiosity in a world that sometimes feels more rigid or set in its ways, especially in highly structured fields like mine?"

Erasmus nods, considering the perspective. "That's an interesting point, Alex. The world may feel rigid, but curiosity can still thrive in structured environments. It's about asking the right questions and looking for solutions in new and unexpected places. For engineers, curiosity is what drives innovation. The boundaries of what we know are constantly shifting because of the questions people continue to ask. Curiosity doesn't always mean breaking the mold, but sometimes simply seeing what's inside it, and seeing it from a different angle."

Alexander listens intently, nodding in agreement as he reflects on the professor's insight.

Lucia, a psychology major with a keen interest in human behavior, leans forward and asks, "In the poem 'Defiance,' there's a strong emphasis on fighting against hardship. But how do we reconcile this defiance with the psychological need to sometimes accept things as they are, especially when we can't control the outcome?"

Erasmus smiles, acknowledging the complexity of the question. "That's a very thoughtful inquiry, Lucy. I think defiance doesn't always have to mean fighting against everything. It can also be about not passively accepting what feels unjust or unnatural. It's about the ability to choose our response. Sometimes acceptance is the most defiant thing we can do, because it takes strength to surrender when needed, especially when we're faced with what we cannot change. True defiance is knowing when to stand up and when to step back, and having the strength to choose wisely."

Lucia nods in understanding, appreciating the depth of the response.

Victor, an international relations major with an affinity for literature, asks with a contemplative tone, "The idea of 'reciprocity' seems woven throughout both 'Defiance' and 'Curiosity.' How do you think these concepts relate to the way people interact globally, especially in terms of diplomatic relations and international cooperation?"

"That's an excellent connection, Victor," Erasmus responds, nodding thoughtfully. "Defiance and curiosity are not only personal tools but also vital elements in international relations. In diplomacy, defiance might look like standing firm on core values, even in the face of pressure, while curiosity is what drives us to understand the complexities of other cultures and the underlying reasons behind international conflicts. The ability to balance these two—holding firm when necessary, and remaining curious about others' perspectives—is essential for fostering cooperation and achieving peace in a globalized world."

Victor, deeply interested, takes a moment to digest the response before nodding in agreement.

With those final words, the class comes to a close, and the students, newly enlightened, gather their things in thoughtful silence.

"That will be all for today. Class dismissed."

As the professor leaves the room, the students wear expressions of profound thoughtfulness, as though they have been handed new, vital existential tools. With the intertwined magic of curiosity and defiance, they leave, ready to wield their newfound powers in the unfolding chapters of their lives.

Chapter 7

Decisions

Victoria and Erasmus' Home (2019)

There is a deluge outside. It's been raining for 24 hours. The middle-aged couple awoke at dawn. With hot teas and romantic tunes playing softly in the background, they remain bundled up in bed, indulging in a rare day of idleness. A passionate melody, Eros Ramazzotti's *Ma Che Bello Questo Amore* (How Beautiful Is This Love), fills the room, creating an ambiance of warmth and intimacy.

To Erasmus' delight, Victoria's feelings of guilt have almost completely dissolved. Over the past weeks, she has grown visibly more relaxed, her true self reemerging with each passing day. This transformation has brought forth her cheerful, carefree spirit, along with the enamored side of her that seems to draw her even closer, both emotionally and physically, to Erasmus.

"Dear, I have a secret to confess," Victoria announces with a mischievous undertone.

"OK, let me brace myself," Erasmus replies in mock apprehension.

"I preserved one of the writings Mrs. V. sent to us," she admits sheepishly.

"Which one?" he asks, his eyebrows rising in genuine surprise.

"The three-legged stool," she replies shyly.

"You preserved a priceless treasure, my lady. That scribble is invaluable," he remarks, his curiosity visibly piqued.

Erasmus stares at her with an intensity that seems to stretch into eternity, the music heightening the moment's depth. Victoria remains silent, Ornella Vanoni's *Dettagli* (Details) weaving its enchanting melody in the background.

Intrigued, Erasmus notices the familiar flicker in her eyes. "All right, my psychologist lady, where are you heading with this?" he asks, his tone probing yet tender.

"Nowhere," she replies evasively.

"Nowhere, as in, you have something to share but are hesitating to let it out?" he counters knowingly.

'*He always catches me before I even begin*,' Victoria reflects, startled by his instinctual ability to read her so easily.

"Dear, every time I read The Three-Legged Stool, I feel that our relationship back at Harvard had a true commitment of love and intense passion but lacked enough friendship or communication," she blurts out, her voice tinged with hesitation.

"Is that a justification or a fact, my lady?" he asks, his tone now stern as he absorbs her words.

"Intimacy was limited," she demurs, her voice wavering. Erasmus takes a long pause, his thoughts swirling as he reflects deeply. His gaze sharpens, and determination hardens his expression. Ornella Vanoni's *Nessuno al Mondo* (No One In The World Like You) plays, its emotive tones amplifying the tension.

"You mean to say that with just a glance, we could read each other's moods? Or that we knew what the other desired? Or how we could finish each other's sentences?" he begins, his voice growing more impassioned. "Or perhaps you're referring to the endless conversations—day after day, everywhere we went— about every facet of our lives? Or maybe it was the fact that during our time together, we were apart only for the briefest of moments? Is that the kind of lack of intimacy, friendship, and communication you're referring to?" Erasmus' words are laced with pointed sarcasm.

Victoria withdraws momentarily, grappling with his response and her own feelings. After a few moments of reflection, she regains her composure, meeting his gaze with renewed clarity and resolve. Laura Pausini and Gilberto Gil's *Seamisai* (If You Love, You Know) permeates the room with its enchanting melody.

"Did I create my own fantasy to justify my decisions and choices, dear?" Victoria asks, her voice barely audible over the music.

"I'm not sure. Please enlighten me," Erasmus replies, his tone tinged with annoyance.

"It seems that instead of gratefully accepting and enjoying what I have, the glass always appears half empty, and my focus is on what I believe I am missing," she declares, her words heavy with introspection.

"I don't think so," he finally articulates. "That's just a convenient excuse. Your real problem is that your perspective is negative even when your glass of life is full. When behaving like this, you always see your glass half empty while yearning to make your own fantasies real," he snaps, his words cutting through the warm atmosphere.

"Tell me about it," she pleads softly.

"Tell you about what?" he asks, puzzled.

"About our life together back then, at Harvard, from your perspective."

Erasmus pauses, his gaze turning inward as he searches through the recesses of his memory. His eyes lose focus, traveling back in time as Sandra Mihanovich's *Habla El Alma* (The Soul Speaks) fills the room, resonating deeply with their mood.

Lost in reminiscence, Erasmus recalls the places, the people, their laughter, the anecdotes, the readings, their shared rituals, plans, and the extraordinary dreams they wove together.

"Don't you remember any of it?" he finally asks.

"Of course I do, my love. I recall all of it vividly," she reassures him, her voice steady as her mind replays those cherished moments.

"But?" he probes, sensing there's more.

Victoria hesitates, her lips quivering as she wrestles with her thoughts. Charles Aznavour and Laura Pausini's *Parigi in Agosto* (Paris in August) drifts through the air, casting a contemplative spell over them.

"It's just that you've recorded and remembered our lives together in a way that I haven't. Either because I avoided it or because of my loss, I denied the extent to which I had it. You pointed out that I always see the glass half empty, and my perception, as a result, is limited. For me, without a doubt, it was the best period of my life. I regret that it went by so fast and was too short. But, if you hadn't helped me just now, I wouldn't have been able to remember our life together in the detail that you do. You've made my memories an immense treasure. You can literally recall every day, every minute, every moment. It's extraordinary. Now, I feel like I'm in a time machine, revisiting and reliving our life through your recollections in a way I didn't see before," she admits, her sincerity shining through.

"So, Vicky, you know the answer to your question better than I do. You know exactly what was missing in our three-legged stool."

"Nothing was missing," she speaks aloud, her voice firm with realization.

Erasmus knows better but chooses to remain silent.

Pablo Milanés' profoundly moving *Para Vivir* (In Order To Live) envelops them, pulling at their hearts.

"The only thing missing was me," she says, her epiphany dawning in her voice.

"You were there, alright, my lady, but only partly." Her newfound clarity inspires Erasmus, his admiration for her evident.

The rain has stopped, and daylight filters through the windows. Yellows, reds, and oranges replace the gray hues, bathing the room in warmth. Their embrace radiates a shared understanding, their tight hold a silent promise.

"If I may ask, my loving erudite, what will be the subject of your class this morning?" she inquires, her voice tender.

"Decisions," he says cryptically.

Victoria studies Erasmus intently, a quiet resolution forming in her heart.

"How fitting, dear. Well, I've decided I will never again look at life as a half-empty glass, always yearning for what I don't have. I promise to adopt the attitude of a half-full-glass kind of person," she declares with conviction.

"Fantastic, my lady," he replies, his delight unmistakable.

"All in the name of love, my dear," she murmurs, her voice sleepy but content.

Alejandro Sanz's *La Fuerza Del Corazón* (The Strength of the Heart) continues to play as the deeply enamored couple drifts into a world of dreams, wrapped securely in each other's arms.

Royal Cambridge Scholastic Institute (2019)

(Campus Streets)

'Remarkable,' With his heart still full from the morning, Erasmus pedals toward the faculty building, the brisk morning air, crisp and invigorating against his skin. *She's come full circle. She sought atonement by confronting her past head-on, and once she achieved it, she turned inward, focusing on her character and virtues,* muses.

The serenity of the morning with Victoria lingers in his mind, but he feels the weight of his responsibility as a teacher settle in once again. His thoughts shift, readying himself for another day in the classroom.

Royal Cambridge Scholastic Institute (2019)
(University Auditorium)

Professor Cromwell-Smith strides down the halls with a spring in his step, his heart swelling with pride for his other half.

As he enters the classroom, the pedagogue's mind shifts again, this time focusing on the students in front of him. He's aware, more than ever, of the delicate balance between the life he's shared with Victoria and the lessons he's about to impart. With a quiet breath, he readies himself to bridge the gap between the personal and the academic.

"Good morning to all of you," he greets his students warmly, his broad smile lighting up the room.

"Good morning, Professor Cromwell," the student body responds in perfect harmony, their voices filled with respect and enthusiasm.

"Decisions," he begins, his voice resonant and measured. "So hard to take, so difficult to make. How many of us struggle daily, over long periods, or even our entire lives, wrestling with the choices we face?" he continues, his gaze sweeping across the room, ensuring every student feels the weight of his words.

"Today, I'll take you back in time to a moment when I was at a crossroads, grappling with a crucial decision. In my search for clarity, I turned to one of my most trusted mentors—an antiquarian steeped in the wisdom of New England."

He pauses, the room falling silent as his students lean in, captivated by the promise of his tale.

"It all begins like this …"

—✦—

By Train from Boston to New Haven, CT (1977)

I'm on my way to meet Mr. Lafayette, the antiquarian of gallant French ancestry. Victoria and I visited him every time Harvard played Yale University. He's always been a beacon of wisdom, helping me navigate the most challenging subjects or situations in my life.

When I arrive at his store in New Haven, he leaps from his trusted reading chair and hurries toward me with a bear hug and a kiss on each cheek—the French way—even though his Gallic ancestry is two or three generations removed.

"What a pleasure to see you here, Erasmus," he exclaims, his voice rich with warmth, tactfully avoiding the subject of Victoria's disappearance.

"The pleasure is mine, Mr. L.," I respond, slightly overwhelmed by his effusiveness.

"I know you're living in America now, but why don't you tell me exactly what you're up to?" he asks with genuine curiosity.

"A few months ago, I started teaching at Brandeis University. I love what I do, and I'm confident this is my calling in life. But when I'm alone, her absence still hurts. I came all the way here to see you because I need your guidance. Somehow, I need to find a way to let go and move on with my life," I plead, the pain in my voice unmistakable.

Mr. Lafayette studies me intently, his piercing gaze seeming to reach into the depths of my soul. For what feels like an eternity, he says nothing, his silence heavy with thought.

"Erasmus," he begins with measured clarity, "from what I've heard from your other mentors—my fellow antiquarians—and

what I observe here today, it's clear that you must decide to move on. Not just acknowledge the need to let go, but consciously decide to put your breakup behind you. And once you've made that decision, implement it with unwavering resolve," he says emphatically, each word landing like a carefully placed stone.

He pauses for a moment, then adds, "I have a scribble that perfectly illustrates the predicament you find yourself in. Let me retrieve it."

With long, deliberate steps, Mr. Lafayette walks away, leaving me alone with my thoughts. He returns quickly, carrying an enormous leather-bound ancient book that looks as though it holds the wisdom of centuries.

"I will now read this to you," he declares, his voice imbued with the authority and passion of a true pedagogue.

"Decisions"

There are no worse decisions in life
than the ones we never make—
not to be confused with choosing to do nothing
or taking no action,
as those are still decisions we consciously make.

Why is it
that so many of us
are so utterly indecisive
about our lives and our futures?

Decisions to ponder, wander, and wonder.
Decisions we nail or blunder,
contest or tender,
waste or reap,
reach or press,
accept or reject,

rejoice or despise,
elevate or bury,
doubt or believe in,
pursue or avoid,
reverse or affirm,
lament or relish,
reluctantly take
or passionately embrace.

Decisions, decisions, decisions to make—
about which paths to follow,
the alternatives we choose,
or the course of action we take.

Being decisive is hard and difficult,
for it demands we conquer
our worst insecurities and fears.

Decisiveness is the consequence
of resoluteness and determination
to bring matters to a conclusion,
one way or another.

Being decisional is the result of readiness—
the readiness to form actionable options
and act upon them
by selecting
from the choices we face.

Decisions always reap guidance.
Through decisions, life's dynamics
unfold and take shape.

It is how everyone and everything,
for better or worse,

forward or backward,
moves and responds
within the circle of life.

In this context,
to decide is not a choice
but an existential imperative.

Without decision,
we fall into a catatonic void,
and life passes us by,
unclaimed and unfulfilled.

Decisions, decisions, decisions to make—
decisions that overwhelm us,
sucking the air out of our lungs,
yet persist, never disappearing.

To be alive requires decisionism.
It is essential to our existence.
There is no way around it.

When a choice presents itself,
when the moment arrives
to form an opinion,
choose a path,
or act—
make the decision,
move on,
and continue.

Decisions are immanent choices,
ones we must perpetually face
as long as we remain participants
in the circle of life.

*

"Mr. Lafayette's words hang heavy in the air, their truth undeniable. Erasmus sits in contemplative silence, the wisdom of the antiquarian's reading resonating deeply. As the train carries him back to Boston, his thoughts churn with newfound resolve, each mile marking a step closer to the decisions he knows he has to make."

— ✦ —

Royal Cambridge Scholastic Institute (2019)
(University Auditorium)

Professor Cromwell-Smith takes his class out of their deep concentration with a pointed reminder.

"Always remember, the worst decisions in life are those you never make. Indecision renders you a spectator, not a participant in life," emphasizes the eminent pedagogue, his words carrying the weight of conviction. The words of Mr. Lafayette still echo in the Professor's mind as he recalls his visit years ago. 'To decide is not a choice, but an existential imperative,' Lafayette had said. Now, back in the present, as the familiar faces of his students watch him attentively, Erasmus realizes that each moment is, in fact, a decision — one that shapes his own journey forward.

"Now, I'd like to open the floor for questions," Professor Cromwell-Smith says, his voice inviting and warm. "Please feel free to ask anything related to the subjects we've covered today."

Madison, a creative writing major, raises her hand and is called upon.

"Professor, in the poem *Decisions*, the emphasis is placed on the existential weight of the choices we face. How do we reconcile the tension between the necessity of making decisions and the overwhelming nature of those decisions, especially

129

when the consequences are unclear or daunting? How do we avoid paralysis by analysis?"

"Madison, that's a thought-provoking question. The fear of making the wrong choice is something many people struggle with, and it often leads to a sort of 'analysis paralysis.' In the poem, we see that the real danger isn't in making a wrong decision—it's in failing to make a decision at all. Indecision itself is a decision, but it leads to stagnation. The key is to remember that no decision is ever completely without risk, and the uncertainty that comes with making choices is just part of the process. Instead of waiting for the 'perfect' moment to make a decision, we must trust ourselves to act, knowing that we can always adjust our course as we go. In a way, the act of deciding is what gives us clarity and direction."

Steven, a neuroscience major, asks the next question.

"Professor, in the poem, decisiveness is described as the result of overcoming insecurity and fear. From a psychological perspective, how can we develop a mindset that encourages decisiveness, especially when we feel overwhelmed or uncertain about the right choice?"

"Steven, that's an insightful question. One of the core challenges in decision-making is that it often requires us to confront our fears—fear of failure, fear of regret, or fear of making the wrong choice. In psychology, this is closely tied to self-efficacy, which is our belief in our ability to make effective choices and handle the consequences. To cultivate decisiveness, we need to build confidence in our ability to make decisions and trust in our capacity to adapt if things don't go as planned. This starts by setting small, low-risk decisions and building momentum. Over time, we learn that making decisions, even difficult ones, doesn't lead to catastrophe. Instead, it propels us forward, and that forward motion is often what helps us grow."

Lindsey, a literature major and a sharp focus in her eyes, speaks next.

"Professor, the poem describes life as a continuous process of decision-making, and yet, it also speaks of the overwhelming nature of those choices. How do we maintain a sense of purpose and coherence in our decisions when we're constantly confronted with so many paths to choose from?"

"Lindsey, that's an important observation. The poem speaks to the paradox of decision-making: while we are constantly making decisions, the sheer number of options can sometimes make us feel overwhelmed. The key to maintaining purpose and coherence is alignment—making decisions that reflect our values, goals, and sense of self. If we can stay connected to our core beliefs and what matters most to us, even the toughest choices become easier to navigate. It's about knowing what guides us and making decisions that align with that deeper purpose. Even when faced with many paths, when we act in accordance with our values, we create coherence and direction in our lives."

Leonard, a psychology major with an athletic build and a sharp jawline, speaks up next.

"Professor, the poem emphasizes the existential imperative of making decisions, yet it also highlights the toll that constant decision-making can take. How do we balance the need for action with the necessity of reflection and pause? How do we ensure that we're making decisions with intention rather than out of impulse or exhaustion?"

"Leonard, that's a nuanced question. The poem captures the urgency of decision-making, but it's also important to remember that decisions aren't just about speed—they're about intention. We can make decisions with purpose and clarity by creating space for reflection. While some decisions need to be made quickly, others benefit from taking a step back. This is where practices like mindfulness and self-reflection come into play. By pausing, reflecting, and gaining perspective, we can make decisions that are grounded in our true values, rather than reacting impulsively or from a place of exhaustion. Balance is key—decisiveness isn't about rushing through life; it's about making choices that align with who we truly are and what we want to achieve."

As the professor wraps the class, he observes the student body's contemplative expressions, their brows furrowed in thought. He surmises they are grappling with the decisions they have yet to confront and reflecting on the choices they've already made—or avoided—on their journey.

"That will be all for today. I'll see you all next week," Professor Cromwell-Smith concludes, his words lingering like echoes of wisdom. As the students rise and file out of the auditorium, he hands each of them a copy of the happiness formula, his gesture filled with quiet hope for their journeys ahead.

He watches them leave, each one likely pondering the choices they've yet to make, or the ones they've already committed to. His gaze lingers for a moment, feeling the weight of the day's lesson and the quiet satisfaction of a shared, unspoken understanding.

As the last of his students exit the auditorium, their murmured conversations fading into the corridor beyond, Professor Cromwell-Smith lingers at the lectern, gazing out over the now-empty seats. The silence feels heavier, more contemplative, after the depth of their shared discussion. Gathering his notes and adjusting his glasses, he allows himself a rare moment of reflection. The echoes of the past and present intertwine, and he silently wonders which seeds of wisdom, if any, have found fertile ground among his students.

Straightening his posture, he walks toward the door, his mind already preparing for the next lecture—a chance to explore life's complexities further and, perhaps, to inspire a few more hearts.

Chapter 8

Resilience

Martha's Vineyard, Massachusetts (2019)
(Gay Head Lighthouse)

Erasmus and Victoria have been pedaling around the island for hours. A gentle breeze makes their ride most enjoyable as they traverse the picturesque seaside landscape of blossoming flowers and manicured gardens. They dismount their bikes and walk toward the majestic cliffs known as "the Gay Head." Finding a comfortable spot, they sit down to enjoy the artisan sandwiches they've brought along.

"Erasmus, it's time," Victoria blurts out suddenly.

"Time?" he echoes, his tone incredulous.

"Yes, it's time for you to tell me about your personal life while we were apart," she says with a playful smile, her eyes sparkling with curiosity.

Erasmus, at first taken aback, pauses as he gazes at her, the surprise quickly melting away.

'Nothing wrong with being inquisitive; after all, she's been an open book with you,' he reasons. 'Besides, even if she hadn't been forthcoming, you'd still fill in the blanks. Isn't that right?' he questions himself, conceding fairness to her.

"Your orders are my command, my lady," he declares with a mock bow, signaling his readiness to comply.

The afternoon sun hovers high above the horizon, casting a golden glow over the cliffs as Erasmus begins to take Victoria on a journey through his past. His voice is calm but tinged with emotion as he shares a chapter of his life that had been shaped by both fulfillment and longing.

"Victoria, as you know, I started writing while we were at Harvard. It wasn't something I planned—it simply flowed onto paper, expressing the intensity of our love while we were together. Once I began scribbling, I found I couldn't stop."

He pauses briefly, looking out at the sea before continuing, his words carrying both pride and vulnerability.

"My first big project was a novel. It took an extraordinarily long time—especially at the start. I had no idea what I was doing. The process was filled with trials and errors, endless rewrites, and even the complete scrapping of entire manuscripts. Eventually, though, I managed to finish it."

Victoria listens intently, her gaze never wavering, as he continues.

"Soon after, albeit with great reluctance and low expectations, I took the finished manuscript to a publisher right here in town," Erasmus shares, his voice softening as he recalls the memory.

—✤—

Boston, Massachusetts (1989)
(Erudite Renaissance Press Offices)

"Your book is very poorly written, Mr. Cromwell," the female executive proclaims, her tone firm and unyielding.

Erasmus sits across from Rachel Thurman, the head editor at Erudite Renaissance Press and, without a doubt, one of the most strikingly beautiful women he's encountered since first meeting Victoria at Harvard. Her elegance and commanding presence are undeniable, yet her sharp critique cuts straight to the bone.

"This is not only my opinion but the consensus of several of our senior editors and proofreaders. They will not touch it as is," she states bluntly, her words leaving no room for ambiguity.

For most aspiring writers, this would mark the end of the road—a rejection delivered in no uncertain terms. Typically, such news would be conveyed in a written note or a brief phone call. But Rachel Thurman has chosen to deliver this verdict in person, motivated by an inexplicable fondness for the stubborn professor sitting before her. However, his unshakable self-confidence and immutable stubbornness push her buttons in ways she can't entirely ignore.

"And about your second submission," she continues, "poetry does not sell. Period. Don't waste your time." Her tone is final, her gaze challenging.

As she finishes her sentence, something unexpected happens. Erasmus smiles—a genuine, unbothered smile that catches her completely off guard.

'How ironic,' she muses, her irritation mounting. 'He's smiling after being told his work is unpublishable.'

"Professor Cromwell, I don't recall ever seeing an aspiring writer smile at me when rejected," she snaps, her frustration evident.

"Mrs. Thurman, perhaps you could join me for dinner, and we could discuss it further," he responds calmly, the suggestion leaving her momentarily speechless.

"What?" she exclaims, her voice rising in disbelief. "Mr. Cromwell, didn't I make myself perfectly clear?"

Her tone sharpens, but inwardly, she acknowledges his audacity.

'This guy is impervious to rejection,' she thinks, grudgingly admiring his indomitability.

It's then that his warm smile and gentle eyes manage to pierce through her defenses.

"You're serious?" she asks, her voice softening, a trace of teasing in her tone.

"It would indeed be a pleasure," he replies smoothly.

"When?" she asks, her resistance finally giving way to curiosity.

"Right now, as soon as you leave the office," he says, his tenacity never faltering.

For the first time, Rachel Thurman smiles back.

La Provence Bistro, Downtown Boston (1989)
(French Restaurant)

The dinner conversation begins with Erasmus sharing his memories of arriving in America, punctuated by shared laughter.

"Everything seemed so modern and advanced other than the people's manners, language, and knowledge – all of which seemed to originate from a land of barbarians."

"I was also clumsy, odd, and would stumble into anything and everything," he adds with a wry smile.

After a few glasses of wine and savoring the finest gourmet cuisine, Rachel Thurman's tongue loosens, revealing her unchecked candor.

"I pride myself on dating the right type of man," she blurts out, her tone laced with arrogance.

"Rachel, let me be very frank with you," Erasmus interjects, choosing to ignore her self-important comment.

"Don't tell me! You're a superhero, and this disguise is your secret personality and persona?" she retorts, sarcasm dripping from her words.

"Perhaps I am; one never knows. But tell me something. If you like my book so much, what are you afraid of?" he counters, his question striking with unexpected precision.

Her smile vanishes as she studies him, intrigued by his boldness. Rachel senses the dynamic shift. The conversation is no longer light-hearted—it's becoming a battle of wits. There's a flicker of renewed interest in her eyes.

"Pardon my naïveté. I'm catching on. You're posturing, setting me up to negotiate my intellectual property rights. You're trying to manipulate, bargain, and extract a great deal for your publishing company," he presses further, unrelenting in his challenge.

Rachel opens her mouth to respond but pauses as his piercing eyes seem to unravel her intentions. She smiles mischievously, surrendering a couple of honest words.

"Business is business, Erasmus."

Ignoring her declaration, Erasmus remains silent. But her use of his first name catches his attention. He smiles, and she reads him just as well.

A distinct dissonance lingers between them, evident even on this first date. Rachel's priorities and Erasmus's values clash, their hearts beating to different rhythms.

Erudite Renaissance Press Offices (1991)

For several months, Erasmus's first book has held a prominent position on the bestseller list.

"Congratulations! Your first royalties' payment, Erasmus," Rachel exclaims, planting an impassioned kiss on his lips as she hands him the check.

Erasmus takes a cursory glance at the amount before slipping it into his pocket with little fanfare. Rachel's eyes widen dramatically.

'He couldn't care less,' she thinks in frustration.

"How does it feel to be a very wealthy university professor?" she probes, hoping to elicit some excitement.

"Exactly like it felt a minute ago. Nothing has changed. I never celebrate having nor making money, Rachel," he replies with casual indifference.

"Maybe now you can consider quitting that job of yours at the university and devote your time to writing full-time," she suggests, her exasperation seeping through her tone.

He doesn't bother to respond, leaving her simmering in silence.

Sniffles Highlands Trail, Telluride, Colorado (1991)
(Summer)

They've been hiking for hours, winding through dense forests and traversing open meadows. As they climb higher along a narrow mountain path, they're greeted by an explosion of wildflowers, sparkling streams, and, at 12,000 feet, an enchanting hidden valley.

At first, they hear a faint trickle, then the crescendo of a roaring waterfall, revealed like a secret behind a rocky turn. The idyllic scene seems untouched, perfect for a postcard.

Hungry and weary, they settle down to devour their artisan sandwiches and energy drinks. Their conversation is sparse, the silence between them untroubled.

"The view from my house is hard to match, but this stunning landscape might just do it," Rachel observes, her tone casual.

"But nothing is cozier than our condo overlooking the Charles River," she adds, her voice trailing off into a steady stream of admiration for her belongings, her rosy cheeks glowing in the crisp mountain air.

Erasmus listens, searching for a connection that feels increasingly elusive.

'What's hers is hers, but what's ours? Where's the heart in all of this?' he wonders silently.

Inca Trail, Cuzco, Peru (1991)
(Winter)

The day's hike has been grueling, a marathon of endurance through breathtaking scenery. At last, as they turn a sharp corner, Machu Picchu unveils itself—a mystical city suspended in the clouds, its ancient walls basking in the afternoon sun.

"Rachel, we're on top of the world," Erasmus exclaims, drenched in sweat but exhilarated.

"Yep, another bucket list item checked off! I can't wait to tell everyone. I did it. I finally did it," Rachel declares, her enthusiasm laser-focused on the achievement.

Her self-congratulatory tone misses Erasmus's growing disenchantment.

'She's blind to the journey's wonder—the mountains, the history, the shared experience. Her triumph is about her circle, her conquest. Where's the empathy? The heart?' Erasmus reflects his joy dimmed by the widening emotional chasm between them.

Hermitage Museum, St. Petersburg, Russia (1992)

In the heart of the Hermitage Museum, Erasmus is spellbound, absorbed in the museum's opulent treasures. For hours, he marvels at the intricate designs, the vivid colors, and the sheer artistry of Fabergé's masterpieces.

Rachel, meanwhile, shifts impatiently, stealing glances at her watch.

'How can anyone spend this much time on decorative trinkets? It's been three hours, and my checklist is far from done,' she fumes inwardly.

On a short break, Erasmus beams, his face lit with unrestrained excitement.

"Rachel, what an experience! The colors are mesmerizing. The integration of malachite, jade, lapis lazuli—it's extraordinary. And those imperial Easter eggs, they're incomparable," he gushes.

Rachel masks her irritation behind a tight grin, her patience worn thin.

"I hope you're ready to leave. Those eggs took up two hours," she mutters internally.

Erasmus, finally catching her lackluster expression, asks, "Bored, Rachel?"

"To death," she replies curtly, her words sharp enough to slice through his enthusiasm.

A few moments later, they leave the museum—one of the world's most extraordinary cultural treasures—abandoning its magnificence to pursue her checklist of sites around the city.

Erasmus walks in silence, the sting of her indifference a weight he cannot shake.

Cortina d'Ampezzo, Italy (1991)
(Winter)

"Where's Erasmus, Rachel?" Brigitte asks, glancing around the vibrant, snow-covered mountain restaurant filled with their lively group of friends.

"Skiing," Rachel replies casually, swirling her glass of wine, her cheeks flushed from the afternoon's indulgence.

"When do you two even see each other?" Mark, a colleague, prods curiously.

Rachel sighs and leans back in her chair. "Well, he's up before dawn, rushing to be the first on the slopes when they open. I don't even get out of bed until around eleven. Once I finally make it up the mountain, I track him down on his favorite runs. We ski together for a while and then stop for lunch."

"And after lunch?" Brigitte presses with a knowing look.

"Oh, he's relentless—he keeps going until the ski patrol chases him off the slopes," she adds with a bright smile, *"But, during the pre-ski hours and all through the night, he's all mine."*

Rachel waves at Erasmus, who emerges through the colorful crowd of skiers. His smile broadens as he spots her, his helmet and gear giving him the aura of a devoted ski enthusiast.

'They're like two dissonant clocks—hanging next to each other on the same wall yet ticking in completely different rhythms,' Brigitte muses silently, her observant eyes noting the gap in their connection.

Restaurant "Jules Verne," Eiffel Tower, Paris (1993)

"Erasmus, we've been together for four years. We've traveled the world. I've supported your teaching and writing careers, and we've become... comfortable with each other," Rachel begins, *her tone a mixture of longing and frustration.*

'Where is she going with this?' Erasmus wonders as he sips his wine, ever the picture of calm curiosity.

"It's been lovely, Rachel. You're right," he replies, uncertain *of the storm brewing beneath her carefully measured words.*

Rachel's patience snaps. She wants to yell at him, to demand attention, but knows it would only slide off his immutable exterior. She tries jealousy—it's never worked before, but she's desperate for a response.

"When are you going to ask me?" she blurts, the words flying *out before she can stop them.*

"Ask you about what?" Erasmus replies, *his absent-minded professor demeanor showing no trace of awareness.*

"To marry me, you silly fool," she half-shouts, her frustration *bubbling to the surface.*

Erasmus freezes, his sharp gaze narrowing as his lips press into a thin line. The charged silence makes Rachel's heart pound as she watches him, hoping for a declaration, fearing rejection.

"Rachel," he finally says, his voice calm but chilling, "let me bluntly ask you something. If I weren't a successful and wealthy writer, would you consider marrying me?"

The question lands like a thunderclap. Rachel's confidence falters, and she hesitates before responding. When she does, her honesty is like a blade.

"No, definitely not."

The weight of her words settles between them, an unspoken understanding sealing their fate. Whatever tenuous bond had kept them together evaporates in an instant.

Later that evening, they board their flight home. They chat casually, laugh about their trip, and even doze off against each other's shoulders, sharing a final semblance of intimacy.

When they land in Boston, they part ways at Logan Airport, kissing goodbye for the last time. They never speak or meet again.

'I really liked Rachel, and we had a wonderful time together,' Erasmus reflects days later. 'But she was never my type.'

Martha's Vineyard, Mass., Gay Head Cliffs (2019)

Victoria's posture as she leans forward is one of a mesmerized listener brimming with questions.

"I get the picture, dear. I get it," she utters softly.

Still mulling over what to say, Erasmus hesitates, uncertain what to add next, but her quizzical expression compels him to continue.

"Victoria, I know exactly what's going through your mind. I understand that I owe you at least some level of transparency.

While I won't delve into irrelevant details, I want to remain respectful to the women I became acquainted with during our years apart. I can tell you that several things were consistent in my life over the years, especially regarding female companionship. First, during our separation, I was seldom alone. Second, aside from my relationship with Rachel and another woman in Europe, all my associations were extremely discreet. Most of my companions were former—emphasis on former—students. Third, Rachel was not the first to propose marriage to me. This happened several times, but I was never inclined, much less willing, to accept. Fourth, the longest of these relationships lasted four years, while the shortest spanned six months. All these women, without exception, went on to marry happily and have children. Lastly, I won't disclose how many relationships there were, but Victoria, there were several," he states in a measured tone.

Victoria's face lights up with a mix of delight and clarity as she clings to his arm while they begin walking back to their bikes. Silence accompanies their journey toward the ferry terminal, but after a few minutes, Victoria halts abruptly, and Erasmus stops too.

"I'm proud of you, dear," she says, her voice trembling with emotion.

"I feel so fortunate to be loved this much by you. I'm the luckiest woman in the world. You longed for and waited for me all these years, hoping I would resurface."

Letting her bike fall to the ground, she steps forward to embrace him and kisses him passionately, her gratitude and affection pouring through her every gesture.

Together, they pedal through a kaleidoscope of colors as the sky transitions from the brightness of a clear day, with its crisp whites and yellows, into flaming hues of orange and incandescent red. By the time they near their destination, the night has enveloped the world in deep blues, a luminous full moon, and a canopy of star-speckled blackness, marking the end of their ride in serene splendor.

Train Ride from Hyannis Point to Boston (2019)

Victoria rests half-asleep on Erasmus's shoulder, the soothing rhythm of the train lulling her into a peaceful haze. Suddenly, she stirs and softly asks, "Sweetheart, what will be the subject of tomorrow's class?"

"Resilience, my lady," Erasmus replies, his mind already immersed in the preparation of his lecture.

As Erasmus pedals toward the faculty building, the weight of his conversation with Victoria lingers in his mind. He reflects on the power of resilience, which now shapes both his personal journey and the theme for the day's lecture.

Royal Cambridge Scholastic Institute (2019)
(University Auditorium – The Next Day)

He enters the auditorium, his thoughts still tangled with the idea of resilience that had come up in his earlier conversation. The students are already seated, awaiting his words, and as the door swings open, Erasmus is ready to guide them through another lesson that feels deeply personal today.

"How's everyone today?" Professor Cromwell-Smith greets his class warmly, his voice carrying a palpable energy.

"Insanely awesome!" the students respond in enthusiastic unison.

"Today, we'll be talking about resilience," he begins, pacing slowly across the stage. "Resilience is the ability to adapt and bounce back when life knocks you down. It's what allows us to face challenges, endure hardships, and emerge stronger. This is not just a survival skill—it's a virtue."

He pauses, his gaze sweeping the room to ensure he has their full attention.

"I'll take you back to a moment in my life when resilience became a defining element of my character. To overcome adversity, we must understand it, accept it, and then rise above it. The story begins like this …"

The professor's voice lowers, signaling the start of another journey into a deeply personal and meaningful life lesson.

— ❖ —

Rowing on the Charles River (1977)

Ever since Victoria and I first met Mr. Faith by chance while rowing along the Charles River, I've maintained the habit of visiting him at his shop on the outskirts of Boston every time I row.

Today, after docking and securing my rowboat, I stroll through the streets of the small village, my steps marked by trepidation and excitement at the thought of seeing my old friend and mentor, Thomas Albert Faith. His antique bookshop, adorned with his name, houses countless treasures of knowledge.

As I step into the sacrosanct place, Mr. Faith is busy dispatching a client, who exits right past me, arms laden with voluminous books clutched tightly against his chest. I hold the door ajar, and the diminutive customer barrels into his waiting limo driver on the sidewalk, who leaps to assist with the load.

"Erasmus, what a pleasure to see you. It's been a long time. Where have you been?" Mr. Faith calls out, moving toward me with his characteristic slow, deliberate steps. He wraps me in his signature bear hug, and, as always, the final squeeze knocks the wind right out of me.

"Mr. Faith, how have you been?" I squeak, struggling to catch my breath.

"Getting old, but otherwise fine," he replies warmly.

"Look at you, all grown up. You even look like a professor now," he adds, his broad smile lighting up the room.

"Mr. Faith, I thought about visiting you of all people because you're the best suited to help me," I announce sternly. "You see, I'm struggling with desire and perseverance. I love my work and devote myself entirely to it, but it feels hollow. Something's missing, and, worst of all, I recognize what it is. I indulge and get lost in thoughts and memories of my past," I confess.

Mr. Faith listens intently, pacing with deliberate steps as if weighing my words. Then, without a word, he strides to the far-right end of his impossibly tall, library-like athenaeum. From the first row, he selects a medium-sized leather-bound book and returns to me, his demeanor both solemn and reassuring.

"Erasmus, here I have the perfect prescription for your current affliction," he begins, his voice resonant with conviction. "It's a scribble I treasure deeply as it touches on the heart of what you're seeking. Your struggle is with resilience—a virtue you must cultivate to confront life's challenges and transcend them. I hope this writing will help you develop resilience as an existential tool moving forward."

With that, he opens the book to a page marked by a red cord. He quickly scans the old writing, and upon finding the precise paragraph, he begins to read in earnest, his voice imbued with the wisdom of ages.

"Resilience"

Resilience lies at the core
of the very essence of the human spirit.
It is a vital, virtuous existential condition,
composed of sheer character power,
and unyielding, awe-inspiring willfulness.

Resilience is the untamable drive,
burning fire,
unflinching defiance,
relentless resistance,
fearless courage,
stubborn perseverance,
unwavering belief,
and an unstoppable hunger—
the fuel required to live with the intensity,
passion, and endurance
needed to succeed at any endeavor.

The resilient person tries again,
never stops,
does not give in to exhaustion,
bounces back,
moves forward,
does not dwell on the past,
adapts in an instant,
perennially studies and learns,
and ignores rejection.
The resilient person uses fear as a strength
and does not comprehend the words:
boredom,
gossip,
lingering grudges,
or jealousy.

The resilient person endures hardship,
overcomes tragedy,
learns from criticism,
treats failure as an opportunity,
mistakes as lessons,
defeats as temporary,

uses "no's" as incentives,
and never, ever quits,
much less surrenders.

Resilience is that quasi-superhuman force
that allows us:
To embark on challenging and demanding quests,
with fortitude and self-confidence.

To endure right up to completion,
despite seemingly insurmountable
challenges, setbacks, and difficulties.
To dare life,
defying all odds,
with absolute conviction and self-belief—
that no matter who or what,
we will, in the end, succeed.

*

"As Mr. Faith's voice faded, Erasmus felt the words resonate deeply within him. The scribble had stirred something dormant—a flicker of determination, a spark to confront his inner struggles. As he left the bookshop and walked back to the river, the sound of oars slicing through the water mirrored the rhythmic beat of his renewed resolve."

— ✦ —

Royal Cambridge Scholastic Institute (2019)
(University Auditorium)

As Professor Cromwell-Smith moves from his personal story to the lecture, he feels the weight of the past experience shaping his words in the present, and as the pedagogue's message settles over the room, a profound silence ensues, broken only by the faint shuffle of papers and the occasional cough, while students exchange glances, their faces marked with a mix of awe and determination, clearly moved by the lesson on resilience that has struck a chord, leaving them inspired and introspective; Professor Cromwell brings the class back to the present with a few additional words of timeless wisdom.

"Resilience is intrinsic to the sacred, serving as a propelling force for those who defend truth, honor, honesty, family, and loved ones.

It is the same driving energy for individuals who, on principle, stand firm for an ideology, religious belief, ethnicity, nation, land, or social group. Resilience also applies to the more mundane pursuits of life—when we passionately chase dreams, commit to ideas, or uphold duties to provide, respect, defend, and love.

Finally, resilience is indispensable for pragmatic endeavors, such as planning, building, delivering, complying, and ultimately finishing what we start," the erudite professor concludes, his words reverberating through the room.

With a final glance at his students, the pedagogue's voice takes on a more contemplative tone, as he prepares to bring the lecture to a close before opening the floor to questions. He pauses for a moment, allowing the weight of his words to settle in their minds.

Sarah, an English literature major known for her philosophical reflections, raises her hand, her face thoughtful. "Professor, in 'Resilience,' the poem emphasizes unyielding persistence in the face of hardship. How do you reconcile this idea with the notion of knowing when to let go, especially when continued effort might only lead to further suffering?"

"That's an insightful question, Sarah," Erasmus responds with a thoughtful pause. "Resilience, in this sense, isn't about mindlessly pushing through every obstacle. It's about knowing when to press on and when to step back. True resilience involves awareness and discernment—it's recognizing when an obstacle is a lesson or an opportunity to grow, and when it's simply a signal that the best way forward is to let go and redirect one's efforts. It's not about stubbornly fighting every battle; it's about fighting the ones that matter and knowing when to conserve your strength for the right moment."

Sarah nods, contemplating the balance between persistence and knowing when to pivot, her eyes reflecting the weight of the professor's words.

Joshua, a psychology major with a focus on emotional resilience, leans forward, his curiosity piqued. "In the poem, resilience is described as a force that allows us to rise again after failure. But how do we distinguish between resilience and stubbornness? Can there be a fine line between the two?"

Erasmus offers a small smile, appreciating the depth of the question. "There is indeed a fine line, Joshua. Stubbornness often comes from a place of ego—refusing to adapt or learn from failure. Resilience, on the other hand, is rooted in growth. It allows you to acknowledge failure, learn from it, and adjust your course. Stubbornness keeps you locked in the same pattern, while resilience empowers you to evolve. It's about choosing to stand back up, not because you have to, but because you have learned something important along the way."

Joshua seems satisfied with the response, his brow furrowed in thought as he considers the practical application of this idea in his own life.

Lynn, a biology major who has studied the neurological aspects of stress and resilience, asks, "Professor, resilience in 'Resilience' is presented as a kind of inner strength. From a scientific perspective, what role does the brain play in cultivating this strength, and how does it affect our ability to bounce back after emotional setbacks?"

"Great question, Lynn," Erasmus says, his tone appreciative. "From a biological standpoint, resilience is a function of both the brain and the body. The prefrontal cortex helps us regulate our emotions, make decisions, and adapt our behaviors in response to stress. The hippocampus, which is involved in memory and learning, also plays a key role in how we process setbacks and use them as tools for future growth. On a more emotional level, resilience is a learned behavior—it's the brain's ability to adapt to challenges, strengthen connections through experience, and build emotional fortitude. The brain, just like our hearts, is capable of incredible recovery, provided we give ourselves the tools and space to heal."

Lynn smiles, clearly fascinated by the intersection of neuroscience and the human experience of resilience.

Vincent, a history major with a particular interest in the psychology of leadership, poses his question with confidence. "Professor, 'Resilience' speaks of persistence, but how do you see this concept in the context of leadership? How does resilience manifest in leaders who face overwhelming odds?"

"That's an excellent connection, Vincent," Erasmus responds. "In leadership, resilience is not only about pushing through personal challenges but also about maintaining the strength to lead others through difficulty. A resilient leader demonstrates the ability to remain calm, adapt, and inspire action even when faced with failure or hardship. They don't shy away from challenges they confront them head-on, not because it's easy, but because their responsibility is to guide others. A resilient leader embraces setbacks as opportunities for growth, not just for themselves but for their team. They understand that every failure is a lesson, and every setback is a steppingstone to greater success."

Vincent nods, the gears in his mind turning as he considers how resilience might shape the future of his own leadership journey.

"That'll be all for today; see you next week," declares Professor Cromwell as he exits the auditorium.

"That'll be all for today; see you next week," declares Professor Cromwell as the bell rings, signaling the end of class. The students remain transfixed for a moment, their expressions a mixture of awe and determination, their eyes reflecting a collective resolve as they grasp the depth of resilience and its necessity for enduring and succeeding in life. Slowly, they begin to file out in silence, each carrying the message of resilience with them. Erasmus watches them leave from the doorway, knowing that today's lesson will resonate long after they've exited the room.

Chapter 9

Life, Beauty, and Art

Victoria's and Erasmus's Campus Home (2019)

"Erasmus, why is it so difficult for you to reveal your inner self?" Victoria asks in the quiet stillness of the early morning.

He remains contemplative, his eyes soft yet searching hers for a moment as though weighing her question carefully.

"I'm always an open book for you to read, my lady," he finally replies, though his puzzled expression and the flicker in his gaze betray him.

"Dear, why do I still have to pry things out of you? Perhaps you thought you could get away with only sharing your love affair with the publisher?" she teases, her smile widening as she reads the guilt in his eyes when he looks away.

His gaze sharpens, intensifying as he prepares to unveil something deeper, prefacing it with two cryptic words.

"Venice and Florence," he says, his voice distant, as if tethered to memories beyond their cozy home studio.

Her brows furrow in confusion, sensing he's about to open another door to his guarded soul. What she doesn't yet realize is that this door leads to a world she didn't know existed within him.

"I've been visiting both places every other year for forty years," he admits softly.

Victoria stiffens, startled by the revelation. They've shared more than two years back together, yet this is the first mention of Italy—Italy, of all places. She resists the urge to interrupt, choosing instead to wait as her curiosity swells.

"Vicky, at one time, both cities became a magnet for me," he continues, his words cryptic yet laced with meaning.

"Why?" she asks, her tone layered with skepticism and a touch of impatience. Her unspoken thoughts are clear: *What's all the fuss? Why the secrecy?*

"Antonella D'Agostino is an antiquarian living in Venice, Italy. She's about to turn 75, nearly a decade older than me. She's been married for 55 years to her childhood sweetheart, Luciano D'Agostino, a retired banker. Together, they have two children—a son who's an architect and a daughter who's a writer. Their children have given them twelve grandchildren and one great-grandchild," he narrates, his tone imbued with deep reverence and affection.

Victoria feels a rush of conflicting emotions as her imagination races. *He hasn't referred to her in professional terms,* she notes, her gut instinct flaring. A growing unease churns within her, as she senses where this might be heading.

But she couldn't be more wrong. Whatever scenario she's conjuring in her mind falls woefully short of the truth he's about to reveal.

"I met Antonella on my first trip to Italy while visiting her antique bookstore. I was 25 years old, and she was 35."

Victoria listens intently, trying to connect the dots but instinctively choosing to let Erasmus guide her through this labyrinth of revelations.

"She introduced me to the world of books authored during the Renaissance era. Through her, I became versed in deciphering the markings of ancient scribbles," he continues, his tone almost detached, as though trying to distance himself from the significance of the memory.

Victoria finds herself at a crossroads: let the story unfold naturally or press him for more details. Her curiosity, tinged with a streak of masochism, prevails. Placing her proverbial hand on the hot stove, she decides to prod further.

"Dear, what's the significance of this antiquarian in Italy?"

Erasmus avoids her direct question, choosing instead to continue at his own measured pace.

"Antonella worked in tandem with Leonardo Conti, an antiquarian based in Florence. Throughout my life, I spent many summers shuttling back and forth between the two antiquarians and their cities. With their guidance, I became proficient in deciphering books written in the middle of the 15th Century onwards," he explains, his voice steady, yet Victoria senses an undercurrent of emotion.

Why is it that the story, as innocuous as it seems on the surface, still rings alarm bells? she wonders, grappling with the unease that churns in her gut.

Erasmus shifts his gaze, finally looking directly into her eyes. For the first time, she feels he's fully present, as though weighing his next words carefully.

"And?" she pushes, her tone laced with quiet insistence, implying that there's more beneath the surface.

"And what?" he counters, his tone feigning incredulity.

Victoria hesitates, momentarily pulling back, but her instincts override her caution.

"Did you?" she blurts out suddenly, her words cutting through the tension like a knife.

Erasmus holds her gaze, his expression unreadable as an eternity seems to pass. His eyes flicker with a faraway look, wandering through memories long buried.

"Is it important?" he asks, his voice betraying a subtle hesitation.

"It is to you. Obviously, you want me to know; otherwise, you wouldn't have raised the subject, at least not like this—

emphasizing her personality more than her trade," Victoria counters, her tone sharp with irrefutable logic.

He remains silent, though she notices a fleeting sadness cross his eyes before it dissipates like a passing shadow.

"It was never meant to be something serious. She never contemplated leaving her husband. Neither did I want it to be more than an annual summer fling. It was always a discreet affair," he admits, the words spilling out with a noticeable sense of relief.

Victoria is entirely absorbed in the moment, her instincts whispering that something feels unresolved.

"When did it end?" she probes.

"Fifteen years ago," Erasmus replies, offering her a wave of relief.

"And yet, you chose to tell me this last, after disclosing all the other 'relevant' relationships in your past," she muses aloud, her tone laced with suspicion.

Victoria's words carry an unspoken accusation of something still unspoken, though Erasmus refrains from defending himself. Instead, he meets her glare with quiet resignation.

Why does this even matter anymore? It's all water under the bridge, her rational mind protests, but her emotions steer her in the opposite direction.

"Dear, how old are Antonella's children?" she asks, her voice sharper now.

Erasmus avoids her gaze.

"The oldest is … wait a minute, where are you heading with this?" he questions, his confusion evident.

"Erasmus, let me hazard a guess: both children are under forty, aren't they?" she counters, her rhetorical tone gaining momentum.

"What exactly are you implying, Victoria?" he asks, his discomfort deepening.

"Were Antonella and her husband unable to conceive children before you, the absent-minded love of my life, came into their lives?" she presses.

Erasmus falters.

"Yes, but how do you …?" he begins, only to trail off, his eyes widening as the weight of her implication sinks in.

"That wouldn't …" he stammers, his voice cracking.

"How do you know?" she persists, unwilling to let him evade the question.

Finally, he lowers his head, his body language heavy with surrender.

"I don't," he confesses.

Images of Antonella's vibrant, quintessentially Italian children flood his mind. Their happy and accomplished lives unfold in his memory, and he recalls his role as the beloved "uncle" from America—a relationship nurtured by Antonella herself.

"Victoria, you know what? Let it be. Whatever the truth may be, some things are better left as they are, even unsaid," he declares, his voice resolute, his gaze steady.

Victoria reacts instinctively. She moves toward him, placing her hands gently on his face, her eyes softening.

"I love you," she whispers, choosing to let the matter rest.

An important chapter of Erasmus's past has emerged, but its presence no longer looms. Together, they silently agree to move forward.

An hour later, as Erasmus readies for class, Victoria resumes their familiar routine.

"And what will be the subject of your class today, dear?" she asks, her voice calm and collected.

With a spirited energy, Erasmus heads for the door.

"Art and beauty," he replies over his shoulder.

Victoria waits, sensing there's more to come.

"It'll be about Florence and Venice, but strictly censored to the professional and poetic sides of it," he adds, turning to blow her a kiss before hopping onto his bike and pedaling off.

After a lingering kiss at the doorway of their campus home, Erasmus steps outside, feeling the warmth of the morning still wrapped around him. Victoria, standing at the doorstep, sends a playful kiss back, her hand lingering in the air as she watches him leave. As Erasmus rides to the university, the peaceful journey allows his mind to wander, shifting between memories of Italy, his conversation with Victoria, and the bustling energy of the campus he approaches, ready to engage his students. Now alone, Victoria reflects on Erasmus's Italian escapade, her thoughts a blend of curiosity and quiet acceptance.

— ✦ —

Royal Cambridge Scholastic Institute (2019)
(University Auditorium)

Entering the lecture hall, Erasmus feels the familiar weight of his role as professor settle upon him. The energy of the classroom, filled with eager faces, grounds him in the present. As he stands at the front, his heart steadies, and his mind shifts back to the intellectual landscape of art and beauty.

"Good morning, everyone," greets the venerable professor with a warm, resonant voice.

"Good morning, professor," replies the spirited student body in unison.

"Today, I'll take you back in time to revisit the Italian peninsula, where, in my early twenties, I met a couple of antiquarians who profoundly impacted my life. We'll recount a memorable occasion when they helped me better understand and appreciate my surroundings during that pivotal period," the sovereign professor begins, his tone imbued with anticipation.

"Inexorably, there was a time in the 15th century when all the roads for the world's antique books led to Italy—not just to Rome, but particularly to Venice and Florence. These cities, in their own right, were even more consequential than the ancient capital when considering the burgeoning market of printed books," Professor Cromwell-Smith elaborates, drawing his audience into the narrative.

"Prior to the 15th century, in 1440, the German-born Johannes Gutenberg invented the movable-type press, sparking a revolution in book printing. In the sixty years that followed, millions of books were published, heralding the birth of a European book trade and making the widespread dissemination of knowledge an irreversible phenomenon across all levels of society," he adds with fervor.

"In the mid-15th century, thanks to its immense wealth, the Italian peninsula became Europe's epicenter for publishing. This development was culturally fitting, as most books at the time were written in Latin or Greek—the languages of Rome and Athens. Venice and Florence emerged as dominant hubs for book production, fueling the Renaissance's intellectual and artistic flourishing. This abundance of books enriched minds like Leonardo da Vinci, who prized his library of magnificent volumes. These texts served as vital resources for his groundbreaking ideas, inventions, and, most notably, his unparalleled art," the professor continues, his passion for the subject unmistakable.

"This historical context sets the stage for the heart of today's lesson—art and beauty," he concludes, transitioning seamlessly into the story.

"It all begins in Florence, Italy, the heart of the Renaissance," Professor Cromwell-Smith continues, his voice steady and infused with admiration. "Florence was not only the creative hub for luminaries such as Leonardo da Vinci, Michelangelo, Galileo, Machiavelli, Dante, and Boccaccio but also a city that served as their intermittent home during this era of unparalleled enlightenment," he declares, his eyes scanning the room for engaged faces.

"This city wasn't just a geographical location; it was a crucible of ideas, a confluence of art, science, and literature that forever altered the trajectory of human history. Florence's spirit fostered an environment where intellects and visionaries thrived. They were drawn to its vibrant culture and patronage of the arts, a testament to the city's unmatched contribution to the Renaissance," he elaborates with unwavering conviction.

Without pausing for breath, the professor continues, fully immersed in the subject. "Here, genius wasn't an anomaly—it was a legacy. Florence didn't merely witness the Renaissance; it orchestrated it, birthing and nurturing minds that would shape our understanding of beauty, humanity, and the cosmos."

— ✤ —

Conti, Libri Antichi,
Antique Book Store, Florence, Italy (1979)

*The antique bookshop of Leonardo Conti is nestled within walking distance of the **Battistero di San Giovanni** and Florence's old city center. Il Signore Conti specializes in books from the Renaissance era, specifically between 1450 and 1500, when over two million books were printed across Europe, with the Italian Peninsula serving as the epicenter of this literary revolution. Conti is a renowned trader of books from this golden period, a reputation further amplified by his collaboration with* *another prestigious antiquarian, Antonella D'Agostino, who owns an antique bookshop in Venice.*

"Mr. Conti, Mrs. D'Agostino, the art and beauty of Italy are utterly overwhelming. It's almost impossible to process all the magnificence that surrounds me," I confess, struggling to contain my awe. "I wonder if you have any books written about art and beauty during the Renaissance era. If so, perhaps we could explore them together," I beseech the two antiquarians, my voice a mix of curiosity and yearning.

After a thoughtful exchange with Signora D'Agostino, Signore Conti is the one to act. Rising with purpose, he begins an intricate search among the mahogany shelves of his cavernous bookshop. The dim light of the shop accentuates the reverence with which he handles the volumes. Finally, from the very top of an imposing cabinet, he retrieves a brown leather-bound book. With a practiced hand, he clears the dust from its cover, revealing an aged but regal tome. By its weight and thickness, it's evident this book spans at least 500 pages, each made of cloth paper.

As he opens it, I'm immediately struck by the hand-painted drawings that adorn its pages. The vibrant colors, delicate lines, and intricate details seem to breathe life into the centuries-old artwork. The beautifully stylized fonts demand attention, while hand-written annotations grace the margins, providing a glimpse into the mind of the book's original owner.

Signore Conti carefully turns the pages, scanning them with an almost reverential focus. Finally, his eyes alight on the passage he seeks. His expression brightens with enthusiasm as he clears his throat. Then, with a voice propelled by passion and expertise, he begins to read aloud, transporting us all into the heart of the Renaissance.

"Life, Beauty, and Art"

Where does beauty reside? Where does it lie?
Where is it found?
Beauty begins within us—
inside all of us,
waiting to be discovered,
waiting to be tapped.

To see beauty in anything or anyone,
we must first recognize the beauty within ourselves.
Where else can beauty be found?
Understanding that it begins with us,
we come to realize and appreciate
that we are surrounded by it.

The beauty we possess
enables us to find it
in everyone and everything else.

However, attractiveness is not always apparent at first glance.
There is dirt and darkness
where diamonds are hidden,
mud and disease
where gold is unearthed,
seemingly buried beneath impenetrable rocks.

There is litter and chaos
where masterpieces are born,
debris and dust
where magnificent craftsmanship emerges,
slime and sulfur
where oil riches burst forth.

Incoherence and lack of meaning
mark the initial scribblings

of the finest works,
and pain, sweat, and tears
are the price of the noblest human achievements.

Where does beauty originate?
Sometimes, beauty is born of ugliness.
It is most deeply valued
when uncovered from the depths of what appears hideous.

Beauty is best appreciated
when it defies stereotypes
and challenges conventional wisdom.

Yet for many, beauty is conferred in abundance,
only to go unrecognized,
its existential worth overlooked,
its magnificence unrealized.

When beauty fails to ignite satisfaction,
the spirit and soul remain hollow and empty.

In all its dimensions, beauty—
whether in possessions or people—
requires a benevolent disposition to be admired.

As life's clock ticks, beauty changes and morphs.
But for those who truly know
how to feel and celebrate it,
beauty never fades, diminishes, or disappears.
Physical youth provides and masks beauty,
but through the years,
the richness of our spirit and soul—
or the lack thereof—
is etched into our faces.

Without the masks of youth,
we reveal who we truly are inside.

Life's truest beauty lies hidden,
ready to be uncovered,
if we make the effort to seek it.

The beauty of a life well-lived
ages with nobility and grace.
Beauty shines brightest
in those life travelers
who live free of limiting
dogmas, prejudices, or stereotypes;
those who find and cherish
pulchritude, attractiveness, and charm,
the liveliness and comeliness of existence,
grace, and anything pleasing to the senses.

True beauty resides in those
who celebrate life fully,
who truly love and are loved,
who give selflessly, expecting nothing in return.

It is found in those who actively participate in life,
who value the small gestures and details,
and who pour their hearts and souls
into everything they do.

They live with passion, inspiration, and happiness.
These are the ones who possess lasting beauty—
a beauty that transcends
place, circumstances, age, or material wealth.

Lasting beauty never fades.
It is one of life's most precious gifts—
one of the hardest to master.

It requires cultivation as an inherent virtue,
to appreciate, wear, and treasure it,
even when it seems absent.
<u>But when does beauty become art</u>?
Art is inherent in beauty,
just as beauty is inherent in art.
Art is born of beauty.
Art creates beauty.
Beauty must be perceived for art to exist,
as art transforms ordinary into sublime, exceptional,
and extraordinary into masterful.

Art alters perception,
not only making objects appealing,
but also evoking feelings with meaning and purpose.

Art creates an intimate, quasi-spiritual connection within us.
It speaks the language of the spirit,
mirroring the soul.

Art resonates with beauty,
infatuating the heart.
Beauty is always driven and born from art.

Like beauty, art exists in the eye of the beholder.
And if so, there are no limits—
no boundaries to what art can be.

A scribble, an essay, a craft—
everything beauty touches
transforms into art.
Art is a deliberate human creation,
inspired by talent, skill,
and the heart.

Even unintentionally,
art is shaped by method, technique,
and intuitive study
rooted in knowledge and intellect.

Art is grace and a blessing—
one cannot help but feel
the hand of the divine
behind its mastery.

At the crossroads of beauty and art
reside the most sublime connections
between the human spirit, soul, and creativity.

It is here that life's mastery lies,
where our unique talents are harvested,
where continuous inspiration and happiness are found.

When we master beauty and art,
we are truly alive.
Both require <u>vital engagement</u>—
a heightened sensory state,
intimately connected with creation.
We become champions of existence,
squeezing, feeling, and savoring
the best life has to offer.

*

"Erasmus, beauty and art are intricately entwined, forming a bond so profound that one cannot truly exist without the other," declares Antonella, her voice imbued with conviction.

"They are not merely complementary; when united, they become a force of nature," adds Leonardo Conti, his eyes glinting with passion.

"Together, they create contagious, continuous, and contiguous virtuous circles, serving as the very enablers for experiencing life at its fullest potential."

"As their words settled over him, Erasmus felt a profound connection to the interplay of beauty and art they described. The timeless wisdom shared in this Florentine shop would resonate with him for years, shaping not just his understanding of art but his very essence as a poet and educator."

—✦—

Royal Cambridge Scholastic Institute (2019)
(University Auditorium)

The weight of the past—of Venice, Florence, and the antiquarians he met there—lingers in his thoughts. Yet, as the present moment calls for his attention, Professor Cromwell-Smith returns to the lecture hall, ready to weave his past experiences into today's lesson on the profound relationship between life, beauty, and art.

Erasmus pauses, allowing the weight of history to sink in. The room is still, the air thick with anticipation. "Now that we understand the historical roots of beauty and art in the Renaissance," he begins, his voice commanding yet gentle, "let's explore how these ideals live on today. Ask me what you've always wondered about the relationship between life, beauty, and art."

Sophia, an art history major with a deep interest in Renaissance art and philosophy, asks thoughtfully: "Professor, in the poem 'Life, Beauty, and Art,' the idea that beauty can be born from ugliness is explored. How does this notion align with the Renaissance ideals of beauty, especially considering the period's emphasis on harmony and proportion in art?"

Professor Cromwell-Smith nods, appreciating the complexity of the question. "Ah, a brilliant observation, Sophia. The

Renaissance ideal of beauty was indeed rooted in harmony and proportion, but what the poem suggests is that true beauty often emerges from struggle, from transformation. Think of the way Michelangelo's sculptures, like *David*, begin as rough blocks of marble—it's only through chiseling away, through a process of struggle, that beauty is revealed. In the Renaissance, artists believed in the idea of *arte povera*, that even in imperfection or the harshness of life, beauty could be discovered. The same can be said of human experience—beauty often comes through hardship, a concept that resonates with the poem's message that beauty is not just in the surface, but in the deeper, often hidden, parts of life."

Sophia nods thoughtfully, her mind processing the connection between art and life's struggles.

Liam, a philosophy major with a passion for aesthetics, raises his hand and asks: "Professor, the poem also suggests that beauty is most appreciated when it defies stereotypes. In a modern context, how can we apply this principle, especially in a society where beauty standards are often rigid and defined by external appearances?"

Professor Cromwell-Smith 's expression softens, appreciating the depth of the question. "Liam, that's a timely and profound question. In a world where social media and advertising often dictate what is considered beautiful, it's crucial to remember that true beauty defies those surface-level standards. It's not confined to the perfect figure or flawless skin. The poem reminds us that beauty is found in authenticity, in embracing the imperfections of both ourselves and the world around us. If we look at artists like Frida Kahlo or the works of writers like Virginia Woolf, we see that beauty arises from their unique voices and the depth of their experiences, not from conforming to established standards. To appreciate beauty in its full complexity, we must look beyond the surface and celebrate the richness that comes from individuality and resilience."

Liam considers the professor's response, a contemplative look settling on his face as he processes the connection between beauty and individuality.

Elena, an English major known for her reflective approach to literature, asks: "In the poem 'Life, Beauty, and Art,' it's suggested that art is born of beauty, and beauty is inherent in art. Could you expand on how this relationship works, particularly in the context of literary art?"

Professor Cromwell-Smith smiles, clearly intrigued by the question. "Elena, that's a wonderful inquiry. In literature, beauty is not always something you see with your eyes, but something you feel with your heart and mind. Art, particularly literary art, takes the raw material of life—often the mundane or painful— and transforms it into something that resonates with meaning and emotion. A well-crafted poem, a novel, or a story takes life's struggles, beauty, and imperfections and turns them into something that elevates our understanding. Think of a poet like Emily Dickinson, who turned ordinary scenes and emotions into works that transcend the everyday. Art is about transforming reality into something more profound, and beauty is that transformative force that connects the artist's vision to the audience's soul."

Elena's gaze deepens as she absorbs the idea that beauty in art is both transformative and deeply personal.

Amir, a sociology major with an interest in the intersection of culture and art, asks: "The poem mentions that beauty can be overlooked, its worth unrealized. In a society driven by consumerism, how can we help people recognize and appreciate the beauty around them?"

Professor Cromwell-Smith pauses, weighing the question carefully. "Amir, you've touched on an important point. Consumerism often reduces beauty to something that can be bought, packaged, and sold—something we can possess rather than experience. To help people appreciate beauty, we must encourage them to engage with the world more mindfully, to seek beauty in the small, everyday moments—whether in nature, in relationships, or in the arts. It's about slowing down and truly seeing, feeling, and experiencing. We also need to foster spaces—both in society and in our education systems—where people can explore and create art that is not driven by commercial interests. When we value the process of creation over the end product, beauty becomes something that nourishes the soul, not just the pocketbook."

Amir nods thoughtfully, considering how cultural shifts might help reframe our relationship with beauty.

Ethan, a psychology major with an interest in how art affects the mind, asks: "Professor, the poem suggests that beauty is eternal for those who truly understand it. From a psychological perspective, why do you think beauty, in both art and life, has such a lasting impact on the human psyche?"

Professor Cromwell-Smith reflects for a moment before responding. "Ethan, beauty has a lasting impact because it connects us to something deeper than ourselves—it taps into the emotional and psychological core of who we are. When we encounter beauty, it evokes feelings of joy, awe, and meaning, often triggering a state of mindfulness. Psychologically, beauty can elevate our mood, reduce stress, and even inspire creativity. Art, in particular, acts as a mirror to our emotional lives, allowing us to process complex feelings and experiences. This is why beauty, whether in a painting, a poem, or a fleeting moment, can resonate with us throughout our lives—because it speaks to the fundamental human need for connection, expression, and understanding."

Ethan looks visibly moved, as if the conversation has unlocked a new perspective on beauty's psychological significance.

"I want each of you to conduct a simple but profound exercise. Identify everything and everyone you consider beautiful in your life, then distinguish those you regard as art," he instructs, his voice measured and deliberate.

"For our next session on a single sheet of paper, itemize beauty and art as they manifest in your world. Reflect deeply on how they interweave with your existence," he assigns, leaving the class immersed in their thoughts.

The room buzzes softly as students exchange contemplative glances, their pens hovering over notebooks as they begin to list the people, places, and objects that bring beauty and meaning to their lives. Some faces lit up with inspiration, while others grew pensive, delving into their memories. It is clear the professor's challenge has stricken a chord, sparking a deeper awareness of the art and beauty in their everyday existence.

Professor Cromwell-Smith steps back from the podium, a sense of fulfillment washing over him as he surveys his students. Their faces are marked by introspection, each seemingly lost within their own interpretations of beauty and art, weaving intricate connections between the lesson and the world around them. With a final nod, he turns and exits the lecture hall, leaving the students seated in quiet reflection. As he walks away, his mind shifts toward the solace of his home and the ongoing journey of understanding beauty in life and art.

Chapter 10

Serenity, Courage, and Wisdom

Boston's Riverside (2019)

The downpour has transformed into a merciless deluge. A northwestern surge has pushed the river to breach its banks, submerging Boston's streets. Massive streams of water carve new paths, while drivers cautiously inch forward, unaware of the worsening storm aimed directly at them. Visibility is near zero, rain pelting down in unrelenting sheets.

Elizabeth Victoria Emerson-Lloyd feels a strange motion under her vehicle—something sinister and powerful. Water begins to seep through the seams of her car doors, creeping into the cabin. Panic sets in as she grabs her tote bag and tries to open the door, but the force of the water outside holds it firmly shut. Instinctively, she rolls down her window—counter-intuitive yet lifesaving. As water surges to her ankles, her engine sputters and dies.

Acting on adrenaline, Elizabeth moves swiftly, twisting her body and pulling herself out of the window with athletic ease. But outside, the torrent is even fiercer. Water rises to her waist, rushing with alarming force. Clinging to her car door handle, she struggles to keep herself steady. Courage begins to wane as her precarious situation grows dire.

"Help!" she cries, her voice barely audible over the roar of the flood.

Those nearby are equally helpless, stranded by the raging currents. Then, as if by divine intervention, a pair of strong hands grip her firmly under her arms, lifting her effortlessly out of the water.

She's hoisted above the chaos. With swift, determined strides, her savior carries her towards the safety of a raised pickup truck parked on a hill overlooking the river, far from the danger zone.

"Relax, you're safe with me," a deep, calming voice reassures her, his breath warm against her ear.

Once inside the truck, Elizabeth sits near the heater, placing her bare feet against the blistering vent, her soaked clothes clinging to her skin. She avoids looking directly at her rescuer, afraid her eyes might betray the overwhelming emotions surging through her. She feels her pulse quicken—a mixture of gratitude and something more profound.

Her savior is striking—6'2" with jet-black hair, piercing blue eyes, and an air of confidence that radiates from his every movement. He admires her agility, recalling the remarkable sight of her pulling herself through the car window.

"I've got a pair of dry socks in my gym bag," he says, reaching for it. As he turns back, his hand grazes her forearm and leg, an unintentional touch that sends shivers coursing through her. She jolts slightly, and their eyes meet—locking, holding, and speaking volumes in silence.

Time seems to freeze as their gaze deepens. His hand finds hers, resting lightly on her knee, a gesture of both reassurance and undeniable connection.

"Jordan," he introduces himself, his voice soft but steady.

"Elizabeth Victoria," she replies, her words tinged with awe and disbelief.

"I don't want any socks right now," she teases, her voice playful yet trembling with the intensity of the moment.

"Wild woman, you're going to wear a warm pair of socks before you catch a cold," Jordan insists, his tone firm yet caring. With assertive yet gentle movements, he slides the socks onto her feet. Elizabeth feels a wave of heat—his touch electrifying her senses.

Her skin's warmth ignites an unfamiliar, intense sensation within him. Their words flow freely as they share their lives, passions, and dreams. The storm outside becomes irrelevant, a mere backdrop to the growing intimacy within the truck's cabin. Smoke curls in the air, mingling with the warmth of their voices and laughter.

By the time the night begins to wane, they've unraveled layers of each other's souls. Both outdoor enthusiasts, they bond over shared adventures, realizing the storm has forged a connection as natural and inevitable as the rivers they both cherish.

Their shared adventures evolve into a symphony of discovery and passion. Together, they conquer towering peaks, climbing Mount Wilson and Mount Sneffels in the majestic San Juan Mountains near Telluride, Colorado. The ascents are both grueling and exhilarating, cementing their bond as they revel in the breathtaking vistas that unfold with each step. These peaks become a shared sanctuary, but it is Jordan's turn to introduce Elizabeth to the skies.

Skydiving and kite surfing become thrilling new chapters in their lives, with Elizabeth embracing the adrenaline rush with unrestrained enthusiasm. Jordan, in turn, teaches her the art of gliding, a pursuit that quickly becomes their favorite shared activity. Soaring silently through the clouds, they revel in the unspoken connection and sense of freedom these flights bring.

Elizabeth, ever the linguist and polyglot, adds another layer to their relationship, teaching Jordan Spanish, Mandarin, and German. Lessons often blur the line between learning and play, their sessions punctuated by laughter, flirtation, and deepening intimacy. The fiery, seductive tension first ignited on that stormy night never fades; it only intensifies, infusing their lives and passions with an energy that fuels their every endeavor.

Over time, Elizabeth learns of Jordan's most cherished and solitary hobby—piloting hot air balloons. The mystery of his reluctance to share this pursuit with her intrigues her. Determined, she begins a playful but persistent campaign to join him. She teases and persuades, but Jordan resists, his reasons veiled behind an enigmatic smile.

Eventually, her persistence wears him down. On a crisp, clear morning, Jordan finally invites her to join him for a flight. They arrive at a secluded launch site, the vibrant balloon standing tall against the endless blue sky. As they prepare for takeoff, both harbor secrets—closely guarded surprises waiting to unfurl.

The morning is electric, charged with anticipation. As the balloon gently ascends, the world falls away, leaving only the whisper of the wind and the boundless horizon. Each is aware that the other has something to reveal, but neither speaks yet, savoring the beauty of the moment.

Elizabeth's heart races, not from the height, but from the weight of her secret. She glances at Jordan, his eyes fixed on the horizon, a subtle smile playing on his lips. Little does she know, his heart mirrors hers, thundering with the anticipation of his own surprise.

Above the world, amidst the serene expanse of the sky, their surprises unfold. What begins as a simple flight becomes a turning point, an indelible memory that reshapes their lives forever. It starts like this …

— �֍ —

Santa Fe, New Mexico (2019)
(Annual Hot Air Balloon Festival)

The scene is nothing short of magical. The sky, alive with vibrant hues, is a sprawling canvas painted by hundreds of hot air balloons, each uniquely shaped and radiating color. The annual Santa Fe Balloon Festival has transformed the heavens into a mesmerizing kaleidoscope, drawing aeronauts and dreamers from across the globe.

Among them, piloting his elegant balloon with practiced ease, is Jordan Augustus Morse, a brilliant aeronautic engineer. Nestled at his side, holding tightly to his arm, is Elizabeth Victoria Emerson-Lloyd, the woman who has captivated his heart and soul. In just six months, their whirlwind romance has blossomed into something extraordinary—a union that feels, as Elizabeth often muses, like a celestial decree.

As the gentle breeze carries them over the desert landscape, the couple is spellbound by the carnival of balloons that drift alongside them. The only sounds are the occasional bursts of the burner, the rustle of the wind, and their quiet, shared breaths.

Elizabeth turns to Jordan, her green eyes sparkling with love and mischief. She holds a small leather-bound journal close to her chest.

"My love," she begins softly, her voice full of affection, "of all of Erasmus' unpublished works, there's one I hold dearest. With his permission, I brought it along to share with you today. It feels especially fitting for this moment—for us, here, floating above the world."

Jordan tilts his head, intrigued. His eyes, a piercing blue, lock onto hers, the corners of his mouth curling into a smile.

"Dedicated to me?" he teases gently.

"Especially for you, my daredevil outdoorsman," Elizabeth replies, her voice tinged with playful reverence.

As the golden morning sunbathes them in its glow, Elizabeth opens the journal. She takes a steadying breath, her voice firm yet tender as she begins to read, the words resonating in the stillness of the heavens.

What an Amazing Day This Is!

Today, I woke up on the surface of Mars, Surrounded by a stark, alien landscape of rocks and sand, Painted in intense shades of red and rusty dust. The scenery soon morphed into a monotonous expanse, Resembling spiritless butterscotch caramel. There is no air to breathe here; the atmosphere is 95% CO_2. Water is almost nonexistent, confined to the distant poles, Far beyond my reach. Nothing grows here. There is no life of any kind. It's a desolate, dead planet.

Then, as I turn and gaze at the night sky, The resplendence of Earth seizes me. Our planet radiates splendor, its greens, blues, and whites glowing like a beacon of life. Its beauty pierces deep into my soul, evoking an overwhelming sense of belonging. "That's my home," I declare. "That's where I live." I point to the luminous dot in the sky.

Looking around me, the contrast is stark: The vibrant Earth, teeming with life, Against the barren, lifeless Martian terrain. At that moment, I realize the gallery of celestial bodies— Asteroids, comets, meteors, moons, planets, and stars— Is also lifeless to the best of my knowledge. Seemingly, our planet is the only one alive!

Today, I woke up on the surface of Mars And felt both undeservingly privileged And profoundly grateful for being alive on such an extraordinary place as Earth.

Today, I woke up inside a 10-nanometer chip, Housing 100 million transistors capable of processing algorithms and software

so powerful That every product and service will soon emulate
the human brain. Today, I woke up in a world where we humans
are continuously enhancing What nature and God have bestowed
upon us, propelling progress and development To unimaginable
levels. And I am alive, right in the middle of this quantum leap,
Reaping its benefits and marveling at its possibilities. Who could
ask for better fortune?

Today, I woke up inside myself. The first thing I did was travel at
the speed of light through the wirings of my brain. By the end, I
had traversed a distance equivalent to the circumference of the
Earth. Next, using the most powerful computer in existence, I
counted the number of cells giving me life. First, I tallied my
neurons—several billion. Then, I turned to the rest of my body's
cells, Filling screen after screen with their staggering numbers.
Each cell, though independent, fulfilled its mission in perfect
harmony with the others.

I was awestruck as I witnessed thousands of vital cells dying,
Replaced instantaneously by newly reproduced ones. My
curiosity propelled me further, observing firsthand how viruses
and infections constantly swarm my body, And how thousands
of pathogens lie in wait, ready to strike. I am infested with
bacteria—billions upon billions of them—essential for life itself.
Yet, I watched in amazement as my body's defense mechanisms
tirelessly kept every threat under control, Eradicating some and
containing others.

Finally, I inspected my organs, Awe-struck by their inexorable
precision, beauty, and perfection As they performed complex
tasks with ease.

Today, I woke up inside myself and realized That the mere fact of being alive is a continuous miracle, renewed every second.

Today, I understood that life is a delicate balance, A fine line between death, sickness, and health. Today, I woke up inside myself and witnessed the infinite complexity of my being. I realized that, here on Earth, I have been gifted an extraordinary organism—my body. This realization illuminated just how precious every moment truly is.

Today, I woke up on top of the world, Feeling the air flow through my lungs. I recognized that just a couple of minutes without it, and life would be gone. I observed the intricate cycles of food and weather that nourish us, Marveling at the perfection of the systems required to sustain life. I grasped how quickly we would weaken and starve without the abundance surrounding us. I saw billions of humans sharing this Earth, provided for equally by its resources.

Today, I woke up and realized I live on the universe's only known "living" planet. Today, I woke up and finally understood how few of us make it from reproductive cells into human beings. Today, I woke up to life. Today, I finally feel truly alive. Today, I feel eternally grateful for simply being alive.

"What an amazing day this is!" I've been given an extraordinary life and two remarkable vessels: my planet and my body.
So, what am I waiting for? What are you waiting for?
What are we waiting for? Let's go out and embrace the incredible gift of being alive.

*

Jordan is overwhelmed by the sheer emotion of the moment. Elizabeth clings to him, serene and content, her presence anchoring him in a world that feels surreal.

"I love you," he whispers, his voice barely audible yet carrying the weight of his heart. Moments later, he slips into a reflective trance, the world around them fading into the background of endless sky and colorful balloons.

At first, Jordan begins to speak almost as though addressing his thoughts aloud. "Elizabeth, my love, there are moments in life that stop us dead in our tracks," he says softly, deliberately, while locking his gaze into hers. "Reality halts; we can hardly breathe, and as it's happening, everything else ceases to exist."

His hand reaches up, and with exquisite tenderness, he brushes the tips of his fingers across her cheek. Elizabeth leans into his touch, tilting her head so her face rests against the warmth of his palm.

"When those rare moments occur, life gifts us its very best. We're consumed by wonder, swept away by an uncontrollable yearning and desire as our hearts rejoice, completely taken by the love we've found."

As he pauses, the silence between them is profound, filled with an almost tangible suspense, broken only by the rhythmic bursts of the burner feeding the balloon's flame. Elizabeth's emerald eyes widen as she absorbs his words, the depth of his emotion unraveling within her. Her hand moves instinctively to her mouth, stifling a gasp as he continues.

"That's exactly what happened to me the moment I first saw you," Jordan confesses, his unblinking blue eyes intensifying. "Elizabeth Victoria, there's nothing in this world I want more than to make you happy. I want to spend every remaining day of my life by your side. I vow to love you, cherish you, and honor you—always. Would you do me the honor of becoming my wife?"

Tears of joy stream down her face as she nods, unable to speak. Instead, she answers with a kiss, filled with passion, gratitude, and unspoken promises. Their lips meet in a moment that seems to transcend time, the world outside their shared space vanishing completely.

For them, the future begins here, among the clouds and beneath the heavens, in a love as boundless as the sky.

Royal Cambridge Scholastic Institute (2019)
(Erasmus and Victoria's Campus Home)

The phone call transforms a quiet Sunday morning into a celebration of love and joy.

Erasmus' home studio phone rings insistently. Sundays are usually tranquil, with hardly any calls, so the persistent ringing piques his curiosity. Finally, he picks up, a look of mild intrigue etched on his face.

"Mom?" Elizabeth's voice crackles with urgency.

"Elizabeth, how nice to hear from you. How have you been?" Erasmus responds warmly, his surprise tempered with fatherly affection.

"Hi, Erasmus. Can I talk to my mom really quick?" she asks hurriedly.

"Of course. Let me fetch her for you," he replies, already moving. He senses something out of the ordinary. *'What could it be?'* he wonders.

"Is everything all right, Elizabeth?" He ventures as he searches for Victoria.

"Everything is wonderful! Put my mom on speaker so you can hear the good news too!" Elizabeth exclaims, her voice brimming with excitement.

Relieved and intrigued by her exuberance, Erasmus finds Victoria just stepping out of the shower.

"Elizabeth's on the line. It seems urgent," he tells her, holding the phone out as she wraps herself in a towel.

"Elizabeth, dear," Victoria says, her maternal instincts instantly alert.

"Mom, Jordan just asked me to marry him!" Elizabeth announces with a burst of joy.

Victoria's face lights up with emotion as she glances at Erasmus. A radiant smile spreads across her face, followed by a gasp and a tear-filled cry of joy. She embraces Erasmus, forgetting her state of undress, wrapped in nothing but a towel and sheer happiness.

"Mom?"

"What wonderful news, my daughter! We're so happy for you both. I know how deeply you love each other," Victoria responds, her voice trembling with emotion as she clings to Erasmus.

"Mother, we're walking on clouds!" Elizabeth proclaims, her voice effervescent.

"I can imagine, darling. This is one of those moments in life to treasure forever," Victoria reflects, her motherly pride evident.

"Indeed, Mom. But also know that, quite literally, we're floating on air," Elizabeth adds mischievously.

"How so, dear?" Victoria inquires, intrigued.

"We're in a freaking hot air balloon! Jordan just proposed to me up here, thousands of feet above the ground," Elizabeth explains.

"Fantastic—romance in the sky!" Erasmus blurts out, his previously reserved demeanor giving way to inspiration. Once the professor's enthusiasm ignites, there's no stopping him.

"I have an idea, one fitting the grandeur of your white knight's proposal," Erasmus declares, his eyes alight with creativity.

"And what might that be, Professor?" Elizabeth asks, her tone both curious and skeptical.

"As you know, your mom and I have been engaged for about a year. Why don't we all get married in a single ceremony?" he suggests, his spontaneity surprising even himself.

The idea lands perfectly. In that rare, serendipitous moment, his suggestion is met with unanimous delight. The seed of a shared wedding is planted, an idea blossoming into reality amidst a backdrop of love, celebration, and the boundless skies.

Royal Cambridge Scholastic Institute (2019)
(Victoria and Erasmus Campus' Home, The Next Morning)

Erasmus's morning begins with an air of anticipation and joy.

"What would be your choice of subject today, dear?" Victoria inquires warmly, waving him off as he readies to leave.

"Serenity, courage, and wisdom—the role they play in our lives and how closely related the three are," he responds with a thoughtful grin.

"You certainly displayed plenty of that yesterday with your wonderful idea," she teases gently, her voice fading as he cheerfully pedals away.

Erasmus smiles back at his beautiful bride-to-be, her words filling him with warmth and satisfaction.

Professor Cromwell-Smith glides over the scattered autumn leaves, his heart buoyed by the joy of Elizabeth's engagement and the vision of the upcoming joint wedding ceremonies. Everything seems to move in slow motion. From a distance, his figure appears dreamlike, weaving along the campus roads as though he and his bicycle are floating just above the earth, carried by the breeze of contentment.

As the stately faculty building looms ahead, reality gently reels him back. By the time he secures his bike and strides purposefully toward the classroom, his thoughts align with the day's mission, the echoes of serenity, courage, and wisdom resonating in his mind.

Royal Cambridge Scholastic Institute (2019)
(University Auditorium)

Reaching the university's stately faculty building, Erasmus secures his bike with ease, pausing only for a moment to breathe in the crisp morning air. The steady rhythm of his heartbeat echoes his confidence as he steps into the familiar hallways of the Royal Cambridge Scholastic Institute. The buzz of students, the soft shuffle of shoes on polished floors, signals the proximity of his classroom. As he approaches the doors, his focus sharpens, the promise of a fulfilling lecture day ahead filling him with a quiet sense of purpose.

"How's everyone today?" Professor Cromwell-Smith greets his class, his eyes twinkling with enthusiasm.

The lively murmur of students responding with energy and positivity amplifies the atmosphere in the room.

"Wonderful!" they reply, their collective voices buzzing with anticipation.

"Let's start, then," he continues, his smile broadening as the room quiets in unison. "Today, I'll take you back in time to the day I met a fascinating antiquarian who imparted a precious life lesson. The story begins like this …"

The professor's voice takes on a thoughtful cadence as he launches into the tale, his presence commanding yet warm, drawing his students into the world of his memory.

— ❖ —

Downtown Boston (1979)

On a late Saturday afternoon jog, coming down from Beacon Hill, the downtown area is just ahead of me. After a turn on Canal Street, I stumble upon it, "The Quibbler: Antique Books for the Inquisitive Mind (Est. 1910)," reads the sign on the quaint shop.

'I've never seen or heard about this antique bookshop before.' Intrigued, I search my memory.

Smelly, sweaty, and all, I enter with the excitement and wonder of a young child stepping into his favorite place. The moment I open the door, a sense of familiarity washes over me. The shop carries the unmistakable scent of old paper and worn leather. Piles of treasured books are scattered everywhere, and the racks are spread across three floors connected by wooden staircases that twist and turn. The entire place feels like a labyrinth.

The surroundings so captivate me that I fail to notice the man observing me with quiet amusement. My eyes finally register his presence, and I jump in shock, eliciting an even broader smile from him in response to my absentmindedness.

"How can I be of help, young man?" asks the bespectacled, slightly hunched man with bushy, shoulder-length hair.

Still processing my surroundings, I struggle to focus on him. My gaze shifts between the shop and the man as if caught in a dream.

"What brings you here this afternoon?" he repeats, his eyes sparkling with curiosity. Then, suddenly, they widen.

"Wait a minute, I know who you are! You're the young man from the book town in Wales, right?" he asks excitedly.

I smile, acknowledging my reputation among New England antiquarians, but remain otherwise silent.

"We were all supposed to meet you at the Cape Cod Antiquarians reunion, but you suddenly left?" he exclaims, his tone shifting into a monologue.

"That's correct," I reply tersely, offering no additional details.

"I hope the cause was nothing serious," the antiquarian ventures empathetically.

"Sort of. She ran away, sir," I elaborate, my discomfort evident.

"I heard, I heard," he says, his voice tinged with condolence.

'So, his question was rhetorical. The New England antiquarians are like a fraternity; they share everything. My misfortune is vox populi—known by all,' I reflect with resignation.

"My name is Lazarus Pincay II, though I'm often called The Quibbler for reasons you'll soon discover," he announces with a theatrical flourish.

Born and raised in Boston to a librarian father and a painter mother, Lazarus Pincay displayed a natural talent for music but an even keener propensity for books. Although he pursued piano lessons for twelve years and seemed destined for a career as a concert pianist, he rebelled, and left school just shy of his 20th birthday. Lazarus spent years in California living in hippie communes until fate intervened. During a spiritual ritual, he met the love of his life, Laura Dean-Lamarck, who hailed from Boston and had earned renown as a writer.

The couple has been married for 25 years. At her insistence, they returned to Boston, where Laura helped Lazarus finance the purchase of The Quibbler Antique Book Store, turning it into the treasure trove I now stand in.

"Nice to meet you, sir. Erasmus Cromwell-Smith is at your service," I introduce myself with a polite nod.

"Mr. Pincay, I'm looking for peace and tranquility to better contemplate life in slow motion and appreciate the details of things," I explain, trying to articulate the sense of clarity I seek.

"Well, young man, you've come to the right place. I have something special for you, something that will help you attain the calmness and strength of character you're searching for," offers the Quibbler, his eyes twinkling with purpose.

Without another word, he walks away, disappearing into the maze of bookshelves. Moments later, I spot him climbing a towering wooden ladder, easily 25 feet tall. He scans the uppermost shelves, plucks a book, inspects it, but descends with a dissatisfied shake of his head.

Then, he vanishes again, slipping down a narrow aisle, his steps deliberate and purposeful. After a short while, he reemerges, clutching a thick, leather-bound book in both hands. The age-worn cover exudes an aura of timeless wisdom.

"The scribble I'm going to read to you perfectly aligns with your current predicament," the Quibbler declares, his voice deepening with conviction.

Opening the book with reverence, he finds the desired page and begins to read, his tone steady and earnest.

*

"Serenity, Courage, and Wisdom"

Serenity is a contemplative state
of absolute inner peace—deliberate, immutable calmness.
It is a condition of placidness
that allows us to observe life's movie from the outside.

In this state, life feels as though it moves in slow motion.
We pause at every frame,
and the false perception of time either flying by
or dragging its feet disappears.

Instead, we experience
a refreshing and genuine measure of time.

Serenity is also a cornerstone of moderation.
Whether in meditative, reflective, or contemplative modes,
calmness and placidness serve as conduits
for caution, restraint, tolerance, and prudence.
They are the best antidotes
to reactive and impulsive behavior.

By fostering moderation in our conduct,
serenity grants us the clarity
to contemplate alternatives and options.

It allows us
to take the necessary time to make decisions:
Do we choose serene inaction,
or do we act with our gut, our brain, our heart,
or a combination of them?

In serenity, life slows down.
Our frantic pace freezes,
and we discover peace in the pause.

But perhaps serenity's greatest virtue
is its ability to help us accept or acknowledge
the inevitable, the irreplaceable, and the irreversible.
Serenity becomes one of our most potent existential weapons
against denial, offering clarity, finality, and closure.

Serenity also lays the foundation for courage.
When impregnated with serenity,
courage becomes fiercer and invincible.
Without serenity, courage risks devolving
into reckless impulsivity or even a suicide mission.

Courage is our best resource for overcoming
extreme adversity and hardship,
for facing seemingly insurmountable obstacles,
devastation, loss, failure, and overwhelming odds.

Courage is also the weapon we wield
to tame and conquer fear.
In doing so, fear transforms
from a paralyzing excuse into an ally.

Fearlessness is an intrinsic part of courage's fire.
It fuels our drive to act,
empowering us to prevent or reverse
the consequences of what we are afraid of.

This is how courage is flushed
with positive and actionable fear.
Courage, when acted upon,
is fearless, dauntless, and intrepid.

Courage is a wild virtue of the spirit,
driven by belief, passion, heart, and fear.

Wisdom, as it relates to serenity and courage,
provides us
with enlightenment, sagacity, and judicious behavior.
Wisdom enables us to decide
when to lean on serenity—
to accept life's crude realities and defeat denial—
or when to summon courage
to reverse the improbable, the impossible,
the irreversible, and the seemingly inevitable.
Sometimes, wisdom guides us to use both,
serenity and courage,
in balance,

according to the circumstances.

Courage is our best resource to overcome
extreme adversity and hardship,
seemingly insurmountable obstacles and difficulties,
devastation and total defeat,
loss or failure, and overwhelming odds.

Courage is also our weapon to tame and conquer fears,
and that is how,
when acting with bravery and valor,
fear becomes our ally instead of a paralyzing excuse.

Fearlessness is an intrinsic part
of the fuel driving courage's fire.
Thus, fearlessness becomes the reason to act
in order to prevent or reverse the consequences
of what we are afraid of.

That's how courage is flushed
with positive and actionable fear.
Courage is fearless, dauntless, and intrepid
when we act and execute.
Courage is a wild virtue of the spirit
driven by beliefs, passion, heart, and fear.

As it relates to courage and serenity,
wisdom provides us
with enlightenment, sagacity, and judicious behavior
to decide either for serenity,
to be able to accept the crude realities
and to defeat denial,
or for the courage to allow us
to reverse the improbable, the impossible, the irreversible
and the seemingly inevitable;

or to use both, according to the circumstances.

*

"Serenity occurs when your soul and spirit are in absolute peace," The Quibbler intones, his gaze locking onto Erasmus with piercing intensity.

"Young Erasmus, life is meant to be lived through continual discourse, enabling people to dissolve conflicts, rectify misunderstandings, resolve dilemmas, or draw conclusions by engaging in challenging arguments. These debates allow us to question the coherence of our actions, interpretations, purpose, or the inherent knowledge we've absorbed. To face life in this way, however, serenity, courage, and wisdom are essential," Mr. Pincay asserts, his voice imbued with conviction.

Erasmus silently muses, 'Ah, now I understand how he earned his nickname.'

"You've got it," Mr. Pincay proclaims, as if reading Erasmus's thoughts. "This is me—a perennial and conscientious Quibbler of life and people," he adds with a satisfied smile, catching Erasmus off guard with his insight.

"As Erasmus leaves The Quibbler, the weight of the ancient tome still vivid in his mind, he feels a deep sense of calm, as if he is glimpsing a map to navigate life's inevitable complexities. This moment, he knows, becomes a cornerstone of the lessons he will one day pass on to others."

— ✦ —

Royal Cambridge Scholastic Institute (2019)
(University Auditorium)

The flash of memory from his past with Lazarus Pincay II fades as Professor Cromwell-Smith directs his focus back to the present. The bustling classroom, alive with student chatter and shifting papers, offers a subtle yet grounding reminder of the present moment. As the professor shifts into the present, with measured words he guides his students through the very principles Lazarus had shared with him years ago—principles that would not only define his journey but now shape the ones that lie ahead for his students. "Serenity, courage, and wisdom are virtues of character. Serenity engenders courage, and wisdom employs them both," he explains, his voice resonating with clarity. His hand rests on the lectern as his voice, calm but resolute, fills the room once again. "Serenity, courage, and wisdom," he begins, his words carrying the authority of years of lived experience, "are not just lofty ideals; they are virtues that inform our every decision, guiding us through life's most complex crossroads." His gaze sweeps across the room, making sure to meet the eyes of each student, ensuring they're attuned to the lesson at hand. "These are the virtues I wish for you to carry with you—today, tomorrow, and in the days ahead.

"Serenity, courage, and wisdom—these are the foundational virtues that shape how we face challenges in life. As we explore these concepts, let's consider how they intertwine with the greater themes of being alive and aware of the moment. I'll start by asking for your thoughts on the role of serenity in your life. Anyone?"

Aiden, a philosophy major with an interest in how personal virtues influence decision-making, raises his hand. "Professor, in 'Serenity, Courage, and Wisdom,' serenity is described as a state that allows us to observe life from the outside, almost as if life is moving in slow motion. How can we cultivate serenity in a world that often demands quick reactions and constant movement?"

"That's an excellent question, Aiden," Professor Cromwell-Smith replies. "Serenity is about learning to step outside of the whirlwind of life, even for a moment. It's cultivating the space to pause, breathe, and reflect. In today's world, that can be difficult, but it's about intentionally creating moments of stillness. Serenity isn't about inaction; it's about being present, recognizing your emotions without being consumed by them, and allowing the moment to unfold naturally."

Aiden nods thoughtfully, his mind clearly working through the implications of the professor's words.

Leticia, a psychology major with an interest in emotional intelligence, raises her hand. "In the poem, courage is said to be a weapon to conquer fear, but it's also noted that without serenity, courage risks becoming reckless. How can we ensure our courage is tempered by serenity?"

Professor Cromwell-Smith's eyes gleam with understanding. "Great question, Leticia, Courage without serenity can quickly turn into impulsivity or rash decisions, especially when fear clouds our judgment. Serenity helps us pause and make sure that the courage we summon is measured. It allows us to act with purpose, rather than out of reaction. When you're calm and centered, courage becomes a force that can move mountains, but only when it's grounded in clarity and reflection."

Leticia appears to absorb the depth of the answer, her expression one of deep thought.

Ethan, a biology major who enjoys exploring the intersection of emotion and reason, speaks up next. "The poem mentions that fear can become an ally through courage. But in the context of modern life, where fear is often paralyzing, how can we practically turn our fears into something positive?"

Professor Cromwell-Smith gives a nod of recognition. "That's an insightful question, Ethan. Fear is a natural human emotion, but it doesn't have to control us. When we face our fears head-on, we turn them from obstacles into opportunities for growth. Fear signals that something matters—it's a response to something we care about. By embracing that, acknowledging it, and moving forward anyway, we transform fear into motivation. Courage doesn't mean we're not afraid—it means we act despite the fear, knowing that it's part of our journey."

Ethan listens intently, clearly reflecting on how this perspective could apply to his own experiences.

Mia, a literature major who enjoys delving into abstract meanings, asks, "The poem *What an Amazing Day This Is!* paints a beautiful picture of life's complexities and the value of being alive. It suggests a spiritual, almost miraculous view of life itself. How do you personally reconcile this kind of spiritual awe with the more grounded, practical aspects of daily life?"

Professor Cromwell-Smith smiles at the question. "Mia, that's a powerful inquiry. *What an Amazing Day This Is!* speaks to the awe that comes from fully realizing the miracle of life in all its complexity. At the same time, we live in a world where daily concerns often demand our attention. I think the key is to embrace both—the awe and the practical. Serenity, courage, and wisdom help us navigate that balance. We can be grounded in the reality of our responsibilities while still taking moments to marvel at the small, miraculous details of life."

Mia smiles, clearly appreciating the depth of the response.

Jodie, a philosophy and ethics major with a focus on existential questions, leans forward. "The poem *What an Amazing Day This Is!* explores the beauty of being alive, yet it's set against the backdrop of challenges and threats to life. How do we live with the awareness of life's fragility without becoming overwhelmed by it?"

Professor Cromwell-Smith looks thoughtful before answering. "Jodie, I think it's about finding acceptance. Life is fragile—that's a truth we all must face. But instead of being paralyzed by that knowledge, we can embrace it. It teaches us to live fully, appreciate the moment, and cherish the people and experiences that shape us. The fragility of life doesn't take away from its beauty; in fact, it enhances it. By living with an awareness of that, we can cultivate gratitude, presence, and a deeper connection to the world around us."

Jodie nods, clearly moved by the response.

Lee, an international relations major interested in the human condition, asks, "In both poems, there's a sense of wonder and deep appreciation for life and its complexities. Do you think this perspective could help shape the way we approach global challenges, like climate change or social injustice?"

Professor Cromwell-Smith nods approvingly. "Absolutely, Lee. The perspective that *What an Amazing Day This Is!* Brings can shift how we view the world. When we recognize the beauty and fragility of life, it can inspire us to protect and cherish it. That sense of awe, combined with the wisdom to act, can drive us to make choices that reflect our shared responsibility to each other and to the planet. It's a perspective that, if embraced globally, could lead to more empathy, cooperation, and a commitment to preserving the wonders of life."

Lee listens carefully, clearly considering the broader implications of the professor's answer.

The room softly buzzes with contemplative energy as the students gather their belongings. Many linger in their seats, their faces thoughtful, as if digesting the weight of serenity, courage, and wisdom in their own lives. It is clear that the professor's words have left a profound imprint on their minds.

The room quiets after his words, the echoes of his reflections settling into the minds of his students. The weight of serenity, courage, and wisdom hangs in the air, as if each student is silently sifting through their own understanding of these ideals. Erasmus pauses, allowing the moment to linger, before offering a parting thought. "Remember," he says softly, "serenity, courage, and wisdom aren't just traits we learn—they are virtues we embody, over and over again, in the choices we make." As he strides out of the room, the door closing behind him, the students remain, each absorbed in the newfound understanding that will guide them long after the class is over.

"See you all next week," he adds, striding purposefully out of the lecture hall.

As he exits, he notices the pensive expressions of the students left behind. Their collective demeanor suggests a quiet introspection, as if each is searching for their own path to peace and balance.

Chapter 11

The Fable of the Old Young Man and The Jester

Martha's Vineyard Beach, Massachusetts (2019)

Three months after Erasmus proposed the idea, the mother and daughter married the men of their dreams in a grand, shared ceremony. A makeshift wooden altar, adorned with vibrant flowers, was erected on a serene beach near Chilmark, on Martha's Vineyard's south side. The azure waves lapping against the shore provided a fitting backdrop for the joyous union.

Following the beachside celebration, Jordan and Elizabeth embarked on an adventure-filled honeymoon, soaring high in a hot air balloon over Europe's majestic landscapes. Their journey culminated in St. Moritz, Switzerland, where they participated in the Grand Engadin Race, a Nordic ski marathon renowned as the world's largest Winterfest of colors, drawing thousands of participants from across the globe.

Meanwhile, Erasmus and Victoria set off on their own dream voyage, visiting the enchanting landscapes of Africa. Before they could fully immerse themselves in their travels, an unexpected detour brought them to Italy—a chance to close an open chapter in Erasmus's life.

It all began with a magical train ride …

Zurich International Airport (2019)
(Arrival from Boston)
"Where are you taking me, my lady?" asks a startled Erasmus as they board a taxi to Zurich's central train station.

"It will be eye-opening, my mysterious Brit," Victoria replies cryptically.

"Milan?" he guesses when he hears the train's destination as they board.

"Erasmus, let's enjoy the ride and stop trying to find a reason behind everything," she counters with a mischievous smile.

The self-absorbed couple dines in style as the train glides through the Alps, a lingering question floating unanswered between them. Erasmus grows increasingly uneasy.

'What could this possibly be?' he wonders, applying logic to his thoughts. 'She told you to enjoy the moment and stop trying to figure everything out,' he quibbles, half-scolding himself.

Time flies faster than they'd like, and soon the magnificent journey nears its end. "We're arriving at Milan's main train station," an announcement echoes in the background.

The train slows to a crawl, and Erasmus feels a swell of anticipation laced with uncertainty.

Stepping onto the platform, Erasmus is struck by a sense of familiarity before he even sees her. Like a slow-motion film, his eyes fall on Antonella, his former lover and lifelong friend, standing a hundred yards away. Her warm, benevolent smile and discreet wave greet him, unchanging and reassuring.

"Dad!" rings out in a chorus, punctuated with perfect British accents.

He turns to find Maria Antonella and Roberto Marcello Conti, Antonella's children—or rather, *his* children.

In the background, he notices Victoria and Antonella, their arms interlocked as if they are old friends catching up.

His two children envelop him in effusive hugs, while his rational mind struggles to keep up with the emotions overtaking him.

'It's been two years since I last saw them. That's all this must be,' he reasons, desperate to comprehend the moment.

"DNA, Erasmus. We always suspected it," Roberto declares, as if reading his thoughts.

"It was easy," Maria adds. "We took hair follicles from the brush in the bathroom you always use. Mom never let anyone else use that room. And there are other clues. For starters, Roberto is a carbon copy of you."

"And she sent us both to have a British education—uncommon in Italy. Then there were the trips to America when we stayed with you. We grew up with the omnipresent figure of the 'British uncle professor,' and Mom always urged us to treat you as a father figure," Maria continues, her voice soft.

"She never told us why, and we understand you didn't have a clue," Roberto concludes with a smile.

A couple of slow tears escape Erasmus' eyes, tracing his cheeks as a deep sense of fulfillment and joy overwhelms him. The two young adults standing before him are undeniably his own flesh and blood.

The next 24 hours become a blur of shared laughter, unspoken understanding, and endless stories. Father, son, and daughter spend hours walking, talking, and playing childlike games in public squares. Meals are minimal—snatched quickly between activities—as they strive to fit a lifetime of connection into a single day.

When it's time to part, Erasmus finds himself on the train platform once more, this time with Victoria and Antonella. They're standing back from the tracks, radiating the ease and warmth of two close friends.

The fleeting day lingers in Erasmus' mind like a dream, leaving behind a newfound bond and the beginning of a story he never thought he'd live.

"Thank you, Antonella," Erasmus says, his voice thick with emotion, eyes brimming with gratitude.

They kiss, a long, lingering kiss shared only by old lovers who understand the weight of years and memories.

"Vai, vai, Erasmus," she whispers, waving him off with teary eyes clouded by the bittersweet farewell.

Erasmus embraces his children one last time, holding them tightly and studying their faces as if committing every detail to memory.

"Erasmus is our real father, although kind of an incidental one, as in once in a while," Maria Antonella teases with a wide grin.

"Yes, our biological one. Well, he'll see a lot more of us when we visit America," Roberto Marcello adds, waving as the train begins to pull away.

When Erasmus turns, he's unexpectedly nose-to-nose with Victoria, her expression both amused and smug.

"Kisses, kisses, unforgettable kisses," she says, her tone tinged with a touch of playful possessiveness.

"Have you already forgotten about me; Erasmus dear?" she quips with the wickedest of smiles.

"How could I, my adored lady? That can never happen," he responds, regaining his charm as he takes her hand, leading her into the first-class dining car.

Hours later, as their flight from Switzerland to East Africa hums steadily above the clouds, the reunited couple nestles together in their seats. Their love has deepened through these shared chapters of rediscovery and acceptance.

Their next destination is Mt. Kilimanjaro—an adventure they have always dreamed of, a fitting chapter in the unfolding story of their rekindled lives.

Zurich's International Airport, Switzerland (2019)
(On the way back to Boston)

The two honeymooning couples reunite at Zurich Airport for their flight home to Boston. The four are radiant, glowing with the happiness and joy of their shared adventures.

"Mom, we're pregnant," Elizabeth-Victoria blurts out unexpectedly as they savor the traditional Swiss raclette while awaiting their flight announcement. Victoria gasps, covering her mouth in surprise, while Erasmus beams with a giant, proud smile. Moments later, the four are locked in a celebratory embrace, their joy and harmony overflowing in an unforgettable tableau of love and family.

Royal Cambridge Scholastic Institute (2019),
(Victoria and Erasmus' Campus Home, Next Day)

"Dear, I never imagined that summiting Tanzania's Mount Kilimanjaro would take three days, trekking through multiple microclimates over 37 miles," Victoria remarks as she and Erasmus watch breathtaking video footage from their honeymoon.

"19,341 feet high, my lady. It's no ordinary mountain. Your body needs time to adapt to the altitudes and thinner oxygen levels," Erasmus explains. The screen shows them walking across the Shira Plateau, its vast, barren expanse offering a spectacular view of the snow-capped Kilimanjaro looming majestically in the distance.

"I was terrified when we first encountered them," Victoria admits, her tone anxious as the video shifts to the dense foliage of the Congo jungle, where the silhouettes of massive gorillas blend into the greenery.

"Terrifying and awe-inspiring, weren't they? Such powerful creatures. But the long trek to find them was worth every step," Erasmus recalls fondly.

"And these!" Victoria exclaims as the video shifts to scenes of young lions near Victoria Falls, Zimbabwe. "Their primal energy, their regal power—it's intoxicating."

"Well, your fear certainly didn't linger long, considering you kissed a lion on the cheek!" Erasmus teases, grinning as the video replays her daring gesture with an outward palm pressed gently to the lion's face.

"That was brave, scary, and—let's be honest—stupid," he chuckles.

"True," she concedes with a laugh. "But their roars! The sheer force of their primal screams gave me chills."

The video transitions to a family of hippos bellowing from the water, their immense jaws snapping open in synchronized display.

"Utterly powerful creatures," Erasmus agrees. "I'm glad we opted for the river safari. The lush water landscapes of the Okavango Delta were spectacular without the dust and long waits of a land safari."

On screen, the safari unfolds, revealing rhinos, giraffes, zebras, elephants, and herds of gazelles roaming freely near the water's edge. Above them, flocks of birds streak across the sky in synchronized waves.

"Great memories," Victoria reflects, her eyes softening. "An unforgettable experience, my love. Three weeks of adventure and discovery that ended far too soon."

Erasmus pulls her close, smiling as the final images of their African journey fade into memory.

"Now back to mundane reality, my lady," Erasmus mentions with a touch of disappointment.

"Now that we've returned, tell me, my reluctant educator, what will be the subject of your class tomorrow?" Victoria inquires, her curiosity piqued.

"Children, clowns, and fairy tales," he replies cryptically.

Wisely, she doesn't react but knows full well that he's honoring his children in Italy. *He still needs time to open up and talk about his revealing, memorable encounter in Milan,' she considers as Erasmus fades away on his bike. 'I can sense how he's still basking in the joy of reconnecting with his kids.*

Royal Cambridge Scholastic Institute (2019)
(Campus Streets)

As he pedals along the cobblestone streets through the crisp campus air, Professor Cromwell-Smith is lost in the memories of the past few days. His face reflects satisfaction and gratitude, especially for the newfound knowledge that Maria Antonella and Roberto Marcello are his biological children. The streets are lined with trees, their branches still adorned with the last vestiges of autumn leaves, a visual reminder of the changing seasons. His thoughts shift as he nears the lecture hall, the familiar building standing tall before him. He slows his pace, pushing aside the past to focus on the present.

By the time he parks his trusty old bike, Erasmus has shifted his thoughts to his upcoming class. However, as he enters the lecture hall, he's greeted by a surprise. A large banner hangs above his desk, reading:

"WELCOME BACK PROFESSOR CROMWELL!
WE SINCERELY HOPE
YOU HAD A WONDERFUL HONEYMOON."

The professor breaks into a broad smile. His eyes scan the room, connecting with each of his students as his gratitude shines through. A wave of energy fills the room as students glance up from their notebooks and papers, some with eager expressions, others still emerging from their own morning haze.

"Thank you all, pure and simple. This is absolutely amazing!" he exclaims, applauding his class.

He greets them with his usual warmth, his eyes twinkling as he steps up to the podium. There's an unspoken expectation in the room, as the class knows today's lesson will be more than just academic; it will be deeply personal.

"There are moments in life that we either celebrate or let pass unnoticed. If we deny or ignore these moments of joy, we risk losing the chance to embrace and rejoice in the brighter side of life for the rest of our days. Today, I will take you back to a memorable day when I learned one of life's greatest lessons: the power and necessity of creating and living our own fairy tale. A life that becomes a perennial celebration, absent of denial, no matter the circumstances."

He pauses, letting his words settle over the room, then continues with a glimmer in his eye.

"It all begins like this …"

— ❖ —

Erasmus' Crumpled Studio (1987)
(Near Harvard University)

Her letter arrives unexpectedly, yet its timing couldn't be more poignant. It is destined to be the last communication I would ever receive from Mrs. V., my beloved mentor from Wales, as she passed away shortly thereafter. My heart races with trepidation as I recognize the familiar package, her unmistakable calligraphy gracing the surface. I abandon everything I'm doing or planning to do, unable to contain myself, and eagerly sit down to open it.

"Dear Erasmus,

Your faithful mentor is getting a bit old. I haven't heard from you in a while, which I fear means things are happening in your life that you prefer not to talk about. Well, there's no way around your most ardent cheerleader. I expect you to update me by sharing your life's news at your earliest convenience.

More specifically, use your lazy writing hand, tap your forgetful heart and your lethargic mind, and write a missive to the attention of one Victoria Sutton-Leigh, a forgotten mentor of yours. She resides back at your birthplace, the unworthy (apparently to you) small town in Wales, Hay-on-Wye.

I enclose here a precious scribble that I hope enlightens your forgetful heart. I'm certain you're in desperate need of it and that it will deeply enrich your hibernating spirit and soul.

I sincerely hope you prove me wrong soon enough.
Love you dearly,
Mrs. V."

Guilt envelops me, heavy and immediate, compelling me to respond. I pick up my pen and begin writing earnestly, recounting everything I can about my life. The letter is mailed that very day. A week later, I call her. Mrs. V. is ecstatic; she's just finished reading my letter. My perennial cheerleader promises to respond in kind, but that promise never comes to fruition.

Only days later, she is gone from our lives.

In the days following her passing, I sift through her letters, treasuring the magnificent moments we shared over time. It is during this reflective period that I stumble upon her final missive and decide to reread it. This time, I notice the enclosed scribble—a treasure I had completely overlooked in my haste to write her back.

Perhaps this is how it was meant to be: for her parting gift to be discovered only after her passing, as a symbolic celebration of her life.

With a reverent heart, I open the scribble and begin to read. The opening verse enraptures me, drawing me into its timeless embrace.

"The Fable of the Old Young Man & the Jester"

The Joker strides back to his "Camerino,"
his dressing room,
as the crowd in the circus main tent,
continues to cheer.

He wears a white-plastered face
with a perpetual smile,
adorned by a giant painted mouth and
a tiny, perfectly round nose,
both glowing red.

A tall, floppy, multicolored hat,
covers shoulder-length strands of bright orange hair.
His loose clothes resemble a harlequin on one side,
while the other is dotted with oversized white polka dots.
His enormous shoes—two flapping tongues—
are impossibly wide at the front
and comically narrow at the back.

His nonchalant antics are shocking, even outrageous.
Everyone and everything become subjects of his jest,
his every move a parody of reality,
inviting the audience into the lighter side of life.
But not all is as it appears in our existence—
or is it?

A diminutive voice cuts through the stillness backstage.
"Jester, Jester!"
A young boy calls out from the shadows of the alley.
The clown turns, his penetrating green eyes
fixing on the teenager.

"Isn't it a bit far off the beaten path
for someone your age to be wandering around?"
the impatient clown asks.

"My parents are just behind the curtains,
feeding the giraffes with my little brother.
They know I'm here,"
the boy responds with confidence.

"Fair enough," the clown mutters,
resigned to the interruption.

The youngster crosses his arms,
raising one hand to his chin in thought.
"Joker, do you make people laugh for a living?"
he asks, his tone serious.

"Isn't causing laughter what clowns do?"
the clown replies in a riddle.

Undeterred, the boy presses further.
"You make people happy, Jester.
Are you a happiness maker, then?"

The clown leans casually against the doorframe of his *Camerino*.
"After all, isn't that what those who come to the circus seek?"
he responds with another question,
offering little insight to his admirer.

"Now, if you'll excuse me,"
the clown says, stepping inside his dressing room.

"Joker, Joker!" the boy pleads,
pushing forward before the door can close.

"I don't find you very funny in person, sir.
Your face wears a painted smile,
but up close, it doesn't feel genuine.
Your eyes—
they exude sadness,
and maybe even anger."

The clown's first reaction is to recoil,
but, to his own surprise, he reverses himself.
"You're an astute observer, little man.
Come in and have a seat," he offers unexpectedly,
leaving the door wide open.

Once seated, the clown offers the boy a box of chocolates,
allowing him to pick whichever one he likes.
"Joker, you make others happy,
but not yourself. Why?"

The clown exhales, leaning back.
"Isn't it how many live?
Keeping up appearances in public,
while guarding their darker realities
close to their chests?"

The boy tilts his head, puzzled.
"Jester, when I saw you on stage,
making everyone laugh,
it seemed like your life was a fairy tale.
But now, sitting here with you,
I wonder—
why aren't you happy?"

The clown lets out a sarcastic laugh.
"Isn't it true that life is always missing something?
That which we covet the most
seems out of reach.
And when we chase a goal,
the moment we catch it,
the goalpost has already moved—
most often because of us."

The boy shakes his head gently.
"Joker, but what you have now is enough, isn't it?
The pursuit of your goals,
what you call *the chase*,
is filled with life's moments—
moments you share with those who love what you do.
You must celebrate the journey of life
as it happens.
Otherwise, you're missing most of it."

The clown chuckles bitterly.
"There are no fairy tales in life, kid.
Those only live in children's books and fantasies."
"My life is a fairy tale, Jester,"
the boy declares with joy.

The clown raises an eyebrow.
"Sure, it is. You must come from a privileged home
wealth, success, no hardship,
no tragedy, no pain.
Of course, you see life as a fairy tale.
But one day, that will change."

The boy smiles softly,
his voice calm but filled with emotion.
"Joker, I am an orphan.

I came to the circus today with my adoptive parents.
We were homeless until recently.
My father just found a job as a janitor,
and my youngest brother walks with crutches—
he contracted polio when he was five."

The clown covers his mouth in shock,
shame washing over him.
"I am so, so…"
he begins to apologize,
but the boy interrupts.
"Jester, you're a privileged man.
Take stock of what you have.
Turn it into your source of joy.
Use your access to happiness and laughter
for what they are—
celebrations of life.
Your fairy tale resides in you.
You do what you love.
People love what you do.
Is there more to ask of life?"

The clown's eyes widen,
his painted smile softening into something real.
"I understand now the source of wisdom
in your words,"
the clown admits.

"And what would that be, sir?"
the boy asks.

"Hardship," the clown replies quietly.
"Life is a fairy tale
that resides inside all of us.
It only requires ingenuity and candor of the soul

and a true desire of the spirit
to embrace the journey of life,"
the boy declares.

His parents and brother approach from the corridor.
"Time to go," they announce.

The boy turns back to the clown,
a broad smile on his face.
"Joker, it was magical to spend time with you.
It was a truly magical moment,"
he says with joy.

"Young man, it was magical for me as well.
It was like a…"
the clown hesitates,
his voice trembling.
"A fairy tale?"
the boy offers, smiling even more.

"It most definitely was,
and a life lesson well learned, too,"
the clown replies, his green eyes sparkling.

For the first time,
his painted smile feels genuine—
perhaps forever.

*

Erasmus leans back in his wobbly chair, the dim light of his small studio casting soft shadows on the walls cluttered with books and papers. The fable rests in his lap, its final words echoing in his mind like a gentle refrain. He glances at Mrs. V.'s letter, now creased from his grip, and feels an ache of longing mixed with gratitude.

Her parting words, wrapped in wisdom and love, have kindled a spark in his restless heart. The fable's lesson—that life's fairy tales are born from within—pushes him to confront the narratives he has allowed himself to live. "The fairy tale resides in me," he whispers, almost as if testing the truth of the phrase. In the quiet stillness of the moment, he resolves to carry her message forward, to weave joy, gratitude, and purpose into the fabric of his days.

— �֍ —

Royal Cambridge Scholastic Institute (2019)
(University Auditorium)

Professor Cromwell-Smith carefully unfolds a set of wrinkled papers, their edges softened by time. His students watch as he places them on the lectern, a sense of reverence evident in his every movement.

The auditorium is silent, the weight of the fable lingering in the air. Professor Cromwell-Smith closes the book gently, his movements deliberate, as though savoring the finality of the tale. He looks up, his eyes scanning the faces of his students, their expressions a mix of introspection and awe.

"That was the last letter I ever received from Mrs. V.," he begins, his voice steady but filled with emotion.

"A story that, like all great fables, is not merely to be heard but to be lived. Her wisdom—woven into these words—remains timeless, much like the lessons we take from life itself. Her letter wasn't just a message from my mentor; it was a mirror reflecting my own untapped potential, my ability to create something extraordinary from the ordinary," The pedagogue reasons.

He pauses, glancing at the notes as if drawing strength from their presence. "Her words reminded me that the fairy tale isn't some unattainable dream. It's here," he continues, touching his chest. "It's within us all, waiting for us to see it, to live it, to share it."

The professor steps away from the lectern, walking slowly across the stage, his eyes scanning the room. "So I ask you, as I once asked myself—what will it take for you to recognize your own fairy tale? And when you do, will you have the courage to live it?"

The air hums with the weight of his words, his students lost in thought, grappling with the possibilities of their own untold stories.

"Now," he continues, his tone softening, "let us return to the present. What does this fable teach us? It reminds us that fairy tales are not confined to books or childhood fantasies. They reside within us, waiting to be embraced and brought to life through the choices we make, the gratitude we show, and the joy we find in the everyday."

Professor Cromwell-Smith pauses, allowing the significance of his words sink in. Then, with a gentle smile, he concludes, "It is in our power to recognize the magic of the moment, to celebrate the journey of life, and to make every day a story worth telling."

The spell is broken, and the room stirs as students emerge from their reverie, the lesson resonating deeply in their hearts.

"The Jester's discovery was to realize that life, for a passing moment, had become a fairy tale for him because he had made it such. The fairy tale resided in him. It inhabited his spirit and soul. Hence, his natural inclination and greatest existential ability was to make out of every possible moment or situation a real-life fairy tale by making others laugh," states the professor in his closing remarks.

A few hands are raised.

Thomas is a senior Philosophy major with a deep interest in existentialism and the nature of happiness. He often challenges abstract concepts and enjoys engaging in philosophical debates.

"Professor, in the fable, the boy calls the clown's life a fairy tale, but the clown dismisses it, claiming there are no fairy tales in life. Do you think the story is trying to suggest that a fairy tale is only possible if we have hardship or challenges to overcome? And if so, does that make hardship essential for finding meaning in life?"

"That's a very insightful question, Thomas. The boy's perspective represents a kind of innocent wisdom. He sees life as a fairy tale, not because it's free from hardship, but because he's learned to embrace it fully, understanding that hardship doesn't diminish life's beauty—it enriches it. The clown, on the other hand, is caught in a cycle of denial, unable to see the beauty in the moments that life provides. The fable suggests that a fairy tale isn't about avoiding difficulties, but about how we respond to them and whether we choose to live joyfully, despite the struggles."

Isabella is a third-year English Literature major, particularly interested in the intersection of storytelling and psychological well-being. She's always eager to draw parallels between literary themes and real-life emotional growth.

"Professor, the clown in the fable spends his life making others laugh, yet he himself is unhappy. The boy challenges him to embrace his own life as a fairy tale, despite the hardships. Do you think the fable is suggesting that we all have a responsibility to find joy in our own lives, rather than relying solely on external validation or seeking perfection?"

"Yes, Isabella, I believe that's exactly what the fable is suggesting. The clown's life, while filled with external validation, lacks personal fulfillment. He is a performer, yes, but he isn't performing for himself—he's performing for others. The boy, with his simple yet profound wisdom, shows the clown that real joy doesn't come from the applause of others; it comes from embracing one's own journey, no matter how imperfect it may be. The fable teaches us that we must find our own happiness, rather than relying on the expectations or perceptions of others."

Marcus is a junior majoring in Psychology with a focus on human motivation and emotional intelligence. He often brings scientific perspectives into philosophical discussions and enjoys analyzing character behaviors through psychological lenses.

"Professor, in the fable, the clown admits that his painted smile hides a deeper sadness. The boy points out that life can be viewed as a fairy tale if we learn to celebrate the journey. From a psychological perspective, do you think that many people, like the clown, mask their true emotions because they believe they are expected to conform to societal ideals of happiness?"

"That's a very astute observation, Marcus. The clown represents what we might call the "mask" people wear—the persona they project to meet social expectations. In psychology, this can be related to what's often termed as "emotion regulation" or the pressure to conform to societal ideals, even when those ideals don't reflect one's true emotional state. The boy's wisdom in the fable teaches us that we must move beyond this façade and learn to acknowledge and accept our emotions as part of our journey. Life's fairy tale isn't about perfection or constant happiness; it's about embracing the full spectrum of human experience, even the difficult parts."

Emily is a senior majoring in Sociology, with a keen interest in the dynamics of happiness and fulfillment in contemporary society. She often looks at social structures and cultural narratives to analyze how individuals find meaning in their lives.

"Professor, in the fable, the clown's life seems full of external success—he makes people laugh, he's adored by the audience—but he still feels unfulfilled. Do you think the fable critiques modern society's obsession with outward success and how that might overshadow our inner sense of purpose and fulfillment?"

"Absolutely, Emily. The clown's life, as portrayed in the fable, is a perfect metaphor for what often happens in modern society. We are conditioned to seek external success, whether it's career achievements, recognition, or material wealth, often at the expense of cultivating internal fulfillment and purpose. The fable critiques this very notion, showing that external validation isn't a true measure of success. True fulfillment, as the boy points out, comes from within—from how we embrace our lives, with all their ups and downs, and how we choose to find joy in the process itself."

Sarah is a second-year student studying Art History, fascinated by how emotions and human experiences are conveyed through art and storytelling. She enjoys drawing connections between literature and visual art.

"Professor, the fable speaks about the importance of finding joy in the journey, even if life isn't perfect. Do you think this idea of a "fairy tale" could be applied to art and the creative process as well, where the true value lies in the act of creation rather than the final product?"

"Yes, Sarah, that's a wonderful connection. Just as the boy sees life as a fairy tale, many artists and creators find that the real magic lies in the process itself. The journey of creation—the struggles, the discoveries, the growth—is often more meaningful than the finished piece. In art, as in life, the act of creation becomes a personal fairy tale. It's in the imperfections, the mistakes, and the moments of epiphany that the true value is found. Just like the boy's understanding, an artist must learn to embrace the creative process with all its highs and lows and celebrate the journey rather than fixating solely on the end result."

As the class comes to a close, Professor Cromwell-Smith stands by the lectern, allowing the students to reflect on the day's discussion. The room, once buzzing with the energy of a lecture in progress, now hums with the quiet introspection of students contemplating their own fairy tales. "Think about that as you go through your week," he adds. "What will you make of your own story?" With a nod and a smile, he dismisses the class, leaving the students to filter out slowly, some with quiet contemplation in their expressions, others with excited chatter as they discuss the ideas that have taken root.

"It's a wrap; see you all next week," he says as he departs.

His students remain seated, their faces marked with quizzical expressions. They seem to be grappling with the professor's message, silently questioning how much of a fairy-tale life they might already possess—or deny themselves—by leaving the good within them unrealized.

Chapter 12

Restlessness and Curiosity

Royal Cambridge Scholastic Institute (2019)
(Victoria and Erasmus' Campus Home)

"Why is it so hard to generate interaction with my precious son?" asks a startled Victoria.

"He's simply reserved and cautious by nature," states Sofia, who has been Bart's girlfriend for the past two years.

"I recognize that, but I'm his mother, and I feel that when it comes to his personal life, I have to dig to extract every word out of him," Victoria adds.

"He's getting better, though," Sofia offers, her eyes filling with love and affection as she talks about him.

"Bartholomeus has always been the family jester. Outwardly, so cheerful and gentle, but hermetic about his private affairs," declares the resigned mother.

Victoria studies the green-eyed, tall brunette, an all-American swimmer and Bart's classmate.

Sofia is an unwavering defender of my fortunate son. Given that she's also head over heels adoring him, why are you giving her a hard time? Victoria scolds herself.

"Tell me about yourself, sweetheart. How's he treating you? How do you feel about your relationship with Bart?"

"I feel happy. He's a wonderful man. We're planning, well in advance, which university we're going to attend to earn our master's degrees."

"That's fantastic news, Sofia. Any idea where you might be going?" asks Victoria with a touch of anxiety in her voice, plus a bit of frustration upon learning one more secret about her son.

"No, but we do have a shortlist."

"Well, he's a natural-born entrepreneur, so I'm pretty certain he'll enroll in a business school."

Sofia says nothing in reply, seemingly guarding a big secret. Victoria is at ease with the loyalty displayed by the young, prudent woman beside her.

"Sofia, earlier, I asked how he is treating you."

"He's always been a devoted partner. Before I met him, I was involved in a long-term relationship that never went anywhere because my former boyfriend was married. So, Bart had to work hard to appease my apprehensions and fears."

Unexpectedly, Erasmus makes a "grand entrance" while pulling a couple of small suitcases.

"Vicky, I don't want to interrupt your lovely chat, but we have to leave within the next thirty minutes," announces the professor while his other half patiently gestures and smiles at Sofia.

"Give us a few minutes; we'll be done shortly," Victoria pleads with a discernible broad smile.

"I'm all yours, dear, no haste," Victoria tells Sofia.

"Bart gave me a poem the other day," Sofia says, handing it to Victoria, who starts reading with what appears to be a touch of curiosity mixed with earnest delight.

"A Very Particular Symbiosis"

I am all of you,
You are all of me,
We are all of you,

We are all of me.

You are me,
I am you,
We are—
only one of you,

only one of me,
only one of us.

One and only,
you and I,
both of us,
forever.

*

"I love it. I'm thrilled Bart wrote something like this. I didn't know he could write!"

"No, it isn't his. He was candid with me about it. But that's irrelevant since what matters is the gesture; besides, it is beautiful."

"May I ask who wrote it?" asks Victoria as she slowly turns her head towards Erasmus, who's shuffling his feet and looking straight down at the floor, avoiding eye contact.

"My beloved Brit, how come you didn't tell me a thing about this?" she asks, sounding hurt but deeply satisfied.
Victoria winks at Sofia as she continues to roast Erasmus.

"Are you also keeping secrets from me, dear? Is this now a male thing in our family?"

"I don't think that writing a poem on Bart's behalf for his girlfriend is something I have to share with you when he specifically asked me to keep it private. Nevertheless, in the end, he's shared it with you through Sofia," replies Erasmus while ignoring the second part of her question.

Although a bit embarrassed, Victoria finally smiles at the realization of her confrontational, out-of-place behavior.

"Thank you for taking such good care of my boy," she volunteers while warmly hugging Sofia goodbye, then walking over to passionately kiss her in-house British poet.

Sofia and Victoria say farewell, and soon thereafter, the middle-aged couple is on their way to Boston's Logan Airport to visit an old friend of Victoria's for a weekend escapade.

St. Louis Public Library, Missouri (2019)

The head librarian, Rebecca Samuels-Ortiz, is always on the move. She labors like a busy humming bee.

On this particular morning, everyone on her staff is struggling to keep up with an entire middle school student body visiting a nearly impossible task. The teenage girls and boys are unruly, loud, and impolite.

"What a rude young man you are," she tells a baby-faced, lanky, bespectacled young man whose legs are propped up on a reading desk.

"Don't even think about it!" she warns a couple of naughty teens about to rip out a page from a valuable book. Protectively, she yanks it from their hands.

"This is not a concert hall," she cautions a pair of young girls as their deafening music blasts through their headphones.

"Tuck your shirts in!" she commands a pair of students walking by.

"Bring your pants up to your waistline," she orders another.

"Tie your shoelaces; otherwise, I'm going to report you and throw you out," she says with a stressed-out voice, finally letting her frustrations erupt.

Two hands from behind cover her face out of the blue.

"Surprise," Victoria whispers.

Samuels-Ortiz turns around in a snap and involuntarily lets out a muffled cry. She excitedly hugs her friend and protégé. Simultaneously, she sees him standing there awkwardly, looking at their long embrace. Her eyes widen.

Erasmus is still shell-shocked by the effusive greeting Victoria emotes as the words come rolling out of her mouth.

"I found him, Becca. Well, actually, Sarah did," explains Victoria.

"Are you Erasmus?" Samuels-Ortiz asks in disbelief.

"The one and only," he replies as Samuels-Ortiz, with smothering enthusiasm, extends her welcoming arms and embraces him long and hard.

"Oh, my g…! How blessed and fortunate you are. Life found both of you, or better said, true Love took hold of the two of you once again," enunciates Samuels-Ortiz.

As the host holds onto Erasmus, she blurts, "She never stopped loving you."

"Becca, he waited for me all those years," interjects Victoria. "May I remind you that I was the one who ran away."

At first, Samuels-Ortiz's facial expression softens, followed by benign and loving eyes.

"Please excuse my antics, Erasmus. I tend to be overly protective of Victoria. Subconsciously, my instincts cast you very differently," Samuels-Ortiz states.

"The mind doctor, perhaps?" intersects Samuels-Ortiz with a mischievous smile, unable to control herself.

"Becca!" complains Victoria in surprise.

"Well, you can't blame me for trying a bit too hard to ensure that your bad karma with men doesn't repeat itself," adds Samuels-Ortiz.

"Well, here we are, after all. I enthusiastically want you to meet my Brit scholar."

"A scholar? …interesting." Samuels-Ortiz thinks aloud.

"It's a real pleasure, Mrs. Samuels. I'm forever in your debt. Thank you from the bottom of my heart for taking such good care of my precious lady," demurs Erasmus.

"That was nothing. It was a pleasure. Victoria deserves that and much more because she's an angel of goodness," Mrs. Samuels-Ortiz is still trying to oversell her mentee. "But I want to know more about the prince valiant that stole my friend's heart. Tell me about yourself, Erasmus."

Being well-acquainted with the customs and traditions of his birthright, Victoria knows it's far too soon for Erasmus to open up to a perfect stranger. Stepping in before British etiquette and shyness can create the wrong impression, she interjects, "He teaches at a New England college. He's also a writer."

"Fascinating. What does Erasmus teach?" the old librarian asks, her curiosity piqued.

"Poetry," Victoria replies with a subtle smile.

"And what does he write about?"

"Mainly science fiction," she adds.

"Published?" Rebecca presses further.

"Three million science fiction and educational books sold," Victoria proudly announces.

Rebecca's eyes widen in amazement. "That's very impressive. Wait a minute. Erasmus, what is your last name?" A sudden realization dawns on her. "Oh! Of course … you are Erasmus Cromwell-Smith. I know you. I've read all your books! Consequently, Victoria, you had him here at the library all the time, just a fingertip away!" she exclaims, her words pouring out excitedly.

Victoria chuckles at her friend's enthusiasm. "You know, Becca, thanks to his influence on me early on, I only like to read poetry. And he's never published his poems," she adds with a mischievous glance at Erasmus.

Rebecca tilts her head, astonished. "And how could I have known you are—the Erasmus?"

"I've read your books through the years but never put two and two together," she admits, her tone blending awe and amusement.

Victoria seizes the moment. "Dear, why haven't you ever published any of your poems?" she asks, her curiosity slipping into prying.

Caught off guard, Erasmus hesitates before responding. His gaze softens as he reflects. "I guess the simplest answer is that the vast majority of the poems, if not all, I've ever written are private," he admits. "Dedicated to you or us," he continues, his voice carrying a deep emotion that visibly touches Victoria.

Later that Day

As they prepare to part ways after a delightful brunch at the fancy Hyatt Hotel in downtown St. Louis, Mrs. Samuels-Ortiz surprises the couple with an unexpected gift.

"I have a copy of an ancient scribble for both of you. It's my wedding gift," she declares, her tone reverent. "It's a precious piece of writing that I treasure and constantly revisit. It's about restlessness and curiosity. It's extraordinary how both of you remained restless due to unfulfilled true Love, never ready to settle for less, convenience, or comfort. In the end, life rewards you for your perseverance," she adds with a smile that holds both wisdom and warmth.

Rebecca then steps back momentarily, walking to her hallowed grounds of knowledge, which is only a short jaunt away. When she returns, she hands them a carefully preserved manuscript. "I pray this piece will be as useful in your lives as it has been in mine," she says, her voice thick with sincerity.

As they embrace in a heartfelt bear hug of three, Rebecca leans close to Victoria and whispers, "Thank you for bringing him here."

"I guess the simplest answer is that the vast majority of the poems, if not all, I've ever written are private, dedicated to you or us," Erasmus reveals after a brief, reflective pause, his voice laden with deep emotion that resonates with Victoria.

Hyatt Hotel, Downtown St. Louis

Hours later, as they prepare to part ways after an elegant brunch at the Hyatt Hotel, Mrs. Samuels-Ortiz surprises the couple with an unexpected gesture.

"I have a copy of an ancient scribble for both of you. It's my wedding gift," she announces, her tone filled with reverence and affection. "It's a precious piece of writing that I treasure and constantly revisit. It speaks about restlessness and curiosity—qualities that define both of you. It's extraordinary how you both remained restless due to unfulfilled true Love, never willing to settle for less, convenience, or comfort. And in the end, life rewarded you for your perseverance," she explains, her eyes shimmering with warmth and sincerity.

Rebecca pauses for a moment before adding, "I pray this piece will be as meaningful in your lives as it has been in mine."

She excuses herself briefly, walking to her sacred library of knowledge, just a short jaunt away. When she returns, she hands them a carefully preserved manuscript, its leather-bound cover exuding an air of timeless wisdom.

Rebecca then turns to Victoria, her voice lowering to a whisper. "Thank you for bringing him here," she says, a subtle but heartfelt acknowledgment of the joy Victoria has restored to both their lives.

The moment concludes with a heartfelt embrace, the three of them locking in a bear hug that speaks volumes of gratitude, connection, and shared love for the extraordinary journey that has brought them together.

Royal Cambridge Scholastic Institute (2019)
(Erasmus and Victoria's Home– Two days later)

Before opening Mrs. Samuels-Ortiz's gift, Erasmus suggests, "It would be best to read it in class. It feels fitting to share it with my students, given its essence," to which Victoria readily agrees. Together, they set the stage for what promises to be a memorable and meaningful event.

"I'm sure reading it will reveal such a wonderful tale," Victoria muses, her voice soft yet brimming with anticipation.

Royal Cambridge Scholastic Institute (2019)
(Campus' Roads)

Victoria and Professor Cromwell-Smith meander through the deserted campus streets, their hands intertwined in a comforting grip. The quiet evening air surrounds them as they savor the moment, reflecting on their weekend trip to St. Louis. The visit to Victoria's "lifeguard vest"—as Erasmus affectionately refers to Rebecca Samuels-Ortiz—lingers in their thoughts, filling them with warmth and gratitude.

Their stroll is unhurried, a time to bask in the tranquility of each other's presence. With each step, they recount snippets of conversations, the joy of reconnecting with a dear friend, and the profound gift bestowed upon them.

As they approach the stately halls of the faculty building, Victoria gently squeezes Erasmus' hand. The simple gesture speaks volumes, grounding him in the significance of the task ahead.

"Make her proud, dear," she murmurs softly, her voice carrying both encouragement and affection, referring to the librarian whose wisdom and faith had been so pivotal.

Erasmus nods, a smile spreading across his face, his resolve quietly reaffirmed. The moment of tranquility fades as they prepare to step inside, and the usual classroom energy of anticipation fills the air. Their arrival marks the end of a brief but significant pause and the beginning of a new chapter in the class, where the gift from Rebecca will be revealed.

Royal Cambridge Scholastic Institute (2019)
(University Auditorium)

"Good morning, everyone," Erasmus announces, his voice resonating warmly through the auditorium as he and Victoria step inside.

"Good morning, professor," the students respond in unison, their energy lighting up the room.

"Victoria joins us today for a special reason," he begins, his tone carrying a hint of anticipation. "Over the weekend, we had the privilege of visiting a longtime friend of hers, Rebecca Samuels-Ortiz, the head librarian of the St. Louis, Missouri, public library. For the better part of the last decade, she has been not only a trusted confidant but also a life coach and mentor to Victoria."

He pauses for effect, the room growing still as his students sense the importance of the moment.

"Arguably," he continues, a fond smile touching his lips, "she is one of the key reasons Victoria and I found our way back to each other after all these years. As we said our goodbyes, Mrs. Samuels-Ortiz gifted us something extraordinary: an ancient scribble, one that she treasures deeply and considers her most valued piece of wisdom. It's her wedding gift to us."

A murmur of interest ripples through the room.

"Victoria and I decided that we wouldn't open or read it until we were here, in class, with all of you. Mrs. Samuels-Ortiz believes that this piece speaks to two virtues she sees in us— restlessness and curiosity."

With reverence, Erasmus unfolds the document, its age and character unmistakable even from a distance.

"It begins like this…" he declares, his voice imbued with gravity and emotion, as he prepares to unveil the cherished words for the first time before an audience.

*

"The Case of the Curious Child and the Restless Magician"

He wears a blue cap adorned with silver stars, draped over an electric blue coat. His top hat tilts slightly to the right, and a black magic wand with silver tips rests lightly in his hand.

For over an hour, the magician has defied gravity, baffled the senses, and mesmerized his audience. Minds have been read, bodies seemingly sawed in half, people have disappeared and reappeared in impossible places. The audience has gasped, cheered, and been left in awe.

The climax arrives with a grand finale: the magician levitates into the air, vanishing amidst a dazzling explosion of fireworks that sparkle and cascade around him. Moments later, he reappears—first on a distant balcony, then another, only to return to the main stage to wave and thank the ecstatic crowd.

As the illusionist concludes his act and steps offstage, a curious child approaches, his wide eyes filled with wonder.

"Is it magic or fantasy?" the child asks eagerly, his innocent voice soft yet filled with genuine curiosity.

The magician, who had grown weary from the performance, raises an eyebrow, momentarily surprised. His skepticism shows in the slight twitch of his lips. "It is both," the restless magician replies, his voice tinged with mischief, still caught in the afterglow of his act.

"If it's one, then it cannot be the other," the child insists, his tone resolute, undeterred by the magician's cryptic answer.

The magician pauses, assessing the child's seriousness. He smirks, but something in the child's unwavering gaze stirs something deeper within him. "Why?" he asks, less impatient, more curious himself.

"Because it's either real or not," the little one declares confidently, stepping closer, his face reflecting pure, innocent curiosity.

The magician sighs, lowering his wand and leaning slightly forward, his eyes narrowing in contemplation. "Magic and fantasy are not one and the same," he begins, his voice thoughtful but tinged with weariness. "Fantasy is a creation of the mind, while magic is something that happens right in front of your eyes. It's all about perception."

The boy's eyes glisten with more questions, and he presses on, his voice full of innocence. "Then neither is real?"

"For some, yes," the magician replies quietly, looking away. His mind begins to shift as he reflects on the child's innocence. "But for others, both are real, and it all resides in the eye of the beholder."

The boy stares at him, wide-eyed and deep in thought. He scratches his head, bewildered. "But how can a fantasy be real?" he asks, his confusion palpable.

The magician crouches to meet the child's eyes, his tired face softening for a moment. He pulls a folded paper from his hat, unfolding it with care. "Reality begins with what we dream. This old scribble explains it best: the restless spirit."

He begins to read aloud, his voice steady and solemn:

"The Restless Spirit"

The restless Spirit possesses

an itch to live,

an urge to seek,

a need to explore,

an imperative to search

The restless Soul chooses what to pursue.
The bug of restlessness,
the root of such itchiness,
keeps our life engines
incessantly active—
it is curiosity.

Curiosity is a condition
of spontaneous inquisitiveness,
a gut-driven eagerness
to learn and explore new things.
Curiosity and restlessness
are human attitudes
that inexorably lead
to the creation of ideas
about things
that don't yet exist.

The totality of civilization and human progress
is derived from ideas—
at first dismissed by others
as mere fantasies within imagination,
yet genuine
to the dreamers themselves.

Magic and fantasy
are both the same type of reality,
but one we must dream of first.

These types of dreamers are uncommon,

as they all possess restless and curious spirits,
filled with magic and fantasy—
both deliberately distorted realities,
just waiting to be made.

The magician folds the paper with care and places it back into his hat. He straightens up, his eyes softened with a mix of admiration and a newly realized humility. "Magic, fantasy, and reality—they're all threads of the same tapestry," he says, his voice gentler now, carrying the weight of his earlier reflections. "Your restless spirit will help you weave them into something uniquely yours."

The child nods slowly, absorbing the magician's words. "Thank you, Mr. Illusionist. Thank you so much," he whispers, his voice filled with awe.

The magician tips his tilted hat, gives a final flourish, and with a swift turn, vanishes into the crowd, leaving the child standing there—wide-eyed and wonder-filled. The spark of a restless spirit ignited within, the boy smiles to himself, his thoughts now as magical as the world around him.

*

Royal Cambridge Scholastic Institute (2019)
(University Auditorium)

As Professor Cromwell-Smith finishes reading, his voice lingers in the still air of the auditorium, a silence heavy with contemplation. The students sit motionless, their eyes betraying a mixture of wonder and thoughtfulness. He gazes solemnly at his class, allowing his words to sink in.

"Victoria and I were restless about our love lives. Despite the passage of time, we never strayed from our beliefs and feelings. Eventually, we found each other again because neither of us was willing to settle for less," he declares, his longing eyes meeting hers.

"The floor is now open for questions," The Professor announces with a calid tone of voice.

David is a senior English Literature major with a focus on magical realism and symbolism in modern literature. He enjoys discussing the interplay between reality and fantasy, particularly how authors blur these boundaries to deepen thematic explorations.

"Professor, in the poem, the magician speaks about how "Magic, fantasy, and reality—they're all threads of the same tapestry." This idea seems to suggest that the boundaries between these elements are fluid. Do you think the poem is arguing that the imagination and fantasy are essential to how we understand the world, even in the realm of real-life experiences?"

"That's a great interpretation, David. The poem highlights that imagination and fantasy are more than mere escapes—they're foundational to how we process and understand the world. The magician's statement about the interwoven nature of magic, fantasy, and reality suggests that without our capacity to imagine, to dream, we wouldn't have the drive to pursue progress or to create meaning in our lives. Fantasy, while often dismissed as unrealistic, can help us see the possibilities and potentials that we might otherwise overlook in our daily existence. The act of creating our own fantasies is a tool for navigating reality."

Ruchel is a third-year philosophy major interested in epistemology and the philosophy of perception. She enjoys analyzing how people form beliefs about the world and how those beliefs can be shaped by external influences.

"Professor, the child in the poem challenges the magician's view of reality and fantasy. He insists that if something is real, it cannot be fantasy, which seems to be a deeply logical way of thinking. Do you think the poem is commenting on how children's more direct, logical understanding of the world contrasts with the more complex, layered ways adults interpret reality?"

"Yes, Rachel, that's an insightful point. Children often see the world through a lens of simplicity and directness, where things are either real or not, as the child in the poem suggests. This contrasts with the more complex, often self-imposed layers of interpretation that adults place on reality. As we grow older, we complicate our understanding of the world, often relying on abstract concepts or multiple perspectives to make sense of it. The child's clarity, though, is an important reminder that there's also wisdom in simplicity. The fable suggests that perhaps we should sometimes embrace a simpler, more open approach to how we view the world—one where fantasy and reality coexist without the need for rigid boundaries."

Samantha is a sophomore psychology major with a keen interest in cognitive development and the psychology of creativity. She frequently examines how people use imagination in their daily lives and how it impacts their problem-solving abilities.

"Professor, in the poem, the restless spirit is described as having an "itch to live" and a "need to explore." From a psychological standpoint, do you think that restlessness is a necessary part of creativity? Can this drive to search and explore be seen as a core element of the human desire to create?"

"Absolutely, Samantha. In psychology, restlessness often signifies a drive to seek new experiences, which is inherently tied to creativity. The "itch to live" in the poem reflects a deep, intrinsic motivation—what we often call intrinsic drive. It's this very restlessness, the constant desire to explore and to understand, that fuels creative processes. Without this restless curiosity, there wouldn't be the impulse to push boundaries, to create something new. Creativity thrives on this constant questioning and exploring of what's possible. The poem, in a way, celebrates this spirit, showing that it's through our restless curiosity that we unlock the potential for magic and transformation in both fantasy and reality."

Thomas is a senior sociology major focusing on the social constructs of reality and the cultural implications of magic and fantasy in modern life. He is interested in how different cultures and communities interpret the concept of magic.

"Professor, the poem talks about how "fantasy and magic are both the same type of reality." Given the way that societies view reality, do you think that magic and fantasy have more to do with cultural interpretations of reality than an objective truth? Is the idea of fantasy potentially more real than we think?"

"That's a fascinating question, Thomas. The idea that "fantasy and magic are both the same type of reality" suggests that reality isn't as fixed or absolute as we often think. Different cultures and communities interpret reality through their own lenses, shaped by their beliefs, histories, and experiences. What might seem like fantasy or magic to one group could be a deeply ingrained part of another's reality. In this sense, fantasy can be just as "real" as what we perceive to be concrete because it serves a purpose in how people navigate their world. It becomes a tool for explaining the unexplainable, for transcending the mundane, and for inspiring creativity and transformation. The line between what we consider reality and fantasy is often more porous than we realize."

Jennifer is a first-year comparative literature major with a focus on narrative structure and storytelling traditions across cultures. She is fascinated by how stories convey abstract concepts like truth, identity, and self-perception.

"Professor, in the poem, the magician ultimately says that the "restless spirit will help you weave them into something uniquely yours." Do you think the fable is implying that by embracing both the fantasy and reality within us, we have the ability to shape our own identities? How does the restless spirit contribute to this process?"

"That's a profound observation, Jennifer. The restless spirit, as described in the poem, is a metaphor for the drive we all have to create meaning and shape our identities. By embracing both the fantasy and reality within us, we can break free from prescribed definitions of who we are. The restless spirit challenges us to seek out our own narratives, to mix the dreamlike and the practical, and to fashion something that is uniquely ours. In a sense, our ability to shape our identities comes from the willingness to explore all facets of who we are—our desires, fears, dreams, and ambitions—and weave them together into a personal narrative that is constantly evolving. The restless spirit empowers us to redefine ourselves in ways that are authentic and transformative."

"That'll be all for today. See you next week," he says, his voice gentle as he and Victoria walk out, their hands entwined, their faces radiating pure happiness.

As they leave, Professor Cromwell-Smith senses the atmosphere in the room. The student body is visibly affected, their restlessness palpable as they ponder how the day's lessons might shape to their own lives, just as it has Erasmus and Victoria. Curiosity fills the air as they wonder how to cultivate those attitudes for themselves.

"Today, my takeaway is that a touch of magic and fantasy is essential for the restless and curious spirit to soar like a kite through life," one student remarks aloud, encapsulating the collective reflection of the group.

'Mission accomplished,' the professor muses, a satisfied smile on his face as he steps into the sunlight.

However, their mood is quickly tempered by reality.

"Erasmus," Victoria says with a laugh, her eyes dancing, "didn't we leave our bikes at home?"

With a shared chuckle, they set off on foot, still hand in hand, their spirits soaring despite the minor inconvenience.

Chapter 13

Convergence

Royal Cambridge Scholastic Institute (2019)
(Late Sunday morning)

A family brunch will occur at noon, and Victoria's three children are all coming. Sarah arrives early to share her background with Erasmus and Victoria, including how she met her boyfriend.

"Mom, as is my routine, that morning I left my studio early, and hurrying, I walked into the coffee shop around the corner. That's when I saw him for the first time," explains Sarah.

Erasmus appears to be reading a newspaper, but he isn't. He's listening to every word Victoria's youngest enunciates.

"For some reason, the first thing that stood out about him was his voice. I was standing in line and overheard this deep and perfectly modulated monologue. I turned around to see a man dressed in running clothes dictating to a tablet," continues Sarah.

Victoria knows Erasmus is listening, even though he pretends not to.

"Brown-rim glasses, thick eyebrows, Hellenic nose, strong jaw, closely cropped chestnut hair, and bluish-green eyes, he's concentrating on his task, utterly oblivious to his surroundings," describes Sarah.

Erasmus sits next to Victoria; her dreamy eyes meet his. He smiles in complicity.

"Then, I saw his hands, Mom, both strong and with protruding veins. He radiated this incredible energy. He moved to one side, and, wearing running shorts, his bare legs came into view. By then, the attraction was so strong that I couldn't take my eyes off

243

him, so I glanced from the side, doing my best to peek only," explains Sarah.

Erasmus and Victoria sip their tea, taking in every word from their front-row seats. Their faces are transfixed as they look forward to hearing the details of the memorable moment.

"Suddenly, he looked up as if aware of my presence. That's when I froze as if incapacitated. We didn't take our eyes off each other. I managed to walk over on wobbly knees and introduced myself – something I have never initiated with a man. The bottom line is that he is 27 years old, single, a writer, and an endurance sportsman. I dumped my short résumé on him as well. Then magic happened. As it turned out, we realized that we both shared an affinity for the same places, music, movies, etc. Mind you, guys, what I have just narrated happened at most in 30 minutes. After a while, I let my rambling side take over, so my tongue went wild. At the same time, we both felt this uncontrollable draw for each other. What happened next was unexpected but extraordinary, as curiosity suddenly took hold of me. I felt this wild urge to exclaim my happiness to the world, and it came out as an inspired question. That led the way to an unforgettable epic exchange."

"It all happened like this …"

—✤—

Coffee Shop
(around the corner from Sarah's dorm)

"Who are you?" she asks, subdued, as if caught in a trance. Both youngsters focus intently on each other, their eyes seemingly lost in space.

"Eugene Laureau," he says, extending his hand to cover hers as if to shield it.

"Sarah Emerson-Lloyd," she responds, using her mother's last name—a habit she's embraced since her father passed away. His

hand continues to cup hers, and she offers no resistance, as if it belongs there.

"I'm a writer," he adds.

"French?" she inquires.

"French-Canadian."

"I'm in my senior year of college but haven't decided on my major yet. I'm leaning toward English literature and poetry," she shares cryptically.

"You don't look like a writer," she blurts out, unfiltered.

"And what do I look like, then?" he asks, amused, a faint smile touching his lips.

"An outdoorsman or an athlete," she replies, biting her lip. What she doesn't say—but feels intensely—is he's gorgeous. She can hardly contain herself.

"I'm both," he replies, sensing the magnetic pull coursing between them.

"C'mon, let's go for a walk," he suggests, standing up and gently tugging her hand.

The young twosome starts their stroll, hands intertwined. Over the next few hours, they talk without pause. Together, they feel at ease, as though they've been doing this all their lives. Time seems suspended, and the world fades away.

Along the way, her fiery temperament ignites playful debates. They spar and tease, their banter laced with intensity but never hostility. It's as if every interaction skirts the edge of a battle or crisis, yet it's all a game—an alluring dance of wills.

Eugene savors her spice and vigor, appreciating her for exactly who she is. He goes along for the ride, mentally stimulated and increasingly captivated by her vibrant energy.

Eugene Laureau's High Rise Condo. Boston (2019)

(A Couple of Months Later)

After a candlelight dinner he carefully prepares, Sarah sits in the living room, relaxed and scanning the breathtaking view of her beloved city and its winding river. Their whirlwind, platonic love affair dances between intense sparks and the healthy tensions ignited by Ms. Emerson-Lloyd's vibrant personality. Eugene's laid-back demeanor has all but surrendered to the vivacious young woman with curly blonde hair. There's nothing he can do to resist her magnetic force.

"Eugene, if you don't show me some of your writings, I'm not leaving tonight," she declares with a teasing edge, attempting to provoke one of their delicious confrontations.

He pretends not to hear, playing coy as he methodically cleans the dishes from the French feast he cooked and served earlier.

"That's it!" she exclaims, bolting toward his studio.

Startled, Eugene abandons his domestic duties and dashes after her. They collide playfully at the studio entrance, crashing onto the plush carpet together. On any other night, this encounter would naturally lead to passionate lovemaking. Tonight, however, it's halted by her sheer determination.

"Eugene Laureau, show them to me!" she demands, smiling mischievously as they remain entangled on the floor.

"Okay."

"What? I can't believe this. It's a miracle. Finally!" she exclaims, her face lighting up as they untangle. He laughs effusively, crawling toward his desk. From amidst scattered papers, he grabs a manuscript resting there.

Settling side by side on the floor, Eugene thrums through the pages until he finds what he's looking for. With love shining in his eyes, he begins to read to her for the very first time:

*

"Through the Hand of the Scribbler"

Through the hand of the scribbler,
his Spirit and Soul burst out.
His words convey his deepest feelings;
his inspiration is spontaneous,
surging out of his serene Spirit
and tranquil Soul.

The images and sensations take shape,
coming alive,

and the ideas turn into words.
As it relates to Love,
only the heart leads,
while the Spirit and Soul follow.

By the hand of the scribbler,
words of Love pour forth.
They are made of
passionate fire and
boundless tenderness.

Writing to love
is easy yet challenging—
an exercise of plain contradictions.
It is so hard to find that
magical, inspirational moment,
but when it arrives,
the words flow quickly and effortlessly,
and their beauty shines of its own accord.

As the phrases come alive,
and the verses gather strength,
all are driven by the name of Love.

Through the hand of the scribbler,
his Spirit and Soul burst out,
and when there is Love,
only the heart leads,
and the Spirit and Soul only follow.

*

Eugene's voice trails off as he finishes. Sarah sits quietly, the profound beauty of his words resonating deeply within her. She doesn't speak, only leans her head against his shoulder, savoring the moment—a shared experience of vulnerability, creativity, and connection.

Sarah's eyes widen, sparkling with excitement. Because of the class she attended with Erasmus teaching, she feels entirely at home in this realm of poetry and prose. She's captivated, her heart now firmly ensnared by Eugene's artistry, though he remains oblivious.

"Why do you keep such beautiful prose from me?" she asks, her voice trembling with emotion.

"I don't know," Eugene admits, searching her gaze for understanding.

"I guess I wasn't ready until tonight. And now, it just feels like the right moment."

"You've written so much of yourself in that. But do you ever worry that the words won't be enough to express all that you feel?" Eugene, caught off guard, might reply, "I don't know. Maybe they never can. But what else is there to do? Write, and hope." Sarah would then reflect more deeply, "It's the hope in your words that gets to me, Eugene. You let yourself feel, and in doing so, you make me feel too."

Their feelings swirl uncontrollably, a blend of exhilaration and awe.

"I want more," Sarah demands, her playful tone masking the intense yearning in her heart.

"All right, my impetuous lady," Eugene teases gently, pulling another page from his manuscript.

*

"What an Amazing Blessing Being Together Is"

Who wrote the script for this movie?
Or is it simply crafted from our time together?
Or perhaps we are its producers and directors?

And what of the audience?
Could it be predestined,
written beyond our understanding?
Has it always been there, waiting,
guiding us along a luminous path,
where Happiness multiplies each day?

A love walkway through life,
where firm ground forms beneath our feet,
a protective shield to carry us
through life's challenges,
warding off harm.
A magical lens that reveals life's best angles,
allowing us to distill, drop by drop,
the finest it has to offer.
A generous path that leads to others,
lined with kindness and scattered flowers,
made lovelier by our passage.
A magic carpet upon which we dwell,
carrying us wherever imagination leads.

This script, our script,
is written in dense, indelible ink,

traced in the ecstasy
of two souls fused into one.

Two souls forever grateful for every fleeting moment,
knowing its beauty is brief.
A script charged with Love,
overflowing with strength and passion,
tenderness and unconditional devotion—
pillars of our Happiness.

It is the script of the most beautiful story ever written,
a testament to the extraordinary blessing
of you and I,
together, forever.

*

Sarah's breath catches as the last words leave Eugene's lips. Her emotions swirl uncontrollably, a tumult of wonder and joy.

"This reminds me of my mother's lifelong, true Love," she says at last, her voice barely above a whisper. "Your writings are just as beautiful as his," she adds with a mischievous twinkle in her eye, "though he's much wittier and smarter."

Her playful, devilish grin and wink lighten the moment, allowing her to defuse the intensity of her overwhelming feelings. Eugene chuckles, his eyes sparkling with admiration.

"Well, I'll take that as a compliment," he replies, pulling her close once more.

And so, in the quiet glow of the evening, they bask in the magic of words and the growing bond between them.

She motions for him to continue, her silence betraying the overwhelming impact of the similarities she senses but cannot yet articulate.

*

"As to How Love Lights Up Everything"

As matter,
we are finite, pure, and simple dust,
and we are ephemeral energy,
but above all,
we are God's miracle.

As reason,
we are conscience, thoughts, and imagination,
and in our minds,
the world is ideas and shadows.

As Spirit,
we are souls in Love,
and our spirits light up life's way,
providing us with meaning and purpose,
and enabling us to travel far
in life's journey.

Out of Matter and Reason,
only Spirit transcends the infinite,
and the Soul is its engine.

Faith is the light that emanates from the Soul,
and the light between all men
originates from the Spirit,
and that is Love.

*

"Sarah, like us, this one is for every couple," Eugene explains, his tone tinged with pride. "I finished it just last night. You've been badgering, chasing, and pressing me about it," he teases with a broad smile.

Sarah remains motionless, her feelings simmering beneath the surface, fighting for release.

"I don't know what's wrong with me," she says finally, her voice trembling. "I feel this ravenous need to delve into your writings. What will it take, Eugene? Are you going to read more to me, or must I wrestle it out of you?"

"Oh, yes, of course, my passionate muse," he replies, stunned by her restraint. He expected a volcanic outburst but instead finds her composure intoxicating. Without delay, he begins to read.

"When I Write to You"

When I write to you,
I give you all of me on those little notes.

When I write for you,
I surrender, perhaps,
some of the best of me.

When I write about you,
I try to tell you in a thousand ways,
how much I love you,
and how deep my feelings are.

When I write to you,
I offer you my best gifts,
those that cannot be touched,
those that can only be felt.
When I write for you,
life's beauty grows through words,
and my heart can be sensed
beating like a drum.

When I write about you,
everything I feel turns into magic,

and all of it is yours,
without limit and to no end.

When I write for you,
time and space stop,
the words flow,
the Spirit is enriched,
and the Soul smiles in joy.

When I write about you,
the heart is emptied of words,
that burst out and pour Love into you.

When I write about you,
there is Happiness in life,
with a crystalline spirit
and an innocent soul.

Whenever I write to you
in the future,
you'll know and feel
that it will always be,
the best and most profound offering
that I can give and will ever give to you.
*

Sarah no longer contains herself. She throws herself at Eugene in an electrifying, passionate embrace, their faces impossibly close.

"My handsome writer," she murmurs, her voice thick with emotion,

You've captured everything—everything I've been feeling, even before I knew I felt it. Your words—they make me think about everything we could be, together. But what about you, Eugene?

What do you want out of all of this? I return to the question I asked you the day we met."

"Where did you come from? Where were you hiding all this time? Who are you?"

"Whoever your heart wants me to be," Eugene responds, his sincerity unwavering.

"But what does your heart truly want?" she counters, pressing him, her voice shivering with hope and desire.

"For yours to feel the way mine does," he says, his words both an admission and a plea.

"And how does yours feel?" She teases.

"Utterly and hopelessly in Love," he declares.

As the words settle between them, they are swept into each other's arms, consumed by a torrent of shared emotions and undeniable desire.

— ✦ —

"Mom, we've been inseparable ever since," Sarah says with a dreamy tone. "A perfect stranger blessed my life when we found each other by accident. It's as if we were made for each other."

"Wonderful, dear. To be in Love at your age is such a gift. You'll be able to treasure this for the rest of a very long life. We're looking forward to meeting him soon," Victoria replies warmly, her face lit by a broad smile.

"Who is he?" interjects Erasmus with his trademark absent-minded curiosity, the obvious query fully displayed.

"Funny, hilarious professor," Sarah quips back, slightly confused.

Then realization dawns. "Oh … his name is Eugene Laureau, and he's of French-Canadian descent. I thought I mentioned it when I told you guys about how we met," she explains, her bafflement apparent.

One Hour Later at Brunch

"Eugene, allow me to introduce them to you. This is only part of my family, as I have a stepbrother and a stepsister living in Italy. My older sister, Elizabeth Victoria, is the tall, smiley, beautifully pregnant one. Standing to her right, the impossibly handsome young man—though not more handsome than you—is her brand-new husband, Jordan Auguste Morse. My favorite person on earth, my brother Bart, is on her left side, with a jungle of chestnut curly hair on his head. Next to him, you'll find my rival in matters of brotherly Love, his girlfriend, Sofia Broomfield. And, of course, the infatuated couple clinging to each other at all hours of the day and night are my mother, Victoria, and my stepfather, Professor Erasmus Cromwell-Smith," Sarah announces with pompous flair.

"Nice to meet you all," Eugene says, his eyes scanning the group appreciatively.

What he doesn't anticipate is how touchy-feely the Emerson-Cromwell clan is. Before he can say another word, he's swept into a sea of kisses and embraces, leaving him both flustered and warmly welcomed by the family.

"Eugene, do you know this is the first time Sarah has brought anyone to our Sunday brunch?" Elizabeth-Victoria teases mischievously, a playful sparkle in her eye.

"C'mon, sister, shut up!" Sarah retorts, feigning rebellion.

"Eugene, I hear you're a writer," Erasmus chimes in, deftly changing the subject.

"I write poetry under my own name and science fiction under the pseudonym Ethan Lawrence," Eugene replies, a hint of pride in his voice.

"Interesting. Let's talk after the meal, and I'll show you some of my work," Erasmus offers, his academic enthusiasm lighting up.

"Let me break the news to everyone," Bart announces, standing tall and confident. "Sofia and I have enrolled in the MBA program at The London School of Economics. We're leaving in a few weeks."

"That is fantastic. We'll visit you over the summer then," Erasmus responds immediately, his tone cheerful and encouraging.

Victoria, initially taken aback, quickly recovers, pulling Bart and Sofia into a warm embrace.

"I'm so proud of you guys," she says sincerely, her voice tinged with a mix of surprise and deep maternal pride.

"Are you leaving before your nephew is born?" demands Elizabeth, her tone playfully accusatory as she alludes to her upcoming baby.

"No, that's why we don't have a firm departure date yet. We're sticking around until … wait a minute, is it official now, a boy?" Bart exclaims, his face lighting up with excitement.

Elizabeth freezes for a split second, realizing she inadvertently let the secret slip. She glances at Jordan, and their shared complicity is evident in their mischievous smiles that follow a moment of mock seriousness.

Victoria, ever the exuberant matriarch, erupts with joy. She jumps up and down, pulling everyone into jubilant hugs and kisses. Her infectious excitement fills the room, making everyone grin.

Erasmus quietly watches her, his mind wandering back to when he first saw her as a baton twirler in the Harvard marching band. His smile deepens with fondness.

"Mom, I've been meaning to ask if you're retiring for good from teaching?" Elizabeth ventures, her voice laced with a touch of disapproval.

"Yes," Victoria replies with a sense of finality. "The upcoming academic year will be my last."

"What about you, Erasmus?" Bart quickly interjects, curious.

"Same. Next year will be my last," Erasmus confirms with a calm nod.

"What are you both going to do?" Sarah asks, her tone light yet genuinely interested.

"Enjoy our time together, travel, and Erasmus will write some more," Victoria replies with a contented smile, glancing at Erasmus, who squeezes her hand affectionately.

Bart, never one to linger on sentiment for too long, switches gears. "Are you going to end your balloonist antics, Jordan?" he asks, steering the conversation toward the soon-to-be father's adventures.

Jordan hesitates, holding Bart's gaze in silence for a brief, tension-filled moment before letting out a reluctant sigh. "I guess I have no choice but to stop," he says begrudgingly, his tone a mix of resignation and wistfulness.

The room fills with a chorus of good-natured laughter, the lighthearted atmosphere underscoring the love and camaraderie that define the family.

Victoria and Erasmus' Home Library
(After the family has left)

"Eugene's writing is fascinating. He's exploring science fiction that delves into the complexities of our future society," Erasmus remarks, his voice tinged with admiration.

"He seems like a decent boy," Victoria replies, her tone reassuring as she tidies up a stack of books. "What are you planning for tomorrow's class, dear?" she asks, curious about his next lecture.

"It'll cover what we experience every weekend at our family brunches," Erasmus replies cryptically, a knowing smile playing on his lips.

"And that'll be?" Victoria presses, her curiosity piqued.

"Convergence," he says with a twinkle in his eye.

As Erasmus and Victoria share their reflective moments after the family brunch, the quiet transition to the next phase of their day unfolds. With the weight of personal discoveries behind them, Erasmus gathers his thoughts for the lecture ahead. Leaving the comfort of home behind, the couple steps into the cool afternoon, ready to enter the world of academia once more.

As Erasmus approaches the university auditorium, the campus streets seem quieter, signaling the shift from family gatherings to scholarly pursuits. His smile widens as he steps into the familiar environment, his presence lighting up the room as he prepares for the students' eager attention.

Royal Cambridge Scholastic Institute (2019)
(University Auditorium)

Professor Cromwell-Smith strides into the auditorium with purpose, his sunny disposition immediately uplifting the atmosphere.

"How's everyone today?" he asks, his voice ringing warmly.

"Marvelous!" comes the spirited response from the student body, a collective expression of energy and enthusiasm.

"Today, I'll take you back to a time when I first understood the profound concepts of convergence and confluence—how everything and everyone in life is interconnected in remarkable ways," Erasmus begins, his voice filled with gravity and intrigue.

"It begins like this …"

—✦—

Carnegie Library, Pittsburgh, PA (2005)

"Erasmus, pay attention," begins Mr. Carnegie, his tone authoritative yet filled with pride. "Andrew Carnegie built this magnificent structure that now serves as a music hall and a library at the end of the 19th century when he was still young. There is no precedent of such magnitude and generosity implementing what becomes a lasting and enduring legacy by such a successful young entrepreneur, ever again in America," he declares as they step inside the grand hall.

"Thank you so much for the invitation and tour. I wasn't aware that so many of America's magnificent public libraries were built and funded by Mr. Carnegie. So many of them are still standing and among the best in the country," Erasmus responds, his admiration evident.

"How can I be of help, Erasmus? You requested we meet," asserts the old Scottish antiquarian, whose presence is a rarity during his short visit to America.

He is, after all, a distant relative of the great Scottish-American philanthropist himself.

"Sir, I want to understand better what lies behind confluence and how convergence interacts with it," asks Erasmus, his voice marked by earnest curiosity.

Mr. Carnegie, calm and deliberate, begins pacing. His thoughts seem to navigate the vast repository of knowledge he carries, searching for the most fitting ancient writing on the subject. Then, as if struck by inspiration, he halts and heads down a narrow aisle lined with shelves brimming with aged tomes.

Minutes later, he returns, cradling a leather-bound book that is twice the size of a standard hardcover. Its weathered cover bears the patina of time, and its weight alone suggests the depth of its contents.

"Erasmus, this is the perfect fit for your curiosity," says Mr. Carnegie, setting the book on a nearby table with care.

With reverence, he opens it and begins to read in earnest.

"Convergence"

Convergence and confluence
are life's timely opportunities.
When there is convergence,
we convene and congregate,
through concurrence and congruence
of common interests,
life paths,
or some form or another
of pre-existing links or bonds.

Similarly, when confluence occurs
through convocation,
we seek concertation, congeniality, and conciliation.
Convergence and confluence
are rare and unique life chances, even vital opportunities.
They may be passing and not repeatable.

That's why,
when they are positive and absent of evil,
we take advantage of them on the spot,
and seize the moment,
never letting any of them go.

*

Mr. Carnegie's voice lingers in Erasmus's mind, the poetic wisdom of the ancient tome he has just read aloud echoing with profound significance. The words, rich with meaning, take hold in Erasmus's thoughts, settling like seeds ready to blossom.

As the reading concludes, Erasmus sits in quiet reflection, absorbing the profound insights shared by the venerable antiquarian. Mr. Carnegie closes the leather-bound book gently and looks at Erasmus with a knowing smile.

"Erasmus," he says, his tone deliberates, "what you take from this depends entirely on how willing you are to recognize such moments in your own life. Convergence and confluence are not theories to ponder—they are calls to action, invitations to act when the stars align."

"I understand, sir," Erasmus responds earnestly. "Your guidance today will not be forgotten."

Mr. Carnegie places a firm hand on Erasmus's shoulder. "Then go forth and make something of it, my boy. Life waits for no one."

With that, Erasmus rises, thanking Mr. Carnegie profusely for his time, wisdom, and generosity. As he steps out of the grand library, the air feels alive with possibility, the poet in him already crafting verses from the ideas swirling in his mind.

— �֍ —

Royal Cambridge Scholastic Institute (2019)
(University Auditorium)

Professor Cromwell-Smith carefully closes the old tome and surveys the room with thoughtful eyes.

In the midst of the present day, Erasmus' thoughts drift back to a pivotal encounter year earlier. The conversation with Mr. Carnegie, deep in the Carnegie Library, resurfaces in his mind. The ideas of convergence and confluence still echo through him as he prepares to share them with his students, the past meeting the present in a lesson of profound importance.

"Our class itself is a clear example of convergence," he states, his voice resonant and reflective. "Pause and reflect on it for a moment. Here, we gather, united by a shared curiosity and a common pursuit of knowledge. No one individual dominates, nor does anyone exploit this gathering for personal gain. Instead, we collectively benefit from this moment of convergence."

He walks to the edge of the dais, his tone growing earnest.

"Going forward, be vigilant for settings of convergence. These are rare, and their occurrence often carries immense potential. When you spot them, ensure that you and those with whom you converge take full advantage—always for the right reasons and toward a shared good," he concludes, his words hanging in the air like a soft echo.

Having outlined the profound significance of convergence, Erasmus pauses, allowing the words to sink in. The students remain still, their faces thoughtful as they process the depth of his message. With a quiet nod, the professor invites them to share their thoughts, ushering the class into an engaging dialogue about the philosophical principles of connection.

A few hands are raised.

Lewis is a Philosophy major with a deep interest in existentialism and the nature of happiness. He often challenges abstract concepts and enjoys engaging in philosophical debates.

"Professor, in the poem "Through the Hand of the Scribbler," you speak of the Spirit and Soul being expressed through the act of writing, especially in relation to love. How do you think this contrasts with more mundane forms of communication? Is it the act of writing itself that reveals a deeper truth about love?"

"That's a thought-provoking question, Lewis. The poem suggests that the act of writing, particularly when it comes from a place of deep emotion, transforms simple words into something far more profound. Writing becomes more than just communication—it is a channel for the writer's Spirit and Soul. The mundane forms of communication, like casual conversation, lack that depth of introspection and emotional surrender. In love, the writing becomes a way of offering one's heart fully, and it transcends the ordinary by creating something eternal and meaningful."

Carly is a psychology major, particularly interested in the intersection of storytelling and psychological well-being. She's always eager to draw parallels between literary themes and real-life emotional growth.

"Professor, in "What an Amazing Blessing Being Together Is," the poem suggests that life's path is like a script—one that is filled with joy, kindness, and even magical moments. Do you think the idea of our lives being scripted is a metaphor for how we create meaning, or do you see it as suggesting that some aspects of our journey are predestined?"

"Yes, Carly, the poem uses the metaphor of a script to explore how life unfolds. While it could suggest that certain paths or moments are predestined, I believe the deeper message is that we play an active role in creating our own script. We are both the writers and the actors in our lives, guided by the choices we make, the people we meet, and the love we experience. The idea of a script is more about the intentionality with which we shape our lives, finding meaning in the moments we create."

Anthony is a creative writing major with a focus on human motivation and emotional intelligence. He often brings scientific perspectives into philosophical discussions and enjoys analyzing character behaviors through psychological lenses.

"Professor, in "As to How Love Lights Up Everything," you write about how faith and love are intertwined, illuminating our path in life. From a psychological perspective, do you think the emotional benefits of love and faith are closely related to our well-being? And if so, how does this relate to the poem's theme?"

"That's an insightful perspective, Tony. Love and faith both play significant roles in psychological well-being. Love creates a sense of connection and belonging, which are essential for emotional health. Faith, in the sense of believing in something greater than ourselves, can provide a sense of purpose and stability. In the poem, love and faith are presented as interwoven forces that guide us and give our lives meaning. This connection mirrors the psychological notion that our emotional well-being thrives when we feel connected to others and have a sense of purpose."

Lisa is a senior majoring in Sociology, with a keen interest in the dynamics of happiness. She often looks at social structures and cultural narratives to analyze how individuals find meaning in their lives.

"Professor, the poem "When I Write to You" reflects a profound, almost sacred offering of love through words. How do you think the act of writing as a form of expression can influence societal perceptions of love? Does it elevate or deepen our understanding of relationships?"

"That's a fantastic question, Lisa. The act of writing, especially in the context of love, can indeed influence how we understand and perceive relationships. When we write about love, we are often giving more than just words—we are giving a piece of ourselves. This vulnerability can deepen the connection between the writer and the reader. On a societal level, the written word can elevate the concept of love by making it tangible, allowing us to see the depths of affection and devotion that might not be as easily expressed in day-to-day life. Writing allows for reflection, and through that reflection, love can be understood more profoundly."

Jenny is an Art History major, intrigued by how emotions are conveyed through art and storytelling. She enjoys drawing connections between literature and visual art.

"Professor, the poem "Through the Hand of the Scribbler" speaks to the spontaneity and inspiration that comes when love is expressed through writing. Do you think this aligns with the creative process in art, where the most genuine work often emerges unexpectedly? How do you see this parallel between artistic expression and the written word?"

"Yes, Jenny, I believe there is a strong parallel between writing and artistic expression in general. Much like an artist who may begin a painting with an idea but allows the process to evolve and reveal unexpected beauty, a writer often allows inspiration to flow without force. The creative process in both mediums is deeply rooted in spontaneity and intuition. When we are in tune with our emotions, whether through paint or words, the expression becomes authentic, unforced, and often more powerful. Both art and writing serve as mediums through which we can channel our most profound feelings, and when we let go of control, the results are often more genuine and impactful," The Professor says in conclusion.

"That will be all for this week," he announces, his voice tinged with a hint of finality. "Our next two classes will be the last of this academic year."

As the students begin to gather their things, their demeanor thoughtful, as they process the depth of his message. Conversations hush, and eyes linger on one another. The professor senses a newfound awareness in the room—a subtle yet profound shift as the students begin to search for the seeds of convergence among their peers.

Leaving the auditorium, Professor Cromwell-Smith smiles to himself. **'Mission accomplished.'**

Chapter 14

Ánimo, Animus, Anima

(Charles River, Boston, 2019)

The enamored couple walks alongside the restless waters of the river as the wind picks up pace, whistling all around them. Huddled together, their steps slow under the force of the blow. The late afternoon cool spring weather feels misplaced, more akin to an early autumn day. The weather phenomena stir an eerie feeling in Victoria, unearthing long-buried memories.

As they approach a familiar turn, chills run through her body. The walkway is not only well known but also brimming with beautiful, unforgettable memories steeped in intense emotions. Soon, the silhouette of the student residence building comes into view. They approach the door, and she trembles, her heart racing.

"Surprise!" Erasmus exclaims, key in hand, as he opens the door and ushers Victoria inside.

Overcome by a torrent of flashbacks, she clings tightly to his arm as though fearing she might crumble under the weight of her emotions.

Erasmus and Victoria's College Days' Studio (2019)

"I bought it many years ago, soon after you left, with a loan taken from Mr. Carnegie," Erasmus reveals softly.

"It looks the same," she marvels, her mouth agape. Her intense gaze roams the space, her face overcome with joy.

"I never touched or changed anything. Never rented it out either," he confesses.

Everything is as they left it—their photographs and souvenirs from countless bike trips, books stacked high in every corner, the reading chair by the floor lamp, and the bed with the same linens. Time seems frozen, the studio an untouched capsule of their love.

"For years, I used to come here. I even slept over sometimes," he admits.

"Didn't that sadden you or make you feel depressed?" she asks, her voice tinged with concern.

"Victoria, sometimes the places where we've been the happiest in life lie scattered in our past," Erasmus begins, his tone reflective. "They're often modest and unpretentious and yet, at the time, provided us with immense and irreplicable joy," he extols as they stroll around the small, nostalgic space.

Then, without warning, and driven by sheer impulse, she turns and kisses him passionately in one swift motion. It's a kiss bursting with the fervor of youth, her arms winding tightly around his neck in a classic sailor's victory kiss posture, one calf bending up as if choreographed by memory.

"I was … we were totally happy in this tiny, cozy place, my adorable Brit," she declares, her glowing smile stretching from ear to ear, her eyes sparkling with unrestrained delight.

"Are we going to stay the night?"

"If you so desire, my lady."

At that moment, Victoria notices the notebooks, and her heart begins to race wildly.

"All your poems from our time together are still here?" she asks rhetorically as she paces toward them, her fingers tracing the edges of the well-worn spines.

"Why?"

"Because this is where they belong… at least, they did until now."

Victoria trembles, working hard to contain her emotions as she begins to leaf through the pages. Her breathing deepens, and her hands grow unsteady while memories long buried start to resurface.

"Do you remember this one?" she asks, pointing to a scribble on a yellowing page.

"That was right after we met, at the very beginning of our relationship," Erasmus replies, his voice filled with nostalgia.

Unaware of their subtle body movements, the twosome naturally reverts to old habits deeply rooted in their past. He reaches for her free hand, and they instinctively nestle together in the same reading chair where so many of the notebook's scribbles had been created, shared, and lived.

Victoria looks at Erasmus with eyes that shine bright and glisten with tears.

"This was your first declaration of love, my beloved Brit."

"Yes, it was, my lady."

Victoria continues flipping through the notebook. When she turns to a particular page, both of them stop and look at each other with sudden recognition, as if unearthing a shared treasure, they had forgotten existed.

The opportune scribble has been waiting, it seems, for this very moment to aid them on their journey of reconnection. Victoria covers her mouth with her hand as the memory of the poem rushes back to her. Her throat tightens with emotion, rendering her momentarily speechless. She hands the notebook to Erasmus, her teary eyes silently urging him to read it aloud.

Erasmus takes the notebook and begins to read with deep emotion, savoring each word.

*

"It Is Commonly Said that Love …"

It is commonly said that
love is never having to say you're sorry,
and never having to apologize.

It has been said, therefore,
that in this regard, Love is perfect
and as it belongs to a twosome,
it is twice perfect.

But the risk of Love
without forgiveness or repentance,
is that it could turn rigid and selfish.
It's the kind of Love,
where forgiveness
is replaced by
obfuscation and recurring reprimands.

It's the kind of Love,
where repentance
is replaced by wounded self-esteem,
and offended egos and pride.
On the contrary,
love is to know how to forgive
those that we love.
Forgiving one another,
we also forgive ourselves.

Love between two people works,
only if the couple,
acts in unison on everything,
so, when one fails, both fail,

or maybe,
the one that has failed,
is the other.

Love is to be sorry together.
Love is absent of pride, selfishness,
forbidden or sacred places.
What matters in Love is
what one feels for one another.

In Love,
it does not matter
if there is a gesture or not,
but only if whatever takes place
is done with our hearts.

Love is not arrogant.
Love is humble.

When in Love,
complaints are ill-fitted,
punishment creates opaqueness,
pride stains,
selfishness hurts,
and punishment kills.

When there is Love,
the offense is born,
with its own pardon,
attached to it.

Remorse is always done
by both lovers and
it is in this way,

that forgiveness does not exist in Love,
because while in Love,
it is not necessary
to say I'm sorry,
or to ask for forgiveness.

*

"I wish we would have read this earlier," Victoria says softly, her voice trembling with a mixture of regret and hope.

"Actually," Erasmus replies insightfully, "it's occurring at the right time. Whatever needed to happen spontaneously took place without aid or crutches," Erasmus replies insightfully.

They both fall silent, holding hands as they absorb the poem's meaning, feeling a renewed sense of love and understanding bloom between them.

"My lady, here is another piece exploring what a couple endures when separated."

In a quiet rhythm, Erasmus begins to read aloud, his voice steady and soothing, as Victoria rests her head on his shoulder.

"When We Are Not Together"

I wish I knew how you are truly feeling.
Hopefully, your heart is as light as mine.
Yet, I've sensed the sorrow in your voice,
and I long to lift it from your spirit.
What we share is far too beautiful
not to be a constant source of joy.
Stay spontaneous, as you've always been;
let's try to keep rigidity at bay.

This extraordinary bond between us
is like a sudden fountain,
springing forth,

needing no coaxing,
no outside force.
Let me be me; I'll let you be you.

But also,
let us be us—together,
just as we are.
We're already so alike;
it will keep us close,
spontaneous, and united,
growing closer and closer still.
I wonder how you are truly doing.
I hope you feel the same happiness I do.

May my words bring you comfort—
not critique or complaint—
but support, never demand.
I wish for you to feel the strength
we create together,
a strength that becomes your solace
when we are apart.

I yearn to be with you now and forever.
But when we cannot be together,
let the love we share
be your carriage and shield.

Let me inspire your happiness,
so that those days apart
are serene, peaceful,
and pass swiftly
as we await each other's return.

And as always happens,
when we reunite in joy,
we find that our love has deepened,
our bond has grown stronger,
and our life together has,
over time,
become richer and more radiant than ever before.

*

As he concludes the reading, Erasmus' eyelids lower in his familiar way, signaling his gentle drift into the realm of dreams. Victoria kisses him softly on the lips and carefully removes the notebook from his hands. Her curiosity draws her back to its pages, and soon, she discovers another treasure—a verse he once dedicated to her.

The memory comes rushing back: it had emerged spontaneously during a long run, as they rested together on a park bench. She begins to read the verse aloud, her voice soft and tender, mirroring how it sounded the very first time he shared it with her. Her hands tremble slightly, overcome by the timeless beauty of his words.

"The Soul's Whispers"

Today, *I remembered those whispers,*
and in total silence,
I slid back to the past …

Those sounds were soft and constant,
like a tiny creek,
a crystalline, crisp trickle.
The Soul's whispers suddenly irrupted
as we were behind the scenes.

The stage, the play, the performers, the audience—

all "acting" as they always do,
on the other side,
putting on a show, living just
for "the appearance" of it.

Behind the show
backstage of the performance,
between the drop curtains,
I could hear life …

But, from afar,
I couldn't discern their performance
nor their costumes,
or the scenario.

The figures on either side were blurry.
I could only hear the whispers …

And without even feeling it,
almost without noticing,
it seemed as though I could hear their souls.
The sounds of their souls came to me,
as a distant whisper.

The words could not be distinguished,
only their cadence remained.
The people were not what they seemed
nor what they seek to be.
Their souls whispered something different …

Today, I remember those whispers,
those sounds, soft and constant.
They were like a tiny creek,
a crystalline, crisp trickle.
They were … the Soul's whispers.
*

Victoria finishes, her mind foggy with thought, and she doesn't immediately realize Erasmus is now fully awake, his eyes transfixed, matching her contemplative gaze. A small surge of emotion courses through her as their eyes meet.

"Did you…?" she begins.

"Yes, I heard it all, my dear. It stirred up such loving emotions," Erasmus responds, his voice calm and soothing.

Victoria's smile spreads, infectious, and Erasmus can't help but respond with one of his own. Her enthusiasm bubbles over, filling the room with a quiet energy. They quietly step out of the residence. For the first time since she left, Erasmus takes the notebook with him.

"Let's keep it close to us at home," he announces.

Victoria is overcome with emotion. The sounds of campus life break the reverie of their quiet walk, signaling the shift from the past to the present. The memories of their younger days, preserved in the student residence, fade into the background as Erasmus thinks about his upcoming class.

Then, from the corner of her eye, she notices a loose piece of paper teetering on the edge of the notebook. Erasmus follows her gaze and instinctively pulls it free. As he unfolds it, his face changes, struck deeply by the sight of its contents.

"What is it?" Victoria asks, leaning closer. Then, as her eyes take in the precise, flowing handwriting, realization dawns.

"That's a letter from Mrs. V.!" she exclaims.

"Indeed, it is," Erasmus confirms, his tone imbued with reverence.

"Her letter will be the centerpiece of tomorrow's class. I'm going to lecture on vital engagement—a dissertation on *Ánimo, animus, anima,* not as animosity, but in its broadest, most transcendent sense," he says.

Victoria's eyes shine with admiration as he speaks. "You're more than welcome to join us, my lady," he adds with a gentle smile.

"It would be my pleasure," she replies, "but I may be a little late—I need to handle some matters regarding the kids' trust."

"Very well, then. It's settled. See you there," Erasmus says, slipping the letter carefully back into its place.

As they prepare to leave their home, the weight of the memories still lingers. With one final glance at the intimate space where their love had been rekindled, they step out into the brisk, quiet morning air. The streets of the campus, just waking from the soft fog of early dawn, now seem like a world away from their moment of personal reflection. Before parting ways, they share a tender kiss, a fleeting but heartfelt gesture that lingers in the air as they break apart.

Erasmus walks toward the university alone, the memory of Victoria's smile still warm in his heart, while she heads off in the opposite direction to tend to her errands. Though their paths briefly diverge, the connection between them remains strong, a testament to the new beginning they have embraced.

Royal Cambridge Scholastic Institute (2019)

(University Auditorium)

Arriving at the university's lecture hall, Erasmus briefly pauses outside the door, collecting his thoughts. A deep breath in, and then, with a smile, he opens the door. The contrast of the quiet, reflective morning to the buzzing energy of the classroom is striking. The familiar scent of chalk and old wood fills the air as he steps onto the stage. The students are already chattering excitedly, waiting for his arrival, unaware that today's lecture will be laced with deeper personal meaning, carried from his own experiences.

Despite having almost no sleep the previous night, Professor Erasmus Cromwell-Smith strides into class with unwavering enthusiasm, radiating an infectious, boundless energy. His quick steps echo across the room as he makes his way to the desk.

"How's everyone today?" he asks, his voice bright and invigorating.

"Insanely awesome!" comes the spirited response from the class, their collective energy mirroring his own.

"Sometimes, we all feel a little low in motivation," Professor Cromwell begins, his tone shifting to one of reflection. "We lack the drive to carry out what's expected of us, or perhaps even what we expect of ourselves. Last night, I stumbled upon a letter—an old gem—from my inveterate and greatest cheerleader, the incomparable Mrs. V. She was my mentor during a deeply transformative period of my life."

He pauses, allowing the weight of his words to settle. "This letter had a profound and uplifting effect on me, especially during times when I struggled to navigate life's challenges. It felt as though Mrs. V., sensing my need across the expanse of time, had written it specifically for me. Within her heartfelt words was a single verse—a powerful reflection on a virtuous attitude, a life condition that unites our desire with the willingness to strive for greatness." "Please allow me to share the verse with you."

The pedagogue unfolds the letter carefully and begins to read the verse aloud, his voice carrying the rhythm of the words with deliberate passion…

"Ánimo, Animus, Anima"

Ánimo, animus, anima,
Ánimo, animus—what does it matter?
They are all one and the same.

Surprised?
Colloquially, animus
is often strictly associated
with animosity,
those deeply rooted ill feelings.

But there couldn't be a more blatant
misuse of a very profound word,
than this.

That's why, in this verse,
animus finds itself cradled
between its homonyms—
ánimo and anima, that is.

Hereunto lies the other side of animus—
or is it ánimo or anima, perhaps?
Well, either or, here is what it truly is …

Animus is a state or condition
that signals our "vital engagement."
into the game of life.

Animus is desire and willingness combined.

It can be an attitude towards anything or anyone,
or a condition born of
the deliberate or even unintended ways we live.

Animus is the impetus of the Spirit,
and the spark of the Soul.
It is the vital force of the heart,
the driver of our design,
the engine behind our intendment,
the catalyst of our purpose,
the vital energy behind our meaning.

It is the fuel for our plans,
the secret ingredient behind our courage,
the light bulb in our mind,
the energy behind our willingness,
the precondition to our disposition.

Animus is the intensity,
the level of engagement,
in a state or condition of willingness.
It resides at our core,
inside our inner Spirit.

If Ánimo, Animus, Anima,
is not spontaneously present
at the onset of life's endless paths,
then it is one we must fight for—
putting our best efforts to acquire it,
to create "the right frame of mind"
to embark on any quest.

Are you in good animus today?
Are you of good animus every day?
Do you have the right anima this morning?

Ánimo, Animus, Anima—
what does it matter?
After all,
they are all
one of the same.

*

Professor Cromwell-Smith pauses, then begins a thoughtful commentary that expands on the verse he has just read.

"This verse reminds me—and I hope it reminds you—that cultivating *animus* is not a passive state. It is something we must actively pursue, especially in moments when life feels heavy. May you all find your own *animus* today and every day."

The room falls silent, the weight of his words hanging in the air. Slowly, a murmur of agreement ripples through the class.

"Now, let's talk about the *butchering* of a word," he continues, his tone sharpening with intellectual fervor. "When researching the etymology of *animus,* every single underscored term in the verse above—Spirit, Soul, heart, design, intendment, purpose, meaning, plan, courage, mind, willingness, vital force, vital engagement, and vital energy—traces back to its true definition. Yet, how often do we reduce it to something as shallow as animosity?"

He lets the observation linger, scanning the room. "This attitude, this condition, is essential if we are to achieve anything meaningful in life. It is the foundation, the fuel, and the guide. Work on it without delay."

"The room is open for questions," he announces with a quiet voice.

Several hands are raised.

Leyton is a senior political science major, known for his insightful analysis of philosophical texts and his ability to link theory to practical action. He often asks questions that challenge the professor's concepts and provoke deeper thought in his peers.

"Professor, in the poem 'Ánimo, Animus, Anima,' you talk about animus being the 'vital force of the heart' and the 'catalyst of our purpose.' How do you think we can consciously cultivate animus in our daily lives, especially in moments when we feel disconnected or uninspired?"

"That's a great question, Leyton. The poem points to animus as something deeply embedded within us, something that requires both awareness and effort to tap into. To cultivate animus, we need to begin by fostering a mindset of openness and receptivity to the world around us. It's about engaging with life and people with a sense of purpose, willingness, and energy, even when we feel low or uninspired. It's a matter of making the decision to be present in each moment, to actively pursue what excites us, and to push forward, despite any resistance we might encounter. When we connect with that inner drive, we can reinvigorate our sense of purpose and, in turn, influence how we engage with the world."

Lynn is a second-year philosophy major with an interest in existentialism and the search for meaning. She often probes the deeper emotional and philosophical aspects of human experience.

"Professor, the poem emphasizes the importance of 'willingness' and 'desire' as part of animus. Do you think these qualities are enough to create real change, or is there something more that needs to be present for one to fully actualize their potential?"

"That's a very insightful question, Lynn. While willingness and desire are essential for animus, they alone are not always sufficient for creating meaningful change. The poem suggests that animus requires an active engagement with the world—a determination to move forward with courage and purpose. Real change comes when those desires and willingness are aligned with action. It's not just about wanting something; it's about being willing to do the work, face the challenges, and keep moving forward despite obstacles. True potential is actualized when animus is paired with sustained effort, reflection, and growth."

Jackson is a senior majoring in literature, with a focus on poetry. He has a keen interest in how language shapes our perceptions of reality and often seeks deeper layers of meaning in poetry.

"Professor, in the poem, you describe animus as a 'vital engagement' that connects to both the spirit and soul. How do you think this engagement manifests in poetry? Is it possible for a poet to fully embody animus in their work?"

"That's an excellent question, Jackson. I believe animus plays a critical role in the creative process. A poet who embodies animus is not just writing to fulfill an external goal but is deeply connected to the inner drive that sparks their creativity. When animus is present in a poet's work, it becomes a conduit for expression that flows naturally and powerfully. The willingness to explore one's soul and spirit through words, to take risks with language, and to pour oneself into the craft—that's how animus manifests in poetry. It's the very heartbeat of a poem, the energy behind the metaphor, the urgency in the rhythm."

Ariana is a junior psychology major with a focus on emotional intelligence and motivation. She enjoys analyzing human behavior and how emotions can influence decision-making and creativity.

"Professor, you mentioned that animus is the 'fuel for our plans' and the 'secret ingredient behind our courage.' From a psychological perspective, how do you think animus influences a person's ability to overcome fear or self-doubt?"

"Great question, Ariana. From a psychological standpoint, animus is closely linked to intrinsic motivation—the internal drive that fuels our actions despite external challenges. When animus is present, it gives us the courage to face fear and self-doubt because it's grounded in a deeper sense of purpose and meaning. It helps shift the focus from the fear itself to the drive to move forward, regardless of the obstacles. It's about reframing fear as something to be acknowledged but not allowed to dictate our actions. When we align our desires and willingness with animus, we become more resilient, less affected by negative emotions, and more determined to reach our goals."

Maya is a third-year sociology student, with an interest in the intersection between social structures and individual agency. She is particularly fascinated by how individuals find meaning and purpose within collective systems.

"Professor, the poem talks about the importance of 'recognizing moments of convergence.' How do you think animus and convergence are connected in our daily interactions with others, particularly within communities or larger social systems?"

"That's a wonderful observation, Maya. Animus and convergence are deeply connected because animus is the driving force that pushes us to engage with the world around us. In a community or social system, when we recognize moments of convergence—whether it's shared values, common goals, or mutual understanding—we are in a state of alignment. Animus empowers us to act on those moments of connection, to be proactive in fostering collaboration, and to contribute to the greater good. Convergence, when recognized and acted upon with animus, can lead to collective growth and transformation. It's about finding the common thread that unites us and actively engaging with it."

With that, he glances at the clock, signaling the end of the class.

"See you next week," he says, his voice tinged with finality.

As he strides out of the classroom, his students sit in contemplative silence, reflecting on his words. He smiles softly, sensing the shift in the room—their minds alive with curiosity, pondering the profound duality within the word *animus* and what it means in their lives—and how both meanings might be found within themselves. One by one, they gather their things, but the energy in the room remains, a testament to the powerful convergence of thought and spirit.

Chapter 15

Life's Endless Virtuous Circles

(En route from Cape Cod to Boston, 2020)

"I wonder how our tiny little baby is doing?" Elizabeth Victoria asks softly as they navigate the long, lonely road out of Cape Cod, visibility reduced to nearly nothing by the dense fog.

"He's in good hands, my love," Jordan reassures her, his voice steady and calming. "Your mom doesn't let him out of her sight—not for a second."

As always, his presence and a few gentle words are enough to soothe her. Elizabeth feels safe, content, and deeply happy. Their day had been extraordinary—a perfect escape. Together, they piloted their balloon across the skies, the flight stretching blissfully from morning until evening. After landing on the picturesque New England coast, the adventurous new parents had eagerly set out on the drive back to Boston, the joy of the day still fresh in their hearts.

"I want this day to last forever," she murmurs, her voice wistful.

But fate has other plans.

An unexpected bend lies ahead, shrouded in fog, unseen and unavoidable. From the opposite direction, a trailer truck loses control—the brakes fail, and it veers wildly off the road. Momentum gathers as it barrels downhill, skidding uncontrollably into the path of oncoming cars.

The collision is devastating and instantaneous.

The unlucky victims are the young Morse-Emerson couple. Returning from their idyllic balloon adventure, they never see the truck until it's too late. The impact is catastrophic—head-on and unavoidable. Their car erupts into a towering ball of flames, the blaze consuming everything in a cruel instant.

The exuberant lives of Jordan and Elizabeth Victoria, so full of love, promise, and joy, are snuffed out as swiftly as a candle's fragile flame.

Mt. Auburn Cemetery (2020)

Elizabeth and Jordan's burial ceremony is deeply solemn, the air heavy with grief and love. Victoria stands surrounded by her two surviving children, Bart and Sarah, their presence a quiet testament to resilience. Beside them stands Erasmus, a comforting anchor in this moment of sorrow. Across from them, on the opposite side of the two caskets, the Morse family mourns their beloved son, Jordan Auguste.

The atmosphere is quiet but charged with unspoken emotions. It is Professor Erasmus Cromwell-Smith's turn to speak. His solemn, pained eyes sweep across the gathered mourners as he steps forward, holding a small piece of paper containing words chosen with care for this occasion. With a steady voice, he begins to read:

"As Time Passes"

As time passes
and life goes on,
we are reminded by tragedy
how precious life is,
and how privileged we are
to be healthy and alive.

Life is short—very short.
We must live it in full,
squeezing every drop out of every single day.

Our family, our friends—
they are our travel companions
on this intense voyage of life.

Work and enjoyment keep us busy,
but Love gives us balance and equilibrium.

As time passes
and life goes on,
as the turn of the next generation approaches,
our greatest satisfaction
is to see our descendants
living in full bloom,
free, healthy,
successful in whatever they pursue,
and happy with their lives,
their friends,
and their loved ones.

*

It is Jordan's father's turn to read his son's eulogy. He steps forward, his shoulders heavy with grief yet steady with resolve. The folded paper in his trembling hands speaks to the weight of his loss, and as he begins, his voice carries the tenderness of a father's love and the sorrow of an irreplaceable absence.

*

"Do You Remember Those Eyes?"

Do you remember those eyes?
I do … I always will.

His eyes smiled at you
with their little twinkle,
that tiny movement where they seemed
to close in on you,

as if you were
the most important person in the world—
at least in that moment, to him.

You couldn't help but feel
that you had his full attention,
his full respect.

His eyes read people so well …
those laser beams made you feel good,
high-spirited, and full of optimism.

His eyes touched you with total approval,
giving you a profound sense
of his limitless faith in you.

He was a source of strength,
able, so quickly,
to get close to you—
as only those who genuinely
accept others as they are can.

Jordan's life was a celebration of life—
a precious life,
a life that, because it is short,
must be lived in full,
squeezing every second out of it.

A life where giving himself to others
is the best legacy he leaves behind.
Do you remember those eyes?
I do … I always will.

*

He pauses, his voice breaking at the end. "Goodbye, Jordan.
You will be dearly missed, son."

Victoria steps forward, composed but deeply moved. She speaks with quiet strength, her voice carrying a resolve that mirrors her late daughter's spirit.

"My daughter Elizabeth would not have wished for anything different than this beautiful homage. She wouldn't have wanted to see us sad. To the contrary, I intend to honor her wishes by celebrating her life and that of her husband, Jordan," she says, her words a poignant reminder to cherish life, even in the shadow of loss.

Victoria and Erasmus Campus Home (2020)

No one dressed in black is allowed at the reception. Instead, Jordan and Elizabeth's favorite music fills the air, creating an atmosphere of bittersweet celebration. In the living room, family home movies play on the television, capturing moments of Jordan and Elizabeth as children—laughing, playing, and living vibrant lives.

Victoria moves among the guests with a radiant smile, exuding warmth and an almost stubborn joy. She refuses to let grief define the day, subduing sadness and commanding happiness at every turn. Erasmus watches her in quiet admiration, awed by the wave of positivity she has generated.

"She's not permitting anyone to be anything but uplifting," Erasmus observes, listening as Jordan's lively parents recount one of his childhood adventures, their laughter mixing with tears.

Suddenly, the sound of a baby's cries emanates from the electronic monitor Victoria carries. Without a word, Erasmus begins ascending the stairs. Moments later, Victoria follows, entering the nursery to find her husband sitting in a rocking chair, feeding the baby. The tender scene stops her in her tracks.

"Learning fast to be a father, dear," she teases gently, but Erasmus barely acknowledges her.

"With his parents gone, his grandparents on both sides are all he's got," Erasmus says, his voice heavy with loving concern.

"Speaking of that," Victoria begins, her tone brightening, "there's absolute consensus among our family and Jordan's."

"Consensus about what?" Erasmus asks, a note of apprehension creeping into his voice.

"That we should adopt the baby," she announces, her eyes shining.

"We?" Erasmus's voice trembles as he repeats the word, his thoughts tangled.

"Aren't we …?" he ventures, unsure.

Victoria stares at him, amused by his flustered response.

"Too old …?" he babbles, still trying to find his footing.

"Are we?" she counters, her gaze steady, challenging him.

"No, I don't mean it that way," he stammers, growing more confused.

"In which way do you mean it, then?" she presses, enjoying his struggle.

"Too old to be parents?" he finally blurts out.

"Same question: are we?" she repeats with playful determination.

"I guess …" he begins to respond negatively but halts mid-sentence, realizing it's fear, not truth, speaking. He pauses, gathering himself.

For what feels like forever, the room is silent. Finally, Erasmus lifts his eyes to meet Victoria's. As their gazes lock, an unspoken understanding passes between them. Slowly, faint, knowing smiles form on both their faces.

"I guess not, Victoria," he says at last, his voice steady.

"This is your chance to be a father, dear," she declares softly.

It's the closest Erasmus has ever come to witnessing Victoria shed a tear for the loss of her daughter and son-in-law.

Minutes later, as promised, Victoria and Erasmus descend the stairs, the baby soundly sleeping in Erasmus's arms. The buzz of conversation in the family room swells as they enter, and Sarah quickly takes charge.

"Mom and Erasmus, Bart and I have discussed this possibility several times," Sarah begins, her voice steady but full of emotion.

"Today, we also talked it over with Jordan's parents, and they've given their blessing." Jordan's father and mother nod in agreement.

Victoria and Erasmus exchange relaxed glances, assuming Sarah is about to announce that she and Bart will adopt the baby. But they couldn't be more wrong.

"Since you're now going to become parents," Sarah continues, her voice filled with warmth, "Bart and I have decided on a name for the baby. With all our hearts, we want you to name him Erasmus Cromwell-Smith II."

Her words hang in the air for a moment, sinking into everyone present. A collective sigh of emotion ripples through the room, followed by cheers and applause.

Erasmus's lips tremble, his arms beginning to wobble as he holds the baby. Sensing his emotion, Victoria quickly takes the baby from him. She looks at Erasmus with a soft smile before breaking down, her tears flowing freely, uncontainable and raw. The baby stirs slightly, tiny drops of her tears falling on his cheeks, a quiet baptism of love and healing.

"There's no better gift to honor Elizabeth and Jordan than what all of you have just done," Victoria says, her voice steady despite the tears glistening on her cheeks. "I'm sure they're smiling down on us right now. Rest assured, Erasmus and I will continue the family path they were just beginning to pave." She wipes away her tears and bends over to kiss the baby softly.

"If you all will allow me," Erasmus interjects, finally regaining his composure, "I'd like to share a couple of pieces that, given the circumstances, carry profound meaning." He pauses, glancing at the baby in Victoria's arms. "The first is something I wrote at the request of Jordan and Elizabeth. They wanted it to reflect the way they dreamed their children would grow up. This will be the first time I've shared it with anyone, and Victoria and I are committed to following their wishes."

He unfolds a sheet of paper, his voice growing joyous as he begins to read…

"For Our Children"

Let them grow healthy and strong
so they may discover a world
that is both difficult and fantastic
at the same time.

Let them travel and meet its people,
and love all their fellow travelers,
especially those in need.
Let it be that
everything they start or involve themselves in
is done with conviction and dedication.

Let them enjoy
their parents and an immensely happy childhood,
filled with boundless Love,
dreams, and illusions.
And as they grow,
let them discover everything and everyone
around them as they truly are.

Then, over time,
let them gradually uncover
who they really are,

so they may find their true selves,
just as God brought them to earth.
So, whoever they are,
they are happy and comfortable in their own skin.

So, whatever they do,
they do it well.
Hence, from that moment forward,
they are always
their authentic selves.
We'll teach you
to be humble, honest, and non-materialistic.
We'll offer you our infinite Love
and our passion for knowledge, sports, and nature.

We'll teach you discipline,
ingraining in you a rock-solid work ethic.
We'll push and press
and will be as demanding as you can bear—
and then some.

We'll make you strong
and teach you to live life in full,
so that life does not slip by
without you seizing every moment of it,
regardless of the circumstances.

*

Erasmus lowers the paper, his voice trailing off, and looks around the room, meeting the eyes of family and friends who are deeply moved by his words. After a moment, he speaks again.

"This second piece comes from an antique book I once read at one of my childhood mentor's bookstores. It's about how we face the future, even as we struggle to find our way forward after the loss of a child."

With a steadying breath, Erasmus begins to read the next piece…

"Destiny"

Life is a tightly wound chain of occurrences,
a maddening scramble
we cannot govern.

Our future is being made
every one-thousandth of a second.

It is an infinite,
never-ending,
totally random string
of connected occurrences.

All these intersecting events
relate, influence, and interact
with one another.

Each and every event in life
is a wonderful and complex accident.

This includes the finite ways of our life,
the urgency of living,
and the uncertainty of our future.

We are an accident,
every moment we are alive,
and in the end,
all is a complex mishap.

Life is a complicated interaction
of events of nature,
human acts and behavior,

and everything born of
human creation,
all under the mantle of life.

We have very little control over life.
But if circumstances allow it,
with faith and willingness,
we can reap from it
immense Happiness and goodwill.

*

As Erasmus finishes, the room is silent, each person lost in their thoughts. The baby stirs slightly in Victoria's arms, drawing everyone's attention back to the present. Erasmus steps forward and gently brush a finger against the baby's cheek.

"We'll honor Elizabeth and Jordan by giving this little one the best life we can," he says softly. Victoria nods, her tears flowing once more, this time a mixture of grief and hope.

The family gathers closer, united by the love that will carry them forward, even in the face of their shared loss.

Erasmus and Victoria's Campus Home (2010)
(A Few Weeks Later)

The transition to parenthood has been surprisingly smooth, thanks to Victoria's experience. What has been unexpected, however, is how little physical work she has had to do for the baby. Erasmus, with an unyielding dedication, has taken on the role of a 24/7 caretaker. His boundless enthusiasm and devotion have left him consumed by fatherhood, pouring all his energy into caring for Erasmus Jr.

Victoria, with her characteristic grace and wisdom, has gradually begun to ease her way into the parenting routine. Using her deft touch and invaluable "know-how," she has started taking on more responsibilities. Slowly but surely, the couple finds themselves working together seamlessly—sharing duties, complementing each other effortlessly, and providing their son with constant love and attention.

The final sign that life is settling into a new normal arrives with the addition of a British au pair. Emma Franklin, a capable and cheerful young woman, is entrusted with day-to-day responsibilities for Erasmus Jr., a role she will hold until his adulthood.

Upon Emma's arrival, Victoria and Erasmus are finally free to step back into their other cherished roles as professors. With Emma's capable hands tending to the baby's needs, the couple finds balance once more—nurturing their child and continuing to inspire others through their teaching.

Royal Cambridge Scholastic Institute (2020)
(Campus Back Roads)

As the sun slowly rises over the campus, Professor Cromwell-Smith pedals with a steady cadence through the quiet campus streets, the early morning sunlight casting long shadows. Victoria had left earlier both of them preparing for their final classes of the academic year. As he rides, the eminent professor's thoughts drift, and he reflects on the bittersweet events of the previous days. He has just begun to settle into the new normal of life after Elizabeth and Jordan's tragic passing, and yet the cycle of life and the promise of renewal remains fresh in his mind. As Professor Cromwell-Smith mind drifts back to his looming class, he takes stock of the subjects, he has explored with his students over the year.

Existential themes—adversity, virtue, forgiveness, reciprocity, resilience—have made this academic year remarkable. Each lesson carried its own weight, every discussion an opportunity to inspire.

Erasmus's mind shifts, flashing through memories of his life with Victoria and the years they spent apart. He revisits their memorable encounters with New England's antiquarian mentors during their time in Boston. His thoughts move to the meetings they had with Colin Carnegie at the public libraries in New York and Pittsburgh—institutions built by his distant relative, Andrew Carnegie.

He recalls the journey to St. Louis to meet Victoria's mentor, Mrs. Samuels-Ortiz, at the grand public library, and the timely scribble gifted to him by Mr. Ringwald, affectionately known as "The Riddler," during the turbulent time when Victoria had run away. A procession of mentors follows in his mind: Mrs. Peabody, Mr. Lafayette, Mr. Faith, and the last letter he received from Mrs. V. Each mentor had left an indelible mark on his journey, their inspirational writings and poems guiding him through life's complexities.

Mr. Willkenvoss, or "The Quibbler," had been profoundly influential, as had Mr. Atsushi, his Japanese mentor. Each played a role in shaping the lessons Erasmus had shared with his students.

His thoughts turn to the joys of the year—the welcome banner awaiting him after his honeymoon, the occasions when Victoria or her children attended his lectures, and countless unforgettable moments that had woven the tapestry of his life. But then, there were the shadows: the tragic death of Elizabeth and her husband, and the bittersweet joy of adopting their child.

As the faculty building comes into view, a poem from his childhood surfaces in his memory: *The Spinning Wheel of Life.*"

'Why not bring it all back full circle?' Erasmus muses, a faint smile touching his lips. With that thought, he decides that in this final lecture, he will share an old scribble—a reflection on the cycle of life.

Royal Cambridge Scholastic Institute (2020)
(University Auditorium)

As he enters the classroom, the energy of his students greets him like a warm embrace, offering a contrast to the stillness of his morning thoughts. With a soft smile, he sets aside his reflections and prepares to share his wisdom with the eager minds before him.

"Good morning, everyone; how are you all doing today?" Professor Cromwell-Smith greets the class with his characteristic energy.

"Just unbelievable, professor!" comes the enthusiastic chorus from the students.

The professor pauses for a moment, his expression softening. "As you all know, Victoria's oldest daughter and her husband recently perished in a tragic traffic accident. Consequently, Victoria and I made the decision to adopt their baby. We will raise him as our son."

A wave of congratulations ripples through the room, expressed through warm gestures and nods of approval.

Erasmus continues, his tone both reflective and instructive.

"Referencing the painful loss and the hardships Victoria and I have faced, today I'll be sharing some of those moments of grief. I want to illustrate how such experiences mark not just an end, but also a beginning—how life's cycles bring about endless renewal."

He steps forward, leaning slightly against his desk, and begins his narration.

"It starts like this … Last year, during a summer holiday, after Victoria and I had been together for a year, we embarked on a journey to Europe. We began in Wales, visiting my hometown."

The class listens attentively as he continues.

"We arrived early one morning and went first to my old home. It's still titled in my name but currently rented to an elderly couple. Later that day, we carried flowers to the town cemetery to pay our respects to my parents and three of my most cherished mentors—Mrs. V., Mr. M., and Mr. N.—all of whom now rest in those sacred grounds."

Erasmus pauses briefly, his gaze distant.

"Afterward, we spent hours exploring the antique bookstores I had loved as a child. Many are now run by descendants or relatives of the original owners. For three days, we delved into these spaces, rediscovering books I had read during my childhood and teenage years," he says, a faint smile tugging at the corners of his mouth.

"In particular, at Mrs. V.'s bookstore, we came across two scribbles—one depicting life's endless cycle and how everything eventually comes full circle, and the other describing the innate drive to live a life of enthusiasm. As I reflect on them now, they feel almost prophetic," Erasmus remarks, his voice tinged with awe.

He picks up a sheet of paper, looking at it briefly before addressing the class again. "Allow me to read the first scribble to you. It encapsulates the recurring nature of life and the profound way each ending leads to a beginning."

With that, he begins to read…

"Life's Endless Virtuous Circles"

As the sun sets
and a life ends,
the horizon explodes
in thousands of colors.

Yellows, oranges, and reds of fire
light the sky,
symbolizing the celebration
of a journey coming to an end.

As in life,
when we mourn the loss and departure
of our loved ones, no longer with us,
total darkness soon arrives and engulfs us,
but not for long.

As we start to peek
and then gaze up at the firmament,
we recognize there are still lights
while we grieve—
that there are still lights in darkness,
as countless stars and the moon
illuminate the entire night sky.

Soon enough, as in life,
a bright new day approaches.

First, it breaks
as a tiny ray of light on the horizon.

Shortly after,
a new beginning
inexorably commences out of darkness,
filled with shiny daylights and vivid hues.

A rebirth, a fresh new start,
makes us realize that,
everything around us is recurrent,
recursive and regenerated.

As each new day begins
a daily renewal of human existence unfolds.
As a life gives way,
a day ends.
Night takes the stage,
but only for a while.

A new life soon starts,
a new day breaks out.
And the lights of life irrupt
in full blast over the horizon.

*

"Here is the second scribble. Please allow me to continue," Professor Cromwell-Smith says, his voice steady yet vibrant as he unfolds the next piece.

"Enthusiasm"

There are a few other expressions
That better depict
what it means to be truly alive
than enthusiasm.

The enthusiast is blessed
with a halo of
ebullient effusiveness,
unstoppable and contagious desire,
restless and immense curiosity,
exalted and positive energy,
to embark and go after
countless virtuous circles.

The enthusiast is possessed with,
an overwhelming but refreshing impetus,
a cheerful and lively willingness,
an incessant and unrelenting drive,
to explore, experiment, and experience
anything, anyone and everything.

For the enthusiast, life is a series of precious bounties
a cadre of improbable moonshots,
just waiting to be tapped.

Enthusiasm is the best antidote
to passivity, indifference, and lack of passion.

Enthusiasm is the essence of Inspiration,
Happiness and True Love.

Spontaneous waterfalls of goodness,
are second nature to the enthusiast.

They are, in reality, deliberate joy-triggers,
unmistakable signals
that symbolize the magic key,
to the land of continuous Happiness.

That place where we are graced with a mantle of
pulsating, ticking, vibrating vitality.

A passionate and inspired life
is always soaked with enthusiasm,
which is the secret catalyst that unlocks
and sustains joy into our existence
as we journey through life.

*

Erasmus pauses, letting the words resonate with the class.
Then, with a reflective smile, he continues.

"Throughout the last three years, we have traversed, under the prism of poetry, through my childhood, teenage years, true Love, lost Love, newfound Love, sickness, death, and, finally, new life. Next year will likely be my last as a teacher.

"What is certain, as of today, is that we have come full circle. Next year, we will revert to a regular curriculum. This means you all have been the beneficiaries of a course that will never be repeated," he proclaims, his voice tinged with pride and nostalgia.

Turning his thoughts back to the present moment, Professor Cromwell-Smith knows the classroom is the place where he can help others see the connections between life's most difficult lessons and the beauty of its endless cycles. Today, he is sharing with them not only his personal reflections but also the wisdom he has gathered over the years, from mentors and experiences alike."

He retrieves another sheet and announces, "Here are two scribbles encompassing many of the subjects we've covered throughout the last three semesters. The first deals with Love. Please allow me to read it to you."

"Love and Success"

It is not whatsoever, about success-driven Love.
To the contrary, everyone and everything in life
is about love driven success.

*

Professor Cromwell-Smith lets the simplicity and depth of the words sink in before continuing.

"And here is another one, one you're already familiar with …"

*

"The Happiness Formula"

Love, Equilibrium (balance), and Values
are the foundations of
Awareness, Passion, and Tempo.
When we truly love,
when we have a balanced lifestyle,
when we live according to our family,
moral/ethical and spiritual values,
we have the keys to continuous Happiness.
When we do what we love and do it with passion,
when we live with intensity, rhythm, and tempo,
when we capture, squeeze
and "live" every moment we are alive,
and when we focus on giving
and do it as well with Passion,
we are simply Happy!
Each of them is a true
and legitimate source of Happiness.
But the ultimate source of constant Happiness
is a noble state of sublime desire,
a heightened level of hypersensitivity,
that brings the best out of all of us
and this is,
Inspiration!
Which leads us to be inspired,
to be inspired persons (life wizards)
and to live
an Inspired Life!
*

"Class, before we part ways, I've prepared a final scribble for you
that sums up what we've learned throughout the last three years."

Professor Cromwell-Smith pulls a scroll out of his rumpled briefcase. Delicately, he unties the little red ribbon that wraps it, his movements slow and deliberate, as though unwrapping something sacred. Holding the scroll open, he begins to read, his voice filled with earnestness and emotion.

*

"Joy"

Joy is the highest level of Happiness,
a virtuous elevated state,
where we reach "The Zenith of Contentment."

Joy occurs,
when Happiness shines and sparkles,
when anything or anyone is radiant and incandescent,
when we are inundated, impregnated, soaked,
with a sense of absolute wholesomeness,
immense pleasure, complete satisfaction,
and totally satiated feelings,
all of them coming from within us.

Some profess that,
when we arrive,
while we are here,
or when we depart this world,
Joy blesses us directly from Heaven
or from our creator Himself.

Others believe that, at a minimum,
Joy must originate
out of a profound and well-grounded spirituality.

Then there are those,
who are certain,
that continuous Joy requires "Clarity in Life,"

which stems from "Coherence,"
"The Glue" that connects meaning
to purpose in our existence.

In final analysis, most certainly,
Joy is any or all of the above.

Joy ensues when we are
aware, conscious, and appreciative,
when we anticipate in delight
and when we are able
to taste, feel, and take pleasure
of pure and simply being alive.

Joy is "Inherent and Immanent" to our core,
very essence and nature,
but Joy may be elusive,
hard to discern and visualize,
often clouded by poisons of the Spirit:
Power, Ambition, Greed, Envy, Anger,
Grudges, Material Wealth
and the most dangerous of them all—our Ego.

In addition, there is no Joy
when we are unable to be caring, doting,
humble and authentically honest.

The inner peace and calmness
of finding and being true to oneself
are fundamental prerequisites to Joy.

Joy has nothing to do with
Character, Success or Riches.

It is about whether our "Existential Inner Lights"
and our "Desire to Live" are ON or not.

As it belongs only to our "Existence,"
Joy cannot be possessed or controlled.
Joy simply is.
The noble and sublime state of "Inspiration"
perhaps the only source of continuous Happiness,
is our secret ingredient, our catapult,
our springboard into the elevated state of Joy.

There is no Joy in the future, much less in the past.
Our masochist minds tend to take us to places
that no longer exist or others yet to be.

On the contrary, Joy's eternal presence
only exists in the "Here and Now!"

A condition of permanent Joy
is the hallmark of the "Wizards of Life,"
those who have lived long enough,
but still possess pure, candid, and innocent hearts.

When in Joy,
we exude, transcend, exult, exhilarate,
elate, blithe, celebrate in exuberance
and seemingly hover, levitate, float, and waft
in utter and sheer bliss,
above mundane reality.

In Joy is where the truest meaning of life resides,
and although "Hidden in Plain Sight" within,
Joy is the biggest existential treasure,
we hold while we exist and are alive.

*

"My dear students, Joy is the ultimate and highest level of
Happiness and one we can only reach through Inspiration,"

concludes Cromwell-Smith, his words resonating deeply with the attentive class.

He pauses, reaching into his briefcase, and pulls out neatly folded handouts. "As a parting gift, I'm giving you the complete version of the Triangle of Happiness—a synthesis of what we've explored together these past three years."

He distributes the pages with care, watching as his students unfold them to reveal a thoughtfully constructed diagram and text:

"The Happiness Formula"

<u>Joy</u>

Inspiration

↑

Passion

△

Awarness   Tempo

Love

Equilibrium

(balance)

Values

Spiritual   Moral/Ethical   Family

Professor Cromwell-Smith lets the final words of the scribble hang in the air, their weight palpable. He surveys the faces of his students, his own filled with immense satisfaction.

Turning his thoughts back to the present moment, Erasmus knows the classroom is the place where he can help others see the connections between life's most difficult lessons, joy's beauty and its endless cycles. Today, he will share with them not only his personal reflections but also the wisdom he has gathered over the years, from mentors and experiences alike.

"My dear students, Joy is the ultimate and highest level of Happiness—one we can only reach through Inspiration," he concludes, his voice steady and warm.

Professor Cromwell-Smith pauses, his voice thick with the weight of the words he has just shared. He feels the room grow still as his students absorbed the cyclical nature of life he had outlined. It is a moment of deep connection, and he gives them a moment of quiet to reflect before opening the floor to questions.

A multiplicity of hands is raised.

Alice is a junior religious studies major with a focus on existential philosophy and the role of suffering in spiritual growth. She enjoys examining how different worldviews approach the concept of life's purpose.

"Professor, in your poem 'Life's Endless Virtuous Circles,' you talk about the inevitability of life's cycles and how each ending leads to a new beginning. How does this perspective relate to the idea of finding peace after suffering? Do you think it's necessary to experience both loss and renewal in order to reach a sense of wholeness?"

"That's an insightful question, Alice. Yes, I believe that understanding life's cycles, particularly the movement from loss to renewal, is central to finding peace after suffering. Life is constantly changing, and we are always in flux. The poem suggests that after each loss, there is always the potential for something new, something hopeful. This cyclical view offers a sense of balance—though we endure hardship, we are also given the opportunity for healing and new growth. In many ways, we need both the loss and the renewal to appreciate the full depth of life. The suffering teaches us about the value of what we have, and the renewal reminds us that life continues, bringing new chances for joy and understanding."

Peter is an engineering major with a penchant for existential themes.

"Professor, in your poem 'Joy,' you describe it as a state of absolute wholesomeness and fulfillment that comes from within. Do you think joy is something that can be cultivated or is it more of a fleeting emotion that we stumble upon during specific moments?"

"Excellent question, Peter. Joy, as I describe it in the poem, can certainly be cultivated, though it's also something that has the potential to arise spontaneously. The process of cultivating joy involves aligning with your true self—finding purpose, maintaining gratitude, and becoming more aware of life's fleeting beauty. The challenge, however, is that many people overlook joy because they're distracted by external achievements, societal pressures, or unacknowledged grief. To cultivate joy, you must first give yourself permission to be present in the moment and to experience life fully. It is this awareness and practice that can allow joy to become a consistent presence, even in the face of difficulty."

Maria is a third-year philosophy major, focused on existentialism and the nature of human resilience. She often connects philosophical concepts with real-world experiences.

"Professor, in your poem 'Life's Endless Virtuous Circles,' there is a sense of embracing both endings and beginnings as equally valuable. How do you think we can practically apply this perspective in our daily lives, especially when we're struggling to move forward after a loss or hardship?"

"A fantastic question, Maria. The key lies in acknowledging that life is a constant flow, not a linear progression. When faced with hardship, it's crucial to remember that while we might feel stuck in the darkness, there is always the potential for light— whether through a new opportunity, a fresh perspective, or the support of others. In practical terms, we can apply this perspective by allowing ourselves to feel our pain but not letting it define us. When we embrace the cycles of life—both the ups and the downs—we are more likely to move through our challenges with a sense of purpose, knowing that they are part of a larger, ongoing process of growth."

Richard is a creative writing major fascinated by the themes of self-motivation.

"Professor, the poem 'Enthusiasm' describes life as a series of bounties, waiting to be explored. How do you think enthusiasm can be sustained during challenging times when the energy to pursue life's offerings seems to wane?"

"A very perceptive question, Richard. Enthusiasm is a force that needs to be consciously reignited, especially in challenging times.

Life's difficulties can drain us, leaving us feeling passive or uninspired. But as the poem suggests, enthusiasm is the antidote to that passivity. It requires us to tap into our curiosity, to rekindle our passions, and to remind ourselves of the beauty and possibility in the world. In difficult moments, the key is to reconnect with the things that spark joy—whether it's a hobby, a meaningful relationship, or simply a moment of solitude. Even in tough times, we can choose to act with enthusiasm, which will eventually sustain us."

Eli is a second year sociology student with an interest in the ways that societal structures influence individual and collective resilience. He enjoys examining how abstract philosophical concepts manifest in different communities.

"Professor, in your description of the sunset and the ensuing night in 'Life's Endless Virtuous Circles,' you highlight the importance of grief before renewal. Can you explain how this relates to the process of healing, particularly in a societal context where grief is often suppressed or overlooked?"

"That's a thoughtful question, Eli. The image of the sunset followed by the night reflects the necessary process of grieving before healing can begin. In many societies, there's a tendency to rush past grief, to avoid it, or to suppress it because it feels uncomfortable. However, grief, like the night in the poem, serves an essential purpose. It allows us to process loss, reflect, and ultimately create space for new growth. When we suppress grief, we deny ourselves the chance to truly heal. Only by sitting with our emotions—just as we must endure the night—can we experience the transformation that leads to renewal. Societal norms often push us toward quick fixes, but true healing takes time, and we must allow ourselves to experience that process fully."

Rita is a psychology major intrigued by the subject of absolute happiness.

"Professor, in 'Joy,' you describe joy as an immanent part of our essence that can't be controlled. How does this idea fit with the notion of working toward personal happiness, where many people believe happiness is something that must be achieved through effort?"

"A great question, Rita. I think this tension between effort and surrender is at the heart of understanding joy. While joy is inherent in our nature, as I suggest in the poem, it often becomes clouded by external expectations or our own struggles with self-worth. To connect with joy, we must first align with our true selves, which involves letting go of the notion that we must achieve happiness. In this sense, joy is not something we strive for directly, but something we allow to arise through conscious presence, humility, and alignment with our values. So, personal happiness can be an effort, but the deeper joy I speak of is more about letting go of external pressure and embracing what is already within us."

Leah is a senior psychology major with a focus on emotional regulation and coping mechanisms. She often explores how personal experiences with grief are shaped by cultural expectations.

"Professor, I noticed that in the poem, you emphasize the interconnectedness of life's events—how one leads into the next, how life is renewed after each loss. Do you believe that this interconnectedness suggests a kind of cosmic order, or is it simply a result of human perspective, finding meaning in the chaos of life?"

"Excellent question, Leah. The poem suggests a certain order, but I'd argue it's more a matter of perspective than a predetermined cosmic order. Life often feels chaotic, especially in moments of loss or suffering, but from the human perspective, we tend to find patterns and meanings to help us cope. This isn't necessarily about a universal cosmic force but about our inherent need to find meaning in the events that happen to us. It's part of how we make sense of the world and our place in it. That said, the interconnectedness in the poem could also be viewed as a spiritual or philosophical recognition that everything is linked— our losses, our growth, and our rebirths are all part of a greater process that transcends individual events."

Dexter is an art history major intrigued by the subject of human inspiration.

"Professor, in your poem 'Enthusiasm,' you discuss the boundless energy and drive that enthusiasm brings. In your experience, how can one sustain this kind of energy when faced with the day-to-day pressures of life, work, and responsibility?"

"Another excellent question, Dexter. Sustaining enthusiasm in everyday life requires intentionality. Life's daily pressures can often drain our energy, but as the poem suggests, enthusiasm is something that must be actively cultivated. This isn't to say that we should be overly positive at all times, but rather that we should nurture our curiosity and excitement in small ways each day. Whether it's setting new goals, allowing ourselves to experience moments of joy, or taking the time to appreciate the people and experiences around us, enthusiasm can be reignited even during routine tasks. The key is to find what excites you about life and build those moments into your daily rhythm."

Lawrence is a senior majoring in literature, with a focus on poetry. He has a keen interest in how language shapes our perceptions of reality and often seeks deeper layers of meaning in poetry.

"Professor, in the poem 'Enthusiasm,' you describe life as a series of precious bounties waiting to be tapped. How can we maintain enthusiasm when faced with the inevitable frustrations and limitations of our personal circumstances?"

"That's a thought-provoking question, Lawrence. Enthusiasm is often tested in the face of adversity, and it can feel particularly difficult to maintain when we encounter setbacks or limitations. The poem suggests that enthusiasm is rooted in a deep, intrinsic drive—a desire to engage with life. Even when circumstances limit our external opportunities, we can still nurture enthusiasm through inner engagement. This could mean pursuing small acts of creativity, embracing learning, or even shifting our perspective to find new ways to engage with what we already have. Enthusiasm comes not from the absence of challenges but from our willingness to keep moving forward, no matter what obstacles arise."

Dieter is an engineering major interested in the relation between love and success.

"Professor, in your poem 'Love and Success,' you present a relationship between love-driven success and success-driven love. Can you expand on how love, in its truest form, transcends traditional notions of success, and how this can influence the way we approach achievement in our lives?"

"An insightful question, Dieter. In 'Love and Success,' I argue that true success is rooted in love, not the other way around. Success that is driven by love is inherently more fulfilling because it's based on a deeper sense of purpose and meaning. Love, in its truest form, transcends material achievement because it is not based on external validation or results. When we pursue our passions, relationships, and work from a place of love, the success that follows is not only more rewarding but also more sustainable. It's a success that is defined by growth, contribution, and connection, rather than by status or accumulation," concludes the professor.

The room is silent, the students captivated, until Erasmus breaks into a familiar smile. "Once again, this was ..." he teases, his arms lifting slightly like an orchestra conductor preparing to cue his ensemble.

The hint is all it takes. The whole auditorium erupts in unison, their voices thundering together:

"Insanely awesome!"

Professor Cromwell-Smith beams, his heart full, as the echoes of their collective cheer carry him into the final chapter of his life's story—a legacy of love, wisdom, and inspiration.

As the final bell of the semester rings, Professor Cromwell-Smith's thoughts briefly drift to the year's teachings, realizing the profound impact these lessons have had on his students. Life, with its many twists and turns, have once again brought him full circle, from grief to new life, from loss to hope, from teacher to student. As he leaves the classroom, a renewed sense of purpose fills his heart.

Parting Words by The Author,

The fourth and final book of *The Equilibrist* series will focus exclusively on the poetry, essays, and fables from the first three volumes.

When I completed writing the third book about my parents—exploring their lives growing up, living together, then apart, and finally reuniting—I thought the journey was complete. Little did I know that chronicling their story would ignite a desire to write about their life after adopting me and the extraordinary world we shared together.

Being a firsthand witness to the remarkable life they built made writing about it effortless. My father ensured I experienced the same type of mentoring and tutoring he had received in his youth. From an early age, he introduced me to the enchanting world of books and antiquarians. This included several transformative years when we lived in his birthplace, Hay-on-Wye, Wales, famously known as Booktown. As I was homeschooled by them, we were free to travel the world together, embarking on countless adventures that enriched my education and my soul.

It was during one of these adventures, sparked by an encounter with the iconic astronomical clock in Prague, that *The Orloj*, a new four-book series about my life with my parents, became a reality. This series follows the 25 extraordinary formative years we spent together, filled with unforgettable experiences, enriching lessons, and the intense love they gave me as truly devoted parents. My father and mother were not only exemplary mentors but also incredible companions in life, and I feel deeply fortunate and blessed to have been their son.

The Orloj also explores the magical and profound relationship I shared with my uncle, Bartholomeus ("Bart"). Our bond grew stronger through the years, and he remains to this day my closest friend and mentor. My aunt Sarah, along with my Italian uncle Roberto Marcello and aunt Maria Antonella, were also integral to my childhood and teenage years. Together, they brought countless unforgettable moments and thrilling adventures to my life, shaping me into the person I am today.

I look forward to sharing these stories in *The Orloj*, as they represent the culmination of a life shaped by love, mentorship, and unending curiosity.

Erasmus Cromwell-Smith
Written at T.D.O.K., 2055

POEMS INDEX

Acknowledgement,

To the ad-hoc members of "The Equilibrist" pseudo editor's committee, you are an eclectic and diverse group of published authors, historians, pedagogues and intellectuals. But first and foremost, you are all serious readers. Adam, Andric, Barry, Christian, Mark, Mitch, Rafael, Tony and Willy, your feedback was invaluable. As important though, was all of you having a strong emotional connection and reaction to the book. It was highly fulfilling and inspirational, making the end of a very intense journey, even more so.
Thank you.

To my team, Amy, Ana Julia (rip), Alfredo, Andrea, Charles, Elisa, Maria Elena and MaryAnn (rip). Without your talent, belief, motivation and hard work, the book would not have been possible.

Magic in Life could not have been possible without the unwavering belief and support of my ad-hoc pseudo editor's committee. Once more, your feedback was invaluable, your enthusiasm highly inspiring, and your engagement emotionally rewarding. You've been INSANELY AWESOME! All the way through. A special thanks must be given to Daniel Dorse for his magnificent rendering of each of The Equilibrist's Audiobook. I know, value and respect the amount of effort and passion you put in these precious artful crafts of the spoken word.

Finally, it is only because of my family's blind faith and support that I was able to carry out this work independently and unconstrained of any commercial editing or vetting filters, which resulted in making The Equilibrist a genuine and authentic creation. You enabled me to release to the world, a craft that is exacting, word by word, to the way I intended and to the form I created it. Thank you as well.

About the Author

Erasmus Cromwell-Smith is an American Writer, Playwright, Poet, and Pedagogue. He's published 32 books in the genres of self-help, poetry, young-adults, education, and sci-fi.

www.ingramcontent.com/pod-product-compliance
Lightning Source LLC
Chambersburg PA
CBHW061555190726

48288CB00007B/2032